Bear Pit

JON CLEARY

Bear Pit

HarperCollins*Publishers*

This novel is entirely a work of fiction. The names,
characters and incidents portrayed in it are the work of the
author's imagination. Any resemblance to actual persons,
living or dead, events or localities is entirely coincidental.

HarperCollins*Publishers*
77–85 Fulham Palace Road,
Hammersmith, London W6 8JB

www.**fire**and**water**.com
Published by HarperCollins*Publishers* 2000
1 3 5 7 9 8 6 4 2

A catalogue record for this book
is available from the British Library

ISBN 0 00 226144 8

Typeset by Palimpsest Book Production Limited,
Polmont, Stirlingshire
Printed in Great Britain by
Omnia Books Limited, Glasgow

For

Benjamin and Isabel

Chapter One

1

Malone switched out the light in his daughter's bedroom.

'Da-ad!'

He switched it on again. 'I thought you were asleep.'

'And I can't sleep with the light on? God, you're so stingy! Can I have the light on while I'm *thinking*?'

'Depends what you're thinking.' He went into her room, sat down in the chair at her desk against the wall. 'Problems?'

'Not really.' Maureen sat up on her bed, nodded at the computer on the desk. 'I thought I'd try my hand at a Mills and Boon romance. There's money in it if you click.'

He turned and read from the computer screen:

Justin unbuttoned Clothilde's tight blouse and her breasts fell out. He picked them up and put them back in again.

'Thank you,' said Clothilde, polite even in passion. 'I'm always losing them.'

'Not much romance there,' said Malone with a grin. 'What follows?'

'Nothing. That's the E-N-D. All I have to do is find sixty thousand words to go in front of it. I don't think I'm cut out for romance – I can't take it seriously.'

'Is that what your boyfriends think?'

She ignored that. 'Maybe I should try grunge fiction. That had a run a while ago.'

'Don't expect me to read it – I get enough grunge out on the job. How's it going at work?'

Maureen was three months out of university and working at Channel 15 as a researcher. It was a television station that put ratings before responsibility, that insisted the bottom line was the best line in any of its productions. It operated with a staff that was skeletal compared to those of other channels, it had no stars amongst its presenters and no overseas bureaux, buying its international material from CNN and other suppliers. Maureen had hoped to go to work for the ABC, the government channel, where, despite harping from Canberra, no one knew what a bottom line was. She had dreamed of working for *Foreign Correspondent* or *Four Corners*, quality shows that compared with the best overseas. Instead she had taken the only job offered her and was a researcher on *Wanted for Questioning*, a half-hour true crime show with top ratings, especially amongst criminals. They wrote fan notes, under assumed names, to the presenter, a girl with a high voice and low cleavage.

'We're doing a special, an hour show on faction fighting in the Labor Party.'

'On *Wanted for Questioning*? The ratings will go through the roof.'

She grinned, an expression that made her her father's daughter. She had his dark hair and dark blue eyes, but her features were closer to her mother's; she was attractive rather than beautiful, but men would always look at her. She had none of his calmness, there was always energy that had to be expended; she would invent hurdles and barricades if none presented themselves. What saved her from intensity was her humour.

'No, this is a one-off special – we haven't been meeting our local quota.' Channel 15 ran mostly American shows; its programme director thought the BBC was a museum. 'The word has come down from the top that we're to pull no punches.'

'Watch out when you get amongst the Labor factions – they're throwing punches all the time. Ask Claire.'

'I have. She's told me where to go and whom to talk to.' Like Malone she knew the difference between *who* and *whom*.

Lisa, her mother, foreign-born and educated, respected English grammar more than the local natives. 'I think she's traumatized at what she's learnt.'

Claire, the elder daughter, had moved out of the Malone house six months ago and was now sharing a flat with her boyfriend Jason. She had graduated last year in Law and now was working for a small firm of lawyers who handled Labor Party business. She was apolitical and Malone and Lisa had been surprised when she had taken the job. With her calm commonsense and her taking the long view, she had told them it was only a first step. She wanted to be a criminal lawyer, a Senior Counsel at the Bar, but first she had to learn about in-fighting. Malone had told her she should have gone into union business, but she had only smiled and told him she knew where she was going. And he was sure she was right.

'There's a State election coming up. Is this the time to start ferreting? You could be accused of bias.'

She grinned again. 'Only the ABC is accused of that. When did you ever hear of a commercial station accused of being biased? The politicians, both sides, know where the majority of viewers are. They're not going to tread on the voters' toes.'

He shook his head; without realizing it, he had trained his girls too well. 'You should've been a cop.'

'I always left that to Claire – remember she wanted to join the Service?'

'I talked her out of it,' he said and was glad. Five years after it had happened he still had the occasional vivid memory of Peta Smith, one of his Homicide detectives, lying dead with two bullets in her back. The Crime Scene outline of her body had once or twice been an image in a dream in which the wraith of Claire had risen out of the outline. 'What have you dug up so far?'

'Some of the inner branches are stacked – they want to topple the Premier before the Olympics. There are three or four starters who want to be up there on the official dais at the opening

3

ceremony. A billion viewers around the world – they'll never have another spotlight like that.'

'Hans Vanderberg isn't going to let anyone take his place. He's got his own gold medal already minted.'

He stood up, reached across and ruffled her hair. Lately he had been touching his children more, as if getting closer to them as he got closer to losing them. Maureen would be gone from the house before too long; and even Tom, the lover of his mother's cooking, would eventually move out. Malone had hugged them when they were small, then there had been the long period when intimacy had become an embarrassment. He was his own mother's son: Brigid Malone hadn't kissed him since he was eight years old. Con Malone had shaken his son's hand on a couple of occasions; when he saw footballers and cricketers hugging each other he said he wanted to throw up. He actually said *spew*; he never used euphemisms if they were weak substitutions. He never used a euphemism for love, for love was never mentioned. In the Malone family while Scobie was growing up it was just understood that it was *there*. There was no need to mention it.

'Take care.'

She looked up at him; there was love in her smiling eyes and he was touched. 'Don't worry about me, Dad. I'm not going to get in the way of any punches. What are you wearing that old leather jacket for?'

'I've been out for a walk. It's a bit chilly.'

'Throw it out. You look like the back seat of a clapped-out Holden.'

'I had a lot of fun in the back seat of a Holden when I was young.'

'Not with Mum, I'll bet.'

No, not with Lisa. The first time he had had fun with her had been in the back seat of a Rolls-Royce in London when she had been the High Commissioner's private secretary. The glass partition along the back of the front seats had been up and the chauffeur had not heard the heavy breathing. He had been a pretty rough-and-ready lover in those days, his Ned Kelly approach as Lisa had called it, but she had been an experienced teacher. She had taken him a long way from the back-seat-of-a-Holden directness. 'You'd be surprised.'

He went out to the kitchen, where Lisa was making tea, their ritual drink before they went to bed. She was measuring spoons of tea into the china pot; no tea-bags or metal pot for her. The kitchen had been newly renovated, costing what he thought had been the national debt; but anything that made Lisa happy made him happy. He took off his leather jacket and looked at it, a faded relic.

'What d'you think that would bring at St Vincent de Paul?'

'A dollar ninety-five,' said Tom, coming in the back door. 'You're not going to give it away? What about your 24-year-old shoes? Vince de Paul might find a taker for them, too.'

'Pull your head in,' said his father. 'Where've you been tonight?'

'Mind your business,' said Lisa, pouring hot water into the teapot. 'He's been out with a girl. There's lipstick on his ear.'

'There's lipstick on both his ears.'

Tom wiped his ears. 'I told 'em to lay off.'

'Them?'

'There was a girl on each ear. It was supposed to be a double-date tonight, but the other guy didn't turn up.'

The banter was just froth, like that on a cappuccino; but, like the coffee's froth, Malone had a taste for it. They were not the sort of family that boasted it had a *crazy* sense of humour; which, in his eyes, proved it was a family that had no real sense of humour. Instead, the humour was never remarked upon, it was a common way of looking at a world that they all knew, from Malone's experience as a cop, was far from and never would be perfect. The comforting thing, for him, was that they all knew when not to joke.

'I was celebrating,' said Tom. 'I made money today. Those gold stocks I bought a coupla months ago at twenty-five cents,

5

there was a rumour today they've made a strike. They went up twenty cents. I'm rolling in it.'

'He'll be able to keep us,' said Malone. 'I can retire.'

Tom was in his third year of Economics, heading headlong for a career as a market analyst. Last Christmas Lisa's father, who could well afford it, had given each of the children a thousand dollars. Claire had put hers towards a skiing holiday in New Zealand; Maureen had spent hers on a new wardrobe; and Tom had bought shares. He was not greedy for money, but they all knew that some day he would be, as his other grandfather had said, living the life of Riley. Whoever he was.

'You'll never retire.' Tom looked at his mother. 'Would you want him to? While you still go on working?'

'All I want is an excuse.'

Lisa was finishing her second year as public relations officer at Town Hall, handling the city council's part in the Olympic Games. For twenty-two years she had been a housewife and mother; she had changed her pinafore for a power suit, one fitting as well as the other. For the first six months she had found the going slippery on the political rocks of the city council, but now she had learned where not to tread, where to turn a blind eye, when to write a press release that said nothing in the lines nor between them. Whether she would continue beyond the Olympics was something she had not yet decided, but she was not dedicated to the job. When one has no ego of one's own there is suffocation in a chamber full of it.

'If he retires, I retire. We'll go on a world trip and you lot can fend for yourselves.'

Tom looked at them with possessive affection. He was a big lad, taller now than his father, six feet three; heavy in the shoulders and with the solid hips and bum that a fast bowler and rugby fullback needed. He was better-looking than his father and he used his looks with girls. If Riley, whoever he was, had a line of girlfriends, Tom was on his way to equalling him. He had the myopic vision of youth which doesn't look for disappointment.

'How come you two have stayed so compatible?'

'Tolerance on my part,' said both his parents.

'They're so smug,' said Maureen from the doorway.

Then the phone rang out in the hallway. Malone looked at his watch: 11.05. As a cop he had lived almost thirty years on call, but even now there was the sudden tension in him, the dread that one of the children was in trouble or had been hurt: he had too much Celtic blood. Was it Claire calling, had something happened to her?

The ringing had stopped; Maureen had gone back to pick up the phone. A moment or two, then she came to the kitchen doorway:

'It's Homicide, Dad. Sergeant Truach.'

2

'I never take any notice of him,' said the Premier, speaking of the Opposition leader seated half a dozen places along the long top table. 'He's too pious, he's like one of those Americans who were in the Clinton investigation, carrying a Bible with a condom as a bookmark. Of course it's all piss-piety, but some of the voters fall for it. We're all liars, Jack, you gotta be in politics, how else would the voters believe us?'

Jack Aldwych knew how The Dutchman could twist logic into a pretzel. It was what had kept him at the head of the State Labor Party for twenty years. That and a ruthless eye towards the enemy, inside or outside the party.

The Dutchman went on, 'The Aussie voter only wants to know the truth that won't hurt him. He doesn't want us to tell him he spends more on booze and smokes and gambling than he does on his health. So we tell lies about what's wrong with the health system. But you don't have to be a hypocrite, like our mate along the table.'

Aldwych usually never attended functions such as this large

dinner. He had been a businessman, indeed a big businessman: robbing banks, running brothels, smuggling gold. But he had always had a cautionary attitude towards large gatherings; it was impossible to know everyone, to know who might stab you in the back. He was always amused at the Martin Scorsese films of Mafia gatherings, backs exposed like a battalion of targets; but that was the Italians for you and he had never worked with them, not that, for some reason, there had ever been a Mafia in Sydney. Maybe the city had been lucky and all the honest Sicilians had migrated here.

Tonight's dinner, to celebrate the opening of Olympic Tower, was a gathering of the city's elite, though the *crème de la crème* was a little watery around the edges. The complex of five-star hotel, offices and boutique stores had had a chequered history and there was a certain air of wonder amongst the guests that Olympic Tower was finally up and running. There were back-stabbers amongst them, but their knives would not be for Jack Aldwych. This evening he felt almost saintly, an image that would have surprised his dead wife and all the living here present.

He certainly had no fear of this old political reprobate beside him; they were birds of a blackened feather. 'Hans,' he said, 'I have to tell you. I always voted for the other side. Blokes in my old profession were always conservatives. Where would I of been if I'd voted for the common good?'

'Jack,' said Hans Vanderberg, The Dutchman, 'the common good is something we spout about, like we're political priests or something. But a year into politics and you soon realize the common good costs more money than you have in Treasury kitty. The voters dunno that, so you never tell 'em. You pat 'em on the head and bring up something else for 'em to worry about. I think the know-all columnists call it political expediency.'

'Are you always as frank as this?'

'You kidding?' The old man grinned, a frightening sight. He was in black tie and dinner jacket tonight, the furthest he ever escaped from being a sartorial wreck, but he still looked like a bald old eagle in fancy dress. 'You think I'd talk like this to an honest man? I know you're reformed –'

'Retired, Hans. Not reformed. There's a difference. Will you change when you retire?'

'I'm never gunna retire, Jack. That's what upsets everyone, including a lot in our own party. They're gunning for me, some of 'em. They reckon I've reached my use-by date.' He laughed, a cackle at the back of his throat. 'There's an old saying, The emperor has no clothes on. It don't matter, if he's still on the throne.'

Aldwych looked him up and down, made the frank comment of one old man to another: 'You'd be a horrible sight, naked.'

'I hold that picture over their heads.' Again the cackle. He was enjoying the evening.

'Are you an emperor, Hans?'

'Some of 'em think so.' He sat back, looked out at his empire. 'You ever read anything about Julius Caesar?'

'No, Hans. When I retired, I started reading, the first time in my life. Not fiction – I never read anything anybody wrote like the life I led. No, I read history. I never went back as far as ancient history – from what young Jack tells me, you'd think there were never any crims in those days, just shonky statesmen. The best crooks started in the Ren-aiss-ance' – he almost spelled it out – 'times. I could of sat down with the Borgias. I wouldn't of trusted 'em, but we'd of understood each other.'

'You were an emperor once. You had your own little empire.' The Dutchman had done his own reading: police files on his desk in his double role as Police Minister.

'Never an emperor, Hans. King, maybe. There's a difference. Emperors dunno what's happening out there in the backblocks.'

'This one does,' said Hans Vanderberg the First.

Then Jack Aldwych Junior leaned in from the other side of him.

'Mr Premier –' He had gone to an exclusive private school where informality towards one's elders had not been encouraged.

The school's board had known who his father was, but it had not discouraged his enrollment. It had accepted his fees and a scholarship endowment from his mother and taken its chances that his father's name would not appear on any more criminal charges. Jack Senior, cynically amused, had done his best to oblige, though on occasions police officers had had to be bribed, all, of course, in the interests of Jack Junior's education.

'Mr Premier, I've got this whole project up and running while you were still in office –'

'Don't talk as if I'm dead, son.'

Jack Junior smiled. He was a big man, handsome and affable; women admired him but he was not a ladies' man. Like his father he was a conservative, though he was not criminal like his father. He had strayed once and learned his lesson; his father had lashed him with his tongue more than any headmaster ever had. He voted conservative because multi-millionaire socialists were a contradiction in terms; they were also, if there were any, wrong in the head. But this Labor premier, on the Olympic Tower project and all its problems, had been as encouraging and sympathetic as any free enterprise, economic rationalist politician could have been. Jack Junior, a better businessman than his father, though not as ruthless, had learned not to bite the hand that fed you. Welfare was not just for the poor, otherwise it would be unfair.

'I'm not. But there are rumours –'

'Take no notice of 'em, son. I have to call an election in the next two months, but I'll choose my own time. My four years are up –'

'Eight years,' said Jack Senior from the other side.

Vanderberg nodded, pleased that someone was counting. 'Eight years. I'm gunna have another four. *Then* I'll hand over to someone else. Someone *I'll* pick.'

'Good,' said Jack Junior. 'So we'll have you as our guest for the dinner the night before the Olympics open. All the IOC committee have accepted.'

10

'Why wouldn't they? Have they ever turned down an invitation?' He had recognized the International Olympics Committee for what they were, politicians like himself. They were more fortunate than he: they did not have to worry about voters.

He looked around the huge room. It had been designed to double as a ballroom and a major dining room; as often happens when architects are given their head, it had gone to their heads. Opulence was the keynote. Above, drawing eyeballs upwards like jellyfish caught in a net, was a secular version of the Sistine Chapel ceiling. Muscular athletes, male and female, raced through clouds towards a celestial tape; a swimmer, looking suspiciously like a beatified Samantha Riley, breast-stroked her way towards the Deity, who resembled the IOC president, his head wreathed in a halo of Olympic rings. Four chandeliers hung from the ceiling like frozen fireworks; there were marble pillars along the walls; the walls themselves were papered with silk. No one came here for a double burger; nor would the room ever be hired out on Election Night. This was the Olympus Room and though gods were in short supply in Sydney, those with aspiration and sufficient credit would soon be queueing up to enter. Bad taste had never overwhelmed the natives.

Jack Junior privately thought the room was an embarrassment; but he was the junior on the board of directors. Still, it was he who had overseen the guest list for tonight, though it had been chosen by his wife. Class in Sydney is porous; money seeps through it, keeping it afloat. Jack Junior and his wife Juliet had not been hamstrung in making out the list. A certain number of no-talent celebrities had been invited; without them there would be no spread in the Sunday social pages, where their inane smiles would shine like Band-Aids on their vacuous faces. The trade union officials and the State MPs from the battlers' electorates, seated on the outskirts like immigrants waiting to be naturalized, were somewhat overcome by the opulence, but they were battling bravely on. After all, they were here only to represent the workers and the battlers, not enjoy themselves, for Crissakes; their wives

11

smiled indulgently at their husbands' attempts at self-delusion and looked again at the seven-course menu and wondered if the kids at home were enjoying their pizzas. The businessmen from the Big End of town were taking it all for granted, as was their wont and want; economic rationalists had to be admired and paid court to, no matter how irrationally extravagant it might be. Business was just coming out of recession from the Asian meltdown and what better way to celebrate than at someone else's expense? Some of them had dug deep when SOCOG had called for help when the Games funds had sprung a leak. The wives, girlfriends and rented escorts took it all in with a sceptical eye. Tonight, if no other occasion, was Boys' Night Out.

The top table was all men. A female gossip columnist, seated out in the shallows, remarked that it looked like the Last Supper painted by Francis Bacon. But four-fifths of the men up there at the long table were ambitious in a way that the Apostles had never been.

The wives of those at the top table, with their own borrowed escorts, were at a round table just below the main dais. The Premier's wife, who was in her seventies, still made her own dresses, a fact she advertised, but, as the fashion writers said, didn't really need to. Tonight she was in purple and black flounces, looking like a funeral mare looking for a hearse. Sitting beside her was Roger Ladbroke, the Premier's press minder, hiding his boredom with the whole evening behind the smile he had shown to the media for so many years. Beside him was Juliet, Jack Junior's wife, all elegance and knowing it. Her dress was by Prada, her diamond necklace by Cartier and her looks by her mother, who had been one of Bucharest's most beautiful women and had never let her three daughters forget it. Juliet's escort was her hairdresser, lent for the evening by his boyfriend.

'Mrs Vanderberg,' said Juliet, leaning across Ladbroke and giving him a whiff of Joy, 'it must be very taxing, being a Premier's wife. All these functions –'

'Not at all.' Gertrude Vanderberg had never had any political or social ambitions. She was famous in political circles for her pumpkin pavlovas, her pot plants and her potted wisdom. She had once described an opponent of her husband's as a revolutionary who would send you the bill for the damage he had caused; it gained the man more notoriety than his attempts at disruption. 'Hans only calls on me when there's an election in the wind. The rest of the time I do some fence-mending in the electorate and I let him go his own way. Politicians' wives in this country are expected to be invisible. Roger here thinks women only fog up the scene.'

'Only sometimes.' Ladbroke might have been handsome if he had not been so plump; he had spent too many days and nights at table. He had been with Hans Vanderberg over twenty years and wore the hard shell of those who know they are indispensable.

'I think you should spend a season in Europe,' said Juliet.

'In Bucharest?' Gert Vanderberg knew everyone's history.

'Why not? Roumanian men invented the revolving door, but we women have always made sure we never got caught in it.' You knew she never would. She looked across the table at the Opposition leader's wife: 'Mrs Bigelow, do you enjoy politics?'

Enid Bigelow was a small, dark-haired doll of a woman who wore a fixed smile, as if afraid if she took it off she would lose it. She looked around for help; her escort was her brother, a bachelor academic useless at answering a question like this. She looked at everyone, the smile still fixed. 'Enjoy? What's to enjoy?'

Juliet, a woman not given to too much sympathy, suddenly felt sorry she had asked the question. She turned instead to the fourth woman at the table.

'Madame Tzu, do women have influence in politics in China?'

Madame Tzu, who had the same name as an empress, smiled, but not helplessly. 'We used to.'

13

'You mean Chairman Mao's wife, whatever her name was?'

'An actress.' Madame Tzu shook her head dismissively. 'She knew the lines, but tried too hard to act the part – and she was a poor actress. Is that not right, General?'

Ex-General Wang-Te merely smiled. He and Madame Tzu were the mainland Chinese partners in Olympic Tower, but there had been no room for them at the top table. Foreign relations had never been one of The Dutchman's interests and it certainly had never been one of Jack Aldwych's. Aware that everyone was looking at him he at last said, 'I haven't brought my hearing-aid,' and sank back into his dinner suit like a crab into its shell. He knew better than to discuss politics in another country, especially with women.

'Ronald Reagan was an actor,' said Juliet.

'He knew the words,' said Ladbroke. 'He just didn't know the rest of the world.'

'You're Labor. You would say that.'

And you're Roumanian, cynical romantics. But he knew better than to say that. Instead, he gestured up towards the top table. 'Your husband and your father-in-law seem to be doing all right with Labor.'

The Aldwyches, father and son, were leaning back with laughter at something the Premier had said. He was grinning, evilly, some might have thought, but it was supposed to be with self-satisfaction. Which some might have thought the same thing.

Then he looked down at the man approaching them through the shoal of tables. 'Here comes the Greek, bare-arsed with gifts.'

'Do we beware?' Jack Aldwych had had experience of The Dutchman's mangling of the language, but he had learned to look for the grains of truth in the wreckage. This Greek coming up on to the dais was not one bearing gifts.

He came up behind Vanderberg, raised a hand and Aldwych looked for the knife in it. But it came down only as a slap on the shoulder. 'Hans, I gotta hand it to you.'

'Hand me what?' Then he waved a hand at the two Aldwyches.

'You know my friends, salt of the earth, both of 'em.' The salt of the earth looked suitably modest. 'This is Peter Kelzo. He gives me more trouble than the Opposition ever does.'

'Always joking,' Kelzo told the Aldwyches: he was the sort who could take insults as compliments.

He was a swarthy man, almost as wide as he was tall, but muscular, not fat. Born Kelzopolous, he had come to Australia from Greece in his teens thirty years ago, found the country teeming with Opolouses and shortened his name to something that the tongue-twisted natives could pronounce. Built as he was, he had had no trouble getting a job as a builder's labourer; shrewd as he was he was soon a union organizer, though his English needed improving. Within ten years his English was excellent and his standing almost as good, though at times it looked like stand-over. He belatedly educated himself in history and politics. He read Athenian history, aspired to be like Demosthenes but knew that the natives suspected orators as bullshit artists and opted to work with the quiet word or the quiet threat. He did not drift into politics, but sailed into it; but only into the backwaters. By now he had his own building firm and other interests, was married, had children, wanted money in the bank, lots of it, before he wanted Member of Parliament on his notepaper. He ran the Labor Party branch in his own electorate and now he was ready to wield his power.

He looked around him, then at Aldwych. He had been one of the subcontractors on the project, though Aldwych did not know that. 'It's a credit to you. I gotta tell you the truth, I was expecting casino glitz. But no, this is classical –' He looked around him again. 'Class, real class.'

'A lifelong principle of my father,' said Jack Junior. 'That right, Dad?'

'All the way,' said Aldwych, who couldn't remember ever having principles of any sort.

Kelzo gave them both an expensive width of expensive caps: he knew Jack Senior's history. 'Just like Hans here.' He patted the Premier's shoulder again. 'You've never lost your class, have you, Hans?'

'Class was something invented by those who didn't have it,' said Vanderberg. 'Oscar the Wild said that.'

'I'm sure he did,' said Kelzo and tried desperately to think of something that Demosthenes or Socrates might have said, but couldn't. Instead, he leaned down, his hand still on the Premier's shoulder, and whispered, 'Enjoy it, Hans. It won't last.'

Then he was gone, smile taking in the whole room, and Jack Junior said, 'I've read Oscar Wilde. I can't remember him saying anything like that.'

'I've never read him,' said Vanderberg. 'But neither has Kelzo. The Greeks haven't read anything out of England since Lord Byron.' Then he turned full on to Jack Junior, the grin almost as wide as Kelzo's smile had been. 'I haven't read anything of him, either. Poets and philosophers don't help us with the voters – Roger Ladbroke keeps me supplied with all the potted wisdom I need. If I started quoting Oscar Wilde, the only voters who'd clap for me would be the homosexuals up in Oxford Street and the arty-crafties in Balmain and they vote for me anyway, 'cause they think I'm a character. The rest of the voters in this city have had it so good for so long, they ain't interested in philosophy or smart sayings, not unless they hear it in some TV comedy. The people out in the bush, they're philosophers, they gotta be to survive, and they're the ones gimme the difference that keeps me in power. I'm the first Labor premier they've ever liked. They think I'm a character, too.'

'And are you?' asked Aldwych Senior from his other side.

The Dutchman turned to him. 'You'll have to ask my minder down there. Roger –' he raised his voice, leaning forward to speak to Ladbroke – 'am I a character? Mr Aldwych wants to know.'

'Every inch,' said Ladbroke, who at times had had to keep the character in recognizable shape.

Further down the top table from the Premier were Bevan

16

Bigelow, the Leader of the Opposition, and Leslie Chung, a senior partner in Olympic Tower.

'Have you ever voted for him?' asked Bigelow, nodding up towards the middle of the table.

'No.' Leslie Chung, like Jack Aldwych, was now respectable, but his past was tainted. He was a good-looking man, still black-haired in his sixties, with the knack of looking down his nose at people taller than himself. Tonight, acting benevolent, he was looking eye to eye with Bigelow. 'But I've never voted for you, either. I give money to both parties, but I vote for the guy with the least chance of stuffing everything up. Some Independent. It amuses me.'

'Does that come from being Chinese?'

Bigelow was a short, squat man with a blond cowlick and a habit of shifting nervously in his seat as if it were about to be snatched away from him; which also applied to his electoral seat, where his hold was marginal. Les Chung, on the other hand, sat with the calmness of a lean Buddha, as sure of himself as amorality could make him. He had made his fortune by turning his back on scruples and now, on the cusp between middle and old age, he was not going to take the road to Damascus. Or wherever one saw the light here amongst the barbarians.

'No, it comes from having become an Australian.' He had been here forty-three years; he didn't say the locals still amused him. 'Even though we call Hans The Dutchman, you couldn't get anyone more Australian than him, could you?'

'I don't know.' Bigelow looked puzzled, a not uncommon expression with him. 'He's not friendly, like most Australians. He's got no friends in his own party, you know that?'

Chung knew that Bigelow had few friends in *his* party; he was a stop-gap leader because his opponents couldn't agree amongst themselves whom they wanted to replace him. 'I don't think it worries him, Bev. They'll never put a dent in that shell.'

Bigelow nodded at the Aldwyches. 'How do you get on with

your partners? When old Jack dies, he's getting on, who takes charge?'

'We've never discussed it. It would be between me and Jack Junior, I suppose. I think I'd get it.' He smiled, 'I'm sure I'd get it. There are other partners, the Chinese ones.' He nodded down towards Madame Tzu and General Wang-Te. 'They'd vote for me.'

'A Chinese Triad?'

'No, just a trio.'

'There's another partner, isn't there?' He could never find a policy to pursue, but his mind was a vault of facts. 'Miss Feng?'

Les Chung looked down at the beautiful girl seated at one of the lower tables with a handsome young Caucasian escort. If he were younger he might have asked her to be his concubine. And smiled to himself at what her Australian answer would have been.

'We Chinese stick together. How do you think you'll go when Hans announces the election?'

'That will depend on his own party hacks. He has more enemies than I have.' Though he spoke without conviction.

'Yes,' said Les Chung, but seemed to be talking to himself.

The evening was breaking up. The Premier and the Aldwyches rose at the top table. Throughout the rest of the room there was a stirring, like the crumbling of two hundred claypans. The waiters and waitresses restrained themselves from making get-the-hell-out-here gestures.

'We'll see you to the door,' said Jack Junior. 'Your car has been ordered. My wife will look after Mrs Vanderberg.'

The offical party moved amongst the tables almost like deity; no one genuflected, but almost everyone rose to his feet. *His* feet: the women, no vestal virgins, remained seated. The Dutchman smiled on everyone like a blessing; if the grimace that was his smile resembled a blessing. He stopped once or twice to shake hands: not with party hacks but with backers of the Other Party: he knew he was being watched by Bevan Bigelow. He

18

introduced Jack Aldwych to the Police Commissioner and the two men shook hands across a great divide while The Dutchman watched the small comedy. There was no one to equal him in throwing opposites together. He did not believe that opposites attract but that they unsettled the compass. It was others who needed the compass: he had known his direction from the day he had entered politics.

Then they were out in the foyer, heading for the doors and the wide expanse of marble steps fronting the curved entrance. Juliet paused to help Mrs Vanderberg with her wrap, another home-made garment, like a purple pup-tent. The two Aldwych men went out through the doors with the Premier, one on either side of him. They paused for a moment while the white government Ford drew in below them. Beyond was the wide expanse of George Street, the city's main street, thick with cinema and theatre traffic.

The hum of the traffic silenced the sound of the shot.

3

'They've taken him to St Sebastian's,' said Phil Truach. 'It looks bad, the bullet got him in the neck.'

'Where's his wife?'

'She's gone to the hospital. We sent two uniformed guys to keep an eye on things there.'

Malone, Russ Clements and Truach were standing on the steps outside the hotel's main entrance. Crime Scene tapes had replaced the thick red ropes that had held back the hoi polloi as the dinner guests had arrived. The hoi polloi were still there, cracking jokes and making rude remarks about the two women officers running out the tapes. Most of the crowd were young, had come from the cinema complexes further up the street or the games parlours; they had come from paying to see violence on the screens and here it was for free. But soon they would be bored, the body gone. Even the blood didn't show up on the maroon marble.

'Who got shot?'

'That old guy, the Premier, Whatshisname.'

'A politician! Holy shit! Clap, everyone!'

Everyone did and Malone said, 'Let's go inside. Are the Aldwyches still here?'

'In the manager's office.'

'What about the dinner guests? I read there were going to be a thousand of them.'

'We got rid of them through the two side entrances. You never saw such a skedaddle, you'd of thought World War Three had started.'

Inside the hotel lobby Malone looked around; it was the first time he had been in the building since halfway through its construction. On one of its upper floors a Chinese girl student had tried to shoot him and had been shot dead by Russ Clements. 'This place is jinxed.'

'Keep it to yourself.' Clements was the supervisor, second-in-command to Malone of Homicide and Serial Violent Crime Agency. He was a big man, bigger than Malone, who lumbered through life at his own pace. He had once been impatient, but experience had taught him that patience, if not a virtue, was not a vice. 'Otherwise the IOC will cancel all its bookings.'

'Phil,' said Malone to Truach, 'let me know what the Forensic fellers come up with. Where did the shot come from?'

'They're still working on that.' Truach was a bony man, tanned tobacco-brown. He looked Indian, but his flat drawl had no subcontinent lilt. 'The guess is that it didn't come from a car. There's no parking allowed out there and the traffic was moving too fast for someone to take a pot-shot at the Premier. How would they know to be right opposite the hotel just as he came out? Ladbroke, his minder, told me there was no set time for the Premier to leave. His car was on stand-by.'

'It could've been a drive-by shooting, some hoons aiming to

wipe out a few silvertails. There was a horde of them here tonight, the silvertails.'

'Maybe,' said Truach doubtfully. 'But if that's the case, I think I'll take early retirement. It's not my world.'

'Where's Ladbroke now?' asked Clements.

'Here,' said Ladbroke, coming in the front doors behind them. In the past hour he appeared to have lost weight; he was haggard, his shirt rumpled, his jacket hanging slackly. 'I've just come from the hospital, I've left my assistant to hold off the vultures. I want to know what's happening here.'

'How is he?'

'They're preparing him for surgery. It doesn't look good.'

The big lobby was deserted but for police and several hotel staff standing around like the marble statues in the niches in the lobby walls. Malone didn't ask where the guests were; the less people around, the better. Keep them in their rooms, especially any Olympic committee visitors. 'Roger, did the Old Man have many enemies?'

Ladbroke was visibly upset at what had happened to his master, but he was case-hardened in politics: 'Come on, Scobie. He's got more enemies than Saddam Hussein.'

'I had to ask the question, Roger. Cops aren't supposed to believe what they read in the newspapers. Let's go and talk to the Aldwyches.'

The manager's office was large enough to hold a small board meeting. Its walls held a selection of paintings by Australian artists; nothing abstract or avant-garde to frighten the guests who might come in here to complain about the service or the size of their bill. There were more scrolls and certificates than there were paintings, and Malone wondered how a hotel that had opened its doors only last week had managed recognition so quickly.

The manager must have seen Malone's quizzical look because he said, 'Those are diplomas for our staff, our chefs, etcetera. And myself. And you are –?'

21

Malone introduced himself and Clements. 'And you are?'

'Joseph Bardia.' He was tall and distinguished-looking, a head waiter who had climbed higher up the tree.

'From Rome,' said Jack Aldwych.

'Paris, London and New York,' added Bardia.

'May we borrow your office, Mr Bardia? We won't be long.'

Bardia looked as if he had been asked could the police borrow his dinner jacket; he looked at Aldwych, who just smiled and raised a gentle thumb. 'Don't argue with him, Joe. Outside. I'll see he doesn't pinch the diplomas.'

Bardia somehow managed a return smile; he hadn't forgotten his years as a waiter. 'Be my guests.'

He went out, closing the door behind him and Jack Junior said, 'Dad, you don't treat hotel managers like that. Two-hundred-thousand-a-year guys aren't bellhops.'

'I'll try and remember that,' said Jack Senior; then looked at Malone and Clements. 'Looks like the jinx is still working.'

'Just what I said, Jack,' said Malone and sat down on a chair designed for the bums of 500-dollars-a-night guests. 'You and Jack Junior were lucky.'

'Do you think the bullet was meant for either of you?' asked Clements. The big man had sat down on a couch beside Jack Junior; the elder Aldwych sat opposite Malone. 'The bullet might of been off-target.'

Aldwych shook his head. 'We're spotless, Russ. Since we finally got Olympic Tower up and running, nobody's troubled us.'

'And we've troubled nobody,' said Jack Junior.

'What about the past?' said Malone. 'Jack, you've got enemies going back to Federation. Now you're top of the tree, respectable, retired from the old game, what if someone decided he had to pay off old scores?'

Aldwych shook his head. 'I don't think so, Scobie. The old blokes who had it in for me, they're all gone. I'm history, Scobie, and so are they. The new lot –' he shook his head again – 'the

22

Lebanese, the Viets, they wouldn't bother with me. They're too busy doing each other.'

Malone looked at Ladbroke, who had gone round the big desk and sat in the manager's chair. He was still shaken by what had happened to The Dutchman, but half a lifetime of working in politics had built its own armour. 'Okay, like I said, the Old Man has enemies. They want to get rid of him before he calls the election, but they wouldn't want to *shoot* him. That would only queer their own pitch.'

'Why?'

'They'd become the first suspects. Who'd vote for them if you proved anything against them?'

'If we prove anything against them, they won't be running for office. We want a list of all those who've been working to toss the Premier.'

Ladbroke frowned. 'I can give you a list, but you won't let 'em know where you got it? I've already been approached to work for them if they get rid of Hans.'

Malone looked at the other three men, raised his eyebrows. 'Aren't you glad we aren't in politics? *Would* you work for them, Roger?'

'No,' said Ladbroke, managing to look hurt that he should be thought venal. 'But I wouldn't tell them that till I'd found another job. And though the Old Man's been a pain in the arse at times, I don't think I could work for anyone else, not after him.'

'You'd be lost out of politics,' said Malone, and Ladbroke nodded. 'What happens if he doesn't recover? He probably won't, not with a bullet in his neck at his age. Not enough to go back to work.'

'Then the Deputy Premier will call the election – it's got to be called, two months at the latest, in March. Our time's up.'

'That's what Hans said tonight,' said Aldwych. 'That his – enemies, we call 'em that? – they reckon his time was up, he'd reached his use-by date.'

'Is the Deputy Premier one of the enemies?' Malone had had no

23

experience of Billy Eustace. He had slid in and out of ministerial portfolios with hardly anyone noticing. He had never held any of the law-and-order portfolios.

Ladbroke pursed his lips. Those in political circles, whether politicians or minders, are wary of discussion with outsiders. Discussion and argument are food and drink to them, but they don't like to share it. 'Billy Eustace? He could be, but I don't know that he has the troops. And he'd never hire a hitman, not unless he got a discount and fly-buy coupons. Billy has the tightest fist I've ever come across.'

'Oh, I dunno,' said Clements, but didn't look at Malone. 'Jack, can we eliminate you and Jack Junior for the time being?'

'For as long as you like,' said Aldwych.

Ladbroke stood up. 'I'd better get back to the hospital. If the Old Man dies –' He bit his lip; it was a moment before he went on: 'I'll let you know right away. Then get the bastard – whether the Old Man lives or dies!'

It was the first time Malone had seen Ladbroke raised out of his laid-back, almost arrogant calm. 'We'll do that. If he regains consciousness, then tomorrow we'll have to talk to him.'

'You'll have to talk to Mrs Vanderberg. She's running things now.'

'How's she taking it?'

'Badly, I think. But she's hiding it. She's as tough as the Old Man. The bastards who wanted to get rid of him should remember that.'

He went out and Malone and Clements stood up to follow him. 'Take care, Jack.'

'You can be sure of it,' said Aldwych.

Out in the lobby one of the Physical Evidence team was waiting. 'We think we've found where the shot came from.'

'Where?'

Sam Penfold was the same age as Malone but looked older. His hair was grey and his thin eyes already faded, as if the search for clues had worn them out. He collected spoor like a hunter, which

24

was what he was. 'Across the road. There's a row of shops, half a dozen or so, rising three storeys. There's a common entrance that leads up to the first and second floors, with a corridor running along the back, connecting them. The rooms above the shops are mostly single tenants. A quick-job printer, a watch and jewelry repair shop, things like that. And –'

Why, wondered Malone, were so many cops these days using theatrical pauses? Were they all training for TV auditions?

'And an alterations and repairs business, the Sewing Bee. It had been broken into. From its street windows you look right across George Street to the steps outside there.' He nodded towards the hotel's front. 'A good marksman with a good 'scope couldn't miss.'

'He did miss,' said Clements. 'Or close enough. The Premier isn't dead.'

'You got anyone over there?' asked Malone.

'Norma Nickles is there and I'm going back. We'll have the place dusted and printed in time to give you prints in the morning. I'm not hopeful, though. We had time to try the door that had been busted. The door-knob was clean, so the guy was probably wearing gloves. All we'll find, I'm afraid, are prints from the staff and customers.'

'Why are you buggers always so cheerful?'

'We're bloodhounds. You ever see a cheerful bloodhound?'

He left and Malone turned as he saw Bardia, the manager, approaching. He had the look of a man who wished he were back in Rome or Paris or London.

'Finished, Inspector?'

'No, Mr Bardia. Just beginning.'

Guests who had been out on the town or visiting friends were coming back, entering the lobby with some apprehension and puzzlement at the sight of the uniformed police and the blue-and-white tapes still surrounding the outside steps. Bardia saw them and smiled reassuringly, as if it was all just part of the hotel's service.

25

Then he turned back to the two detectives. 'The police will be here for – days?' He made it sound like *months*.

'No. Tomorrow, yes. But after that things should be back to normal for you.' Then he looked beyond the manager into a side room off the lobby. 'Excuse me.'

He crossed the lobby into the side room and Clements, left stranded, took a moment to recover before he followed him. Les Chung, Madame Tzu and General Wang-Te looked up as the two Homicide men approached. They all had the bland look that Malone, a prejudiced cynic, thought only Orientals could achieve.

'We meet again.' Two years before he had met Madame Tzu and General Wang-Te on a case that had threatened to ruin any chance of Olympic Tower's being a successful venture. The same case on which the Chinese girl, screaming at him, un-bland as a cornered animal, had tried to kill him. 'Murder seems to bring us together.'

'Is he dead?' The bland look dropped from Les Chung's face.

'No, but he may soon be – they're not hopeful. It was attempted murder.'

'It wasn't – what do you call it? – a drive-by shooting? A random attack?'

Madame Tzu might have been asking if the Premier had been attacked by a wasp. It was impossible to tell her age within ten years either side of the true figure; but whatever it was, she wore it well. She had a serenity that was a sort of beauty in itself; men would always look at her, though not always with confidence. Men, particularly the natives, tend to be cautious with serene women: it is another clue in the feminine puzzle. She wore a simply cut gold dinner dress, a single strand of black pearls and an air that didn't invite intimacy.

'No, Madame Tzu, it wasn't a random shooting. They knew whom they were after. You and General Wang are staying here at the hotel?'

General Wang-Te had sat silent, not moving in his chair. He was a bony man on whom the skin was stretched tight. Last time Malone had met him he had worn cheap, round-rimmed spectacles that appeared to be standard government issue in China then; tonight he wore designer glasses, rimless with gold sidebars, Gucci on the Great Wall. As he looked up at Malone the light caught the lens, so that he appeared sightless.

'The general is,' said Madame Tzu. 'We're directors, remember.'

'Owners,' said Wang-Te, speaking for the first time.

'Where are you staying?' Malone asked Madame Tzu.

'I still have my apartment in the Vanderbilt. I'm not a hotel person.' She made it sound as if five-star hotels were hostels for the homeless.

Clements spoke to Chung. 'Have you had any threats against the hotel, Les?'

Chung was one of the richest men in the city, but the two detectives knew his past history. Years ago, before Clements had joined Homicide, he had arrested Leslie Chung on fraud charges. Chung had got off, but ever since he had been Les and not Mr Chung. Arrest doesn't breed friendship but it makes for a kind of informality. It is a weapon police officers always carry.

Chung shrugged as if he had been facing threats all his life; they were dust on the wind. 'One or two. The usual nutters – anti-development, anti-foreign investment, that sort of stuff. But they don't go around *shooting* people.'

'Then you'd say this had nothing to do with the hotel? Or the whole Olympic Tower project?'

'Nothing,' said Chung, and Madame Tzu and Wang-Te together added a silent nod.

'Do you have any enemies in China?' Malone asked them.

They didn't look at each other; it was Madame Tzu who said, 'Of course. Who can claim that in one point two billion people all of them are friends?'

She's smothering her answer with figures. 'So, eliminating all

27

the nutters and the one point two billion of your countrymen, would you say the shooting was political?'

The three Chinese gave him a blank stare: the Great Wall of China, he thought. He wanted to scrawl the *graffiti* of a rough remark on the Wall, but that would be racist. Not, he was sure, that any of them would care.

At last Les Chung said, 'I think it would be politic to say nothing.'

Madame Tzu and General Wang-Te, like intelligent puppets, nodded.

Malone grinned at Clements. 'Wouldn't our job be easy if cops could be politic?'

'Let's go home,' said the big man. 'I'm tired.'

When the two detectives had gone, Madame Tzu said, 'If Mr Vanderberg dies, what happens?'

'Nothing that will affect us,' said Les Chung. 'Our bookings are solid till after the Olympics. By then the whole complex will have established itself.'

General Wang-Te was wishing he knew more of history beyond the Middle Kingdom. The history of this country where he sat now had begun only yesterday. 'Do Australians do much political assassination?'

'All the time,' said Les Chung, who knew nothing of the Middle Kingdom, but knew even the footnotes in the history of his adopted country. He was not a man to put his foot into unknown territory. 'But only with words, not with bullets or knives. To that extent they are civilized.'

'What a wonderful country,' said Wang-Te and sounded almost wistful.

4

Out in the lobby Malone said, 'Let's go across the road and look at that place – the Sewing Bee?'

They crossed the road with the traffic lights. Traffic was six deep across the roadway stretching back several hundred metres; a drive-by, random shooting in this congestion was not even a theory. They walked up to the row of shops opposite the huge block of Olympic Tower. The footpath still had its late-night crowd, mostly young; groups moving slowly with arrogance and loud voices, challenging with their shoulders, high on group courage. One of them shouldered Clements, an oldie, and the big man grabbed him and swung him round.

He shoved his badge in the youth's face. 'You wanna try that again, son? Just you and me, not your army?'

The youth was as tall as Clements, but half his weight. He wore a baseball cap, peak backwards: it seemed to accentuate the blankness of his face. He had stubbled cheeks and chin and a mouth hanging open with shock. His big eyes flicked right and left, but he was getting no support from his six companions. They had no respect for the police badge, but Clements, despite his age (Jesus, he must be *middle*-aged!), looked big and dangerous.

At last the youth said, 'Sorry, mate. I slipped.'

'We all do that occasionally,' said Malone. 'Let him go, Assistant Commissioner. He's only young and not very bright.'

Clements let go the youth and walked on beside Malone. 'Assistant Commissioner?'

'You think kids are impressed by a senior sergeant? He'll live for a week on how he tried to push an assistant commissioner out of the way.'

'I hope none of the seven Assistant Commissioners get to hear of it.'

The entrance to the rooms above the shops was between a pinball parlour and a shabby coffee lounge. They climbed the narrow stairs and came to a long lighted corridor that ran along the back of the half a dozen offices. They passed the Quick Printery; R. Heiden, Watch & Jewelry Repairs; and Internet Sexual Therapy. They came to the open door of the Sewing Bee.

The alterations centre had two rooms side by side, both with windows opening on to George Street. Sam Penfold and Norma Nickles were in the main room with a woman with close-cropped hair and a belligerent expression, as if she blamed the police for breaking into her establishment.

'This is Mrs Rohani, the owner,' said Penfold. 'We called her and she's come in from Kensington.'

'Anything stolen?' Malone asked.

'Yes!' Mrs Rohani had a softer voice than Malone had expected; breathy, as if every word had to be forced out. 'He took my strongbox, twelve hundred dollars. Out of my desk. He forced the drawer open.'

Malone scanned the room. Clothes hung on long racks, queues from which the flesh-and-blood had been squeezed; dresses, jackets and trousers waiting to see *The Invisible Man*. There were four sewing machines, all with that abandoned look that equipment gets when its operators have gone home. On a wall was a big blow-up of a *Vogue* cover, circa 1925, like a faded icon.

Malone looked back at Penfold. 'Any prints on the desk?'

Penfold in turn looked at Norma Nickles, who said, 'There are prints everywhere, but I dunno whether they are his. Mrs Rohani has four girls working here and clients come in all day, men as well as women.'

She was a slim, blond girl who looked even slimmer in the dark blue police blouson and slacks. She had been a ballet dancer and occasionally she had a slightly fey look to her, as if adrift on Swan Lake. But she could gather evidence like a suction pump and Malone knew that Sam Penfold prized her as one of his team.

'I've come up with something on that window-sill, though. A distinctive print and Mrs Rohani remembers the man it belongs to.' She led Malone to the window, pointed to the sill that had been powdered. 'Four fingers, the tip of the third finger missing – he must of leaned on the sill as he looked out. Mrs Rohani remembers him being interested in looking across at Olympic

Tower, though she says he wasn't the first and he probably won't be the last.'

Malone turned back to the owner. 'What was he like? When did he come in?'

'Three – no, four days ago. Man about forty, my height, on the stout side but not much. That was why he was here, wanted his pants taken out. Brought 'em in last week—' She took a puffer out of her handbag, sucked on it. She was an asthmatic: the situation had taken the breath out of her. She put the puffer away, went on, 'He came in four days ago to pick 'em up. Both times he walked across to the window, said how much he admired Olympic Tower. Said he used to be an architect. If he was, he couldn't of been too successful. His pants were fifty-five dollars off the rack at Gowings. People come in here, I know more about 'em than the census-taker.'

Malone wondered what she thought of him in the Fletcher Jones blazer and polyester-and-wool trousers bought at a sale, his usual shopping time, three hundred dollars the lot, free belt and socks. Did she guess he turned lights out when people were not using them, just lying there, thinking?

'We'll need a list of all your clients for the past month,' said Clements.

Mrs Rohani looked dubious. 'Ooh, I dunno. I've got some prominent people, they come in here, they don't want it known they're having alterations. You know, their hips have spread, the men's bellies have got bigger –'

'I'll know where to come,' said Clements. 'But in the meantime we need that list. We don't put confidential information on the Internet –'

'Women as well as men clients?'

'Everyone. Their names and addresses. Particularly that man with the fingerprints on the window-sill.'

'How long will it take you to trace him if he has form?' Malone asked Penfold.

'Once back at the computer, six minutes, anywhere in Australia.'

31

Malone, a technological idiot, marvelled at the way the world was going. 'Remember the old days?'

Then his pager buzzed. 'May I use your phone, Mrs Rohani?'

He crossed to the phone on a nearby desk, dialled Homicide. He listened to Andy Graham, the duty officer, then hung up and looked at Clements and the other two officers.

'The Premier's dead. He died twenty minutes ago on the operating table.'

Mrs Rohani took out her puffer again, sucked hard on it. Malone had a sudden feeling that air had been sucked out of the city.

Chapter Two

1

Claire rang next morning at 7.15. 'I've just heard the news on the radio. The Premier – it's unbelievable!'

'It's a shock,' said Malone, but didn't sound as if it was too much of a shock. He was not callous, but he had grown accustomed to murder and the circumstances of it. 'It's going to shake things up a bit.'

'Is it what!' Then she said, and he caught the cautious note in her voice: 'Are you on the case?'

'Yes. Why?' She said nothing and he got impatient with her: 'Come on, Claire! Why are you asking?'

'Haven't I always asked?'

Women! Daughters and wives in particular: 'Don't start sounding like your mother –'

Lisa came down the hallway, paused and gave him the look that only wives and long-time lovers can conjure up. He put his hand over the mouthpiece.

'It's your daughter –'

'I gathered that. Why is she sounding like me?'

He waved her on; not dismissively, for Lisa would never take dismissal. She raised her middle finger, said, 'Is that the right gesture?' and went on out to the kitchen.

'Who was that?' asked Claire.

'Your mother. Come on – why are you so concerned that I'm on the case?'

'Dad –' He could see her, usually so articulate, fumbling with words at the other end of the line. Perhaps if she were still living at home she would be more direct; moving out had widened the distance between them in more ways than one. He could no longer read her face, not at the end of a phone line. 'Dad – yesterday – I don't think I should be telling you this –'

'Righto, I'll hang up. But if I find you're withholding evidence of any sort –'

'You would, wouldn't you?'

'Bring you in?' He sighed. 'Yes, I think I would.'

'Well –' He had never known her to be so reluctant to voice an opinion. She had been a lawyer since she was twelve years old: bush lawyer, Bombay lawyer, Philadelphia lawyer: she would have argued with both Jesus Christ and Pontius Pilate. 'Dad, yesterday Norman Clizbe and Jerry Balmoral came into the office – you know them?'

'Only by name. I've never met them.'

They were the secretary and assistant-secretary of the Trades Congress. The Congress had been going for almost a hundred years, a minor opponent of the major union organization, the Labor Council; then suddenly, about twenty years ago, it had found a new lease of life, had grown in strength and influence and now was on a par with the Labor Council in the affairs of the State Labor Party. It had developed a taste for power, like the re-discovery of a long-neglected recipe.

'Mr Clizbe went into the partners' office and Jerry Balmoral came into mine. I think he thought he could do a line with me.'

'Should I say *Yuk*?'

'Go ahead. He's got enough conceit for a talk-back host. Anyway, he chit-chatted, then he said – and I quote –'

A lawyer through and through. 'Go ahead. Quote.'

'"Would your father handle a political murder or would that be a job for the Federal police?"'

'Let me get this straight before you go on. Is this lawyer-client confidentiality?'

'I wouldn't be telling you this if it were. It was chit-chat.'

'Did you ask him why he was asking such a question?'

'Yes. He said it was just a question that had come up in a discussion on police policy.'

'What's a trade union organization doing discussing police policy? Why did he ask *you*?'

'He said he knew I was your daughter.'

'What did you say?'

'About being your daughter? Nothing. But I told him it would be a State police case and I asked him again where the subject had come up.'

'What'd he say to that?'

'He just laughed and I got the charm bit – yuk! He said the question had been asked the other night at a branch meeting.'

'He say which branch?'

'No. He then asked me if I was free for dinner last night. I said no, I got more of the charm bit and he then went into the partners' office. He's such a smartarse.'

'How's Jason?'

'What sort of question is that?'

'I didn't mean *he's* a smartarse – forget it. Keep what you've told me to yourself, don't mention it in your office, especially to your bosses. To nobody, understand?'

'Yes, Inspector.'

'In your eye. Take care.'

He hung up and went out to the kitchen to breakfast. 'What did Claire want?' asked Lisa.

'She just wanted to know if I'm on the Premier's murder.'

'If you are,' said Maureen, 'don't ask me anything we've dug up in our investigation.'

'I'll let Russ drag you in and hang you by your thumbs if we find you know something we don't. Don't expect any favours.'

'Are we going to sit around this table and you're not going to tell us anything?' said Lisa.

'We know nothing at this stage,' said Malone, pouring fat-free milk on his Weet-Bix, then slicing a banana on it. In his younger days he had been a steak-and-eggs man for breakfast, but he had reached an age now when he had to watch that the waistline didn't hide the view of the family jewels. 'Except that he was shot, we think by a hitman.'

'Where from?' asked Tom.

'From a window right across the street,' said Maureen, and Malone gestured at the fount of knowledge, the TV researcher. 'I've been on to our night crew. They were inside, in the ballroom, and missed what went on outside. They didn't even get a shot of the Premier lying on the front steps.'

'Tough titty,' said Malone.

'Your friend, Mr Aldwych, the old guy, threatened to smash our cameraman's face in.'

'Jack was always public-spirited.'

'I don't think you'll have to look outside the Labor Party,' said Tom, reaching for his third piece of toast. 'From what I've read they're cutting each other's throats. They're stacking certain branches with new members, building up cash funds –'

'What are you reading?' asked his father. 'Economics or Politics?'

'These days, our lecturer says, you can't separate them. He's a chardonnay Marxist. I need a new cricket bat.'

'What does a fast bowler need a *new* bat for? I used any old bat lying around. I'll give you mine – Pa's still got it, I think.'

'You're really tight-arsed about money, aren't you? You give a new meaning to anal-retentive.'

'Hear, hear,' said Maureen.

'Does your Marxist lecturer teach you to talk to your dear old dad like that? How much do you want?'

'A hundred and forty bucks. There's a sale on.'

'You're going to be a good economist. You're learning how to spend other people's money.'

36

Then the phone rang again; it was Gail Lee, the duty officer. 'It's on, boss. You're wanted for a conference with senior officers at the Commissioner's office at nine o'clock.'

'Righto, Gail. Tell Russ I want everything collated by the time I get back from Headquarters.'

'Everything? What have we got so far?'

'Bugger-all.' He grinned without mirth to himself; there would not be much smiling over the next week or two. 'But get it all together.'

Tom went off on his bicycle to his holiday work, stacking shelves at Woolworths. Maureen took the family's second car, a Laser, and Malone drove Lisa into town in the Falcon.

'I'm going to be busy.' Her work as public relations officer on the council's Olympic committee was becoming burdensome now as the Games got closer. 'Eight months to the Olympics opening and we have a political assassination. How do I put a nothing-to-worry-about spin on that?'

There were several bad jokes that could answer that, but he refrained. 'We don't know if this has anything to do with the Olympics –'

'I'm not suggesting it has, not directly. But every politician in the State wants to be sitting up there with the IOC bosses when the torch comes into the stadium. Half of them would offer to carry the torch just to have the cameras on them. Hans Vanderberg is up there in Heaven or down in Hell, wherever he's gone –'

'Hell. He's down there now asking the Devil to move over, the real boss has arrived.'

'Wherever. But he's spitting chips to see that someone else is going to take his place. Even Canberra is trying to muscle in. That official dais is going to be so crowded –'

'I can't look that far ahead.'

He kept his place in the middle lane of traffic; road rage was replacing wife-beating as an expression. A young driver in a BMW coupé shouted at him; a girl in a Mazda on his other side yelled something at Lisa. She turned her head and gave the girl a wide smile and what her children called her royal wave, a turning of the hand just from the wrist. The girl replied with a non-royal middle finger.

'Ignore them,' said Malone.

'Who? The drivers?'

'No, the politicians. Whatever you put in your release, don't mention anyone in Macquarie Street. Put your Dutch finger in the dyke and hold it there.'

He dropped her at Town Hall, then drove up to College Street and Police Headquarters. As he entered the lobby he was met by Greg Random, his immediate boss. 'We sit and just listen, Scobie. No comment unless asked.'

Chief Superintendent Greg Random had never been guilty of a loose word, unlike Malone. He was tall and lean and as weather-beaten as if he had just come in from the western plains. He was part-Welsh and though he couldn't sing and had never played rugby nor been down a coal mine, he was fond of reciting the melancholy of Welsh poets.

As they rode up in the lift Malone asked, 'Why here and not Police Centre?'

There was no one else in the lift, so it was safe to be frank and subversive. 'This is His Nibs' castle. Does the Pope go to the Coliseum to declare his encyclicals?'

'We're going to get an encyclical today?'

'You can bet on it.'

The big conference room was full of uniforms and silver braid. Both Random and Malone were in plainclothes, the only ones, and seated in the corner of the room they looked like suspects about to be questioned.

The Deputy Commissioner and all seven Assistant Commissioners were in the room, plus half a dozen Chief Superintendents and five Superintendents. Malone had never seen so much brass since his graduation from the Police Academy. Then Commissioner Zanuch made his entrance.

He never came into a room; he *entered*. He was a handsome man, something he admitted without embarrassment; there was no point in denying the truth of the mirror. He was vain and an ambitious climber amongst the social alps; he was beginning to see himself as a public monument. He was also highly intelligent, remarkably efficient and no one questioned that he was the best man for the position. Commissioner of Police in the State of New South Wales was not for the unconfident. He would always have enemies on both sides of the law.

He sat down at the top of the long table. 'You've read the papers, heard the news, gentlemen. The talk-back hosts have told us how we should conduct the case and they'll get louder as the week goes by. We have never been faced with a case as serious and wide-reaching as this one.'

'We've decided it's political?' Assistant Commissioner Hassett was Commander, Crime Agencies. He came from the old school, the sledgehammer on the door, the boot up the bum, but he was shrewd and he ran his command with a loose rein and a ready whip.

'No, we haven't, Charlie, not yet.' He looked across the room at Random and Malone. 'What have you got so far, Chief Superintendent?'

'Very little, sir. Perhaps Inspector Malone can fill you in.'

Thanks, mate. 'We have a couple of slim leads, sir. A handprint that may turn up something. A man who was in the shop from where the shot was fired, he was there twice this past week admiring the view from the window. We're trying to trace him. I expect to hear from Fingerprints this morning if he's got any record.'

'Have you started questioning anyone yet?'

A few loose words slipped out: 'Macquarie Street, sir? Sussex Street?'

'Oh Gawd,' said Charlie Hassett and six other Assistant Commissioners gave him silent echo.

Commissioner Zanuch was not entirely humourless. 'Inspector

39

Malone, let us fear not to tread, but nonetheless, let us tread. Carefully, if you can.'

'Yes, sir.' Malone felt every eye in the room was on him. 'I think I'd rather be in Tibooburra.' The back of beyond in the Service.

'Wouldn't we all.'

The Commissioner was enjoying the situation; over the next few days his Police Service would be the power in the land. The Government would be fighting its war of succession; the Opposition, seeking backs to stab, suddenly looked up and saw opportunity on the other side of the Assembly. Murder creates a vacuum, no matter how small and for how short a time. The vacuum now was large and Commissioner Zanuch stepped into it, secure that he was the tenant by right.

'Strike force will be set up, unlimited personnel. Call in all the men you want,' he told Hassett.

'What about us?' asked the Assistant Commissioner, Commander Administration, and all his colleagues nodded.

'We're united on this,' said Zanuch. 'A team. This is political – or it's going to be. I presume you've all got your political contacts?'

All the Assistant Commissioners looked at each other before they all nodded. None of them had achieved his rank by virgin birth. The net of political contacts in the room could have strangled a purer democracy than that of the State in which they served. They were honest men but they knew from long experience that honesty was a workable policy, not necessarily the best.

'Work those contacts. If you come up with anything, pass it on to Charlie. What shall we call the task force? We have to give it a name for the media – they love labels. They don't know how to handle anything that's anonymous.'

'How about Gold Medal?' The Assistant Commissioner, VIP Security Services, was a humourist, sour as a lemon. With VIPs, a breed that never diminished, it was difficult to be good-humoured.

'That will only rile the Opposition,' said the Assistant Commissioner, Internal Affairs. 'They could be our bosses in two months.'

'Let's be brutal,' said the Commissioner. 'We'll call it Nemesis.'

'The TV reporters will ask us what that means.'

'Tell 'em it means their channel bosses,' said Charlie Hassett and everyone laughed.

The meeting rolled on and at last Random and Malone were released. They said nothing to each other as they went down in the lift, but as they walked out into the glare of the January day Random said sombrely and unexpectedly, 'We'll miss The Dutchman.'

Malone looked across the street to Hyde Park, where old men played chess and draughts on tables beneath trees. Kibitzers stood behind them, offering advice, like retired minders. Hans Vanderberg had gone before retirement had consigned him to a bench somewhere, playing old games in his mind, surrounded by ghosts he had defeated with every move.

'Where will you set up the Incident Room?'

'At Police Centre. I'll move in there, you report to me direct. Where are you going to start?'

'I don't know, depends what they have for me when I get back to the office.' He sighed. 'Wouldn't it be nice to be on holiday right now? Walking the streets of Helsinki.'

'Why Helsinki?'

'Can you think of anywhere that's further away and still has decent hotels?'

Malone went back to Strawberry Hills, to Homicide's offices. The area had been named after the English estate of Horace Walpole, near-silent member of parliament but compulsive correspondent; he wrote mailbags of letters and Malone sometimes wondered how he would have reacted to the cornucopia of the internet. The offices were spacious and always neat and clean, a tribute to Clements, an untidy man with a contradictory passion for housekeeping, except on his own desk.

41

Phil Truach, looking in need of another one of his forty cigarettes a day, was waiting with good news: 'Fingerprints have traced that hand-print on the window-sill. A guy named August, John August. He did three years for armed robbery down in Pentridge and he'd been acquitted before. He's got enough form.'

'Anything on him recently?'

'The Victorians say they haven't heard of him for nine years. They say on his form he wasn't a hitman, but you never know.'

'Is his name on the Sewing Bee's list of customers?'

Russ Clements had come into Malone's office, taken his usual place on the couch beneath the window. Though the couch was only four years old, he had dented his imprint on it at one end. He gestured at the typewritten list in his hand. 'There's no August. The name here is John June.'

Malone shook his head at the folly of criminals. 'Full of imagination. What's the address?'

'None. Just a phone number.'

He gave it and Malone punched it. He listened for a moment, said, 'Sorry, wrong number,' and hung up. 'Happy Hours Child-Care Centre.'

'What?' said the other two.

Malone repeated it. 'Possible hitman running a day-care centre? It's a switch.' He reached for the phone book, found what he wanted. 'The Happy Hours Child-Care Centre, Longueville. I think I'll take one of the girls with me. That'll look better than two big boof-headed cops turning up to frighten the ankle-biters. What else have you got, Russ?'

'Another list.' Clements held it up. 'All the political bods we should look at. You want boof-headed cops on that?'

'We'd be the only ones they'd understand.' He stood up, sighed. He was sighing a lot these days, as if it were a medical condition. 'I'm not looking forward to the next coupla weeks.'

'It's all in a good cause.'

'Did you ever think you'd say that about The Dutchman?'

'No,' said Clements. 'But the old bugger stood by us when we needed him. I think we owe him.'

Malone collected Gail Lee and drove out to Longueville. Gail, half-Chinese, was slim and good-looking, a shade of coolness short of beautiful and as competent as any man on Malone's staff of nineteen detectives. She drove a little too fast for Malone's comfort, but he would have been a poor passenger with the driver of a hearse.

Longueville is a small suburb on the northern shore of the Lane Cove river, one of the two main rivers that flow into Sydney Harbour. It is now a pleasant area of solid houses in their own grounds, though some of the more modern ones are as conspicuous as circus tents in a cemetery. The suburb is a quiet retreat that has no major highway running through it. Once, long ago, it was thickly wooded with cedar and mahogany and populated, according to gossip of the times, by murderers and other assorted criminals. Today, if there are any criminals in the area, they are hidden behind accountants, the new forest for retreat.

The Happy Hours Child-Care Centre looked as if it might once have been a scouts' or a church hall. It stood in a large yard shaded by two big jacarandas and a crepe myrtle. There were sandpits and playground equipment and a dozen or more small children in the yard. There were shouts of laughter coming from the hall, kids in a happy hour.

While Gail went looking for someone in charge Malone moved into the yard and stood looking at the children there. He was not naturally a child-lover, but the behaviour of the very small always fascinated him. Sometimes, but only occasionally, he saw in them what he would have to face when they grew up. He believed that the bad seed could show in sprouts.

Half a dozen sat in a tight circle under one of the jacarandas, bound by giggles as by a daisy chain. Malone smiled at them and they smiled back.

'You like it here?'

They all nodded, heads under their blue sun-hats going up and down like a circle of semaphores.

Malone looked at the large name-tabs pinned to their yellow smocks. There were Justin and Jared and Jaidene and Alabama and Dakota and Wombat Rose – 'Wombat Rose? That's a nice name.'

She was four or five, a cherub with a wicked glint already in her big blue eyes. 'Me mother wanted to call me Tiger Lily, but that was taken, she said.'

'No, I like Wombat Rose better.' Then he saw the small boy sitting by himself under the other jacaranda and he crossed to him. 'Why are you sitting on your own over here?'

'They won't talk to me.'

'Why?'

''Cos me name's Fred.'

Before Malone could laugh Gail Lee came out of the hall with a woman. 'This is Mrs Masson, the owner.'

She was in her forties and feeling the heat and the children, two pressures that rarely have a woman looking her best. She was good-figured and had thick brown hair and large brown eyes, but today, one guessed, was not one of her good days.

'Police?' She frowned, making another subtraction from her looks. 'What do you want? Here?' She gestured at the innocence around them. 'Has someone been trying to get at the children?'

'Nothing like that, Mrs Masson. We're actually looking for a Mr June. We'd like a word or two with him.'

'John? My partner?'

'He's a partner in the Centre?'

'No, no, he's my partner in that other –' She gestured. 'We live together. De facto, if you like, but I hate the term.'

'Me, too. Where could we find him?'

'What's it about? Go and play, kids.' The children had gathered round the three adults, eyes and ears wide. 'Go and play ball with Fred.'

44

Fat chance. Fred got up and went into the hall, taking his isolation with him.

'We'd just like to ask him some questions –'

'Are you a policeman?' asked Alabama or Dakota.

'Kids –' Mrs Masson was losing patience with the children or the police officers or both – 'inside!'

'Is she a lady cop?' asked Wombat Rose.

'Inside!'

Malone and Gail Lee hid their smiles as the children, taking their time, made their way into the hall. Suddenly the yard was bare, threatening; the playground equipment looked like torture machinery. Mrs Masson said, 'You're not local police, are you?'

'No.' Malone added almost reluctantly: 'We're from Homicide.'

'Homicide?' She frowned again. 'You're investigating a murder or something?' Malone nodded. 'And you want to talk to John about it? Why?'

'We're not accusing him of anything, Mrs Masson.' This route was well-worn: telling the innocent party things they didn't know. 'We think he can throw some light on a case we're working on. How long have you known John?'

'I dunno – five, six years. We've been together ever since I opened this –' she swept an arm around her; it looked as if she wanted to sweep it away – 'four years ago. It's a struggle since the government took money out of child care –'

'John doesn't work here?'

'No, he has his own one-man business – he's a carpenter and general handyman. I can get him on his mobile –'

'No, we don't want you to do that –'

She frowned yet again; then her eyes opened wide. 'It's serious, isn't it? What's he done, for God's sake? Jesus –' She turned; a young Asian girl stood in the doorway of the hall. 'Not now, Ailsa – not now!'

'Mr June is on the phone –'

45

'I'll take it,' said Gail Lee and moved quickly to the doorway, pushed the girl into the hall and disappeared.

Mrs Masson was silent for a long moment. A cicada started up, the first Malone had heard this summer; it was like a drill against the ear. Then Mrs Masson seemed to gulp, as if she were drowning in disappointment. 'What's he done? Are you going to tell me?'

'How much do you know about him? How much has he told you about himself before he met you?'

She walked slowly, almost blindly, across to a backless bench under one of the trees, the seat where Fred had sat in his exclusion. She sat down and Malone sat beside her, straddling the bench. Inside the hall a game had been started, the children laughing like a mocking chorus while the cicada had been joined by what sounded like a hundred others.

'He came from Melbourne, he said he'd been married before but it broke up after a couple of years. He has a mother down there, but I've never met her.'

'Has he been a good – partner? A good husband?'

'I've been married before. John is twice as good as the legal husband I had. I love him – does that answer your question? Now tell me what he's done.'

She looked at him pleadingly, but he turned away as Gail came out of the hall. 'Mr June is on his way. He'll be five minutes – he's coming from Lane Cove.'

'What did you tell him?'

'I said there was some trouble with one of the children.' She looked at Mrs Masson's angry frown. 'I'm sorry –'

The frown now seemed to be permanent, like a scar. 'For Christ's sake, tell me what he's done. You come here, upsetting everyone and everything –'

'We haven't done that, Mrs Masson,' said Malone quietly. 'We've upset you and I'm sorry about that. But no one else. Just let's wait till Mr June gets here.'

They sat, while the laughter and screams came out of the hall

46

and a magpie carolled in the jacaranda above them and a couple of mynahs chattered at it to get lost. The cicadas suddenly shut up and the other sounds seemed to increase. Then abruptly Mrs Masson stood up, looked at her watch, said, 'It's time for their morning snack,' and walked, almost ran, into the hall.

'It's never easy, is it?' said Gail.

'What?'

'Telling them what they don't know. Don't want to know.'

'Never.'

Then two minutes later the van drew up in the street outside. A man got out and came hurrying into the yard. Malone and Gail crossed from the bench to stand in his way as he headed for the hall doorway. 'Mr June?'

He pulled up sharply. 'Yes. Are you the child's parents? What's happened?'

'No, Mr June, we're not.' Malone produced his badge. 'Can we have a word? Over here under the trees.'

June hesitated, then followed them. There was nothing threatening about him, though Malone had not been sure what to expect. He was medium height, running a little to fat, with a round pleasant face and thinning black hair that needed a cut. He was dressed in overalls that, with inserts showing, had been let out at the seams; a pair of gold-rimmed glasses hung on a string round his neck. His left hand had the top joint of the middle finger missing.

'What's the charge?'

'None so far. We just thought you could help us with our enquiries.'

'Shit, that old one!'

'You've heard it before, Mr August?'

For a moment there was no expression at all, as if he were alone without thought. Then abruptly his face clouded, he rolled his lips over his teeth. 'I gave that name away nine years ago –'

'Why?'

'I wanted to make a new start. I've done that –'

Then Mrs Masson came out again into the yard; hurrying, as if running away from the children. She rushed straight at August, grabbed his left hand, stood holding it as if he were another of her charges. 'What's it about, John? What do they want?'

'They just want to ask me some questions. I – I saw something the other day – I didn't tell you about it –'

'What?'

He was a practised liar; he had been living a lie for nine years. 'A couple fighting – they just want me to tell them what I saw –'

'Someone's dead? They said they were from Homicide—' One could almost see her mind racing, she was defending – what? She looked at Malone. 'Is someone dead?'

'Yes. We'll just take Mr – Mr June back to our office. He'll be back here within an hour.'

'Why can't you ask him the questions here?' She was still clinging to his hand. She's a mother, Malone thought, but where are her own kids?

Then the children came spraying out of the hall, a yellow-smocked torrent. Justin, Jared, Jaidene, Alabama, Dakota, Wombat Rose: even Fred joined the circle round the adults. Twenty or thirty other children milled around. They all stared at the adults, innocent as cherubs but ears as wide as devils'. Wombat Rose looked up at Malone and winked at him with both eyes.

'Come on, Mr June. We'll have you back here in an hour.'

'I'll come with you, John –'

He took his hand from hers, put it against her cheek. 'It'll be all right, sweetheart. Don't *worry*, I'll be back, it's *okay*.'

It was difficult to tell if he was trying to tell her something. Was there some secret between them? But she just looked at him blankly, shook her head as if to deny that everything was *okay*.

Malone, Gail Lee and August/June went out of the yard, trailed by a dozen kids as far as the gate. Mrs Masson still stood under the jacaranda tree; the tiny splurge of yellow smocks leaked away from her, leaving her high and dry and alone.

48

August looked back and waved with the hand that was his mark.

'I'll follow you,' he said, moving towards his van.

'No, lock it, John. We'll get you back here.'

'That's a promise?' For a moment something like a smile hovered around his small mouth.

'No, John. Depends what you have to tell us.'

Gail drove the unmarked police car and Malone sat in the back with August. They had been travelling for ten minutes before August broke his silence. 'Now we're away from Lynne, tell me why you've picked me up.'

'We're questioning a list of clients from the Sewing Bee. Your name was on the list.'

He laughed. 'The fat and the thin, a list of all those needing alterations? Come on—' Then he sobered, looked quizzically at Malone. 'This hasn't got something to do with what happened to the Premier last night?'

'What makes you think it has?'

He shook his head. 'You don't catch me like that. Yeah, I was at that place, the alterations centre, what's it called? The Sewing Bee. I remember standing at the window, having a look at the place across George Street, Olympic Tower. What I've read, what was on radio this morning, Hans Vanderberg was standing at the front of the hotel when he was shot, right? He was shot from the Sewing Bee, that what you're saying? So what am I supposed to know?'

He wasn't belligerent, just curious. Malone had met other hitmen and they had all had a characteristic coldness, sometimes blatant, other times subdued. It was a job, with most of them part-time: you killed the target, collected your pay, went home. One or two of them had been show-offs, mug lairs, but they did not last long; sooner or later someone hit them. August, if he was the hitman in the Vanderberg case, was out of character.

There was silence in the car again till they reached the Harbour Bridge, where they were held up by a long bank-up of traffic.

August looked out at the mass of cars and trucks, immobile as rocks.

'Can you imagine what it's gunna be like during the Olympics?'

'I'm leaving town,' said Malone. 'I'm going to Tibooburra.'

'What about you, miss?' August could not be friendlier, more unworried.

'I have seats for all the main events at the stadium.' Gail glanced at Malone in the rear-vision mirror. 'My father bought them. He said we're to be one hundred per cent, dinky-di Aussies for two weeks.'

'I'm one of the fifty thousand volunteer helpers,' said August.

'Doing what?' Shooting whoever is on the official dais on opening day? Malone, against reason, was becoming irritated by August's apparent lack of concern.

'Helping the disabled. Getting them seated, things like that. I like volunteer work. I do Meals on Wheels in my van once a week.'

Are we bringing in the wrong bloke? But you had to start somewhere and this man was the only one with a record. Malone made no comment and they drove the rest of the way to Strawberry Hills in silence. As they rode up in the lift to Homicide's offices August said, 'You're making a mistake, you know.'

'We sometimes do, John. But once we've eliminated them, we usually come up with the right answer.'

'Are there any reporters here?'

'We don't encourage them.'

'Do me a favour? After I've convinced you I know nothing about all this, don't let them know you've had me in here. I want to protect Lynne and her day-care centre.'

Gail took August into one of the interview rooms and Malone went into his office to see what was on his desk. Clements followed him. 'Why'd you bring him back here instead of taking him to Police Centre and the incident room?'

'Because that's where the media are hanging out. I don't want them asking questions or guessing till we've got something definite.'

'He admitted anything?'

'Nothing. Anything further come in?'

'We double-checked the Sewing Bee list, everyone on it has been interviewed. He's the only one with form, if you exclude Charlie Hassett.'

'*He's* on the list?'

'Three uniforms being let out at the seams. He's already been on to me. If I let it slip to the media, he's demoting me to probationary constable . . . There's more come in from Victoria on August. One of those acquittals he got was for attempted murder – his first wife's boyfriend. What's he like?'

'He's a carpenter and handyman, that's his trade. In his spare time he does Meals on Wheels.'

'Holding a gun at their heads to make 'em eat it?' Then he smiled sourly. 'Why am I so cynical about reformed crims?'

'Has anyone been down to Trades Congress headquarters?'

'With the crowd we've got working on this, you can bet *someone*'s been down there. But nothing's come through on the computer yet.'

'Ring Greg Random, tell him to tell everyone to lay off. That is for you and me soon's I finish with our friend inside.'

He went out to the interview room. August sat comfortably on one side of the table and Gail sat opposite him. The room was sparsely furnished: table, four chairs and the video recorder. August gestured at it, casually:

'You gunna turn that on?'

'Not unless you want us to.' Malone sat down. 'We'll do that if we decide to charge you.'

'What with?'

'Murder of the Premier.'

August looked around him, as if looking for an audience for this comedy. Then he sat forward, suddenly serious. A strand of the thinning hair had fallen forward and he pushed it back.

51

'Inspector Malone, I'm not a murderer –'

'You tried to murder your first wife's boyfriend.'

August waved a curt hand. 'The jury didn't think so. We had a stoush, a fight over a gun, *his* gun, not mine, and it went off.'

Malone couldn't contradict this; he hadn't read the transcript of the trial. Perhaps he should have done a little more homework. 'What did you feel when he got the bullet and you didn't?'

'Glad. What would you feel? The guy was sleeping with my wife . . . Let's get down to why you think I murdered Mr Vanderberg. Because I've got form? I've had none for the last nine years, I'm clean –' He folded his hands together, looked down at them. 'I came up here, changed my name, made a new start. I met Lynne, we hit it off and I moved in with her . . . You've got nothing on me, Inspector, except my past.'

'Where were you last night around eleven o'clock?' asked Gail.

'Home.' Then he smiled wryly. 'Alone. Lynne was at some parents' meeting and didn't get home till midnight. Earlier, I'd been up at Lane Cove town hall, a meeting on aged care. More volunteering . . .' He smiled again; he could not have been more relaxed. 'I got home around ten, waited up for Lynne and we went to bed, I dunno, twelve-thirty, around then.'

'What did you do between getting home at ten and Lynne's arrival? Watch television?'

He smiled again; he was not cocky, but there was a growing confidence. 'You don't catch me like that, Constable. No, I rarely watch TV after ten o'clock. I read, old crime thrillers – d'you read crime novels?'

'No,' said Gail.

'I do – occasionally,' said Malone. 'What did you read last night?'

'Elmore Leonard, one of his early ones.'

'Which one?' asked Malone, who always read Leonard.

'I can never remember titles.'

'Try, John.'

The smile now was fixed. '*Switch*, that was it. The one about the guy on the toilet that's got a bomb attached to the seat – if he stands up, he's a goner. Very funny. Embarrassing, too.'

'That was *Freaky Deaky*. I'd have thought you'd remember a title like that.'

'I told you, I'm no good at titles. For years I thought I'd read *The Maltese Pigeon.*'

'Nice joke, John, but let's be serious. We'd like a look at your bank account and Mrs Masson's.'

'Why?'

'The price for knocking off the Premier wouldn't have been small change. The hitman might've been paid in cash, people don't write cheques for those sort of jobs. The hitman would have to deposit it somewhere. He wouldn't cart fifty thousand around in a brown paper-bag –'

'Fifty thousand?' He seemed genuinely interested in the amount. 'You think that's what he got?'

'Maybe more. I don't know the price for political assassination – it may be more, much more. Do you need money, John?'

'Who doesn't? But I wouldn't kill anyone for it.' He was still calm, still unoffended.

Malone so far had no doubts; but he had no conviction, either. An open mind did not mean it was non-adhesive: fragments occasionally stuck that gave a hint of a recognizable picture. At the moment it was like trying to paint a picture on water.

'Why would I kill Hans Vanderberg? I voted for him in the last election. I'd do the same at the next. He was sly and conniving and half the time you didn't believe what he said, but he got things done.'

'Who'd you vote as? John June?' asked Gail.

'Yes. The Electoral Commission can't always check on whether you are who say you are. They were satisfied I was an honest citizen – which I am.'

'But John August, the real you, might not care one way or the other?'

53

August just looked at her, the mere shadow of a smile on his lips, and Malone said, 'Detective Lee has a point. Which bank do you and Mrs Masson use? We can get a court order –'

'There'll be no need for that.' This time his voice was snappy. 'I'll give you permission to look at mine. But you'll have to ask Lynne about hers –'

'We'll do that. We also want a release from you in the name of John August. Just in case you have *two* bank accounts.'

August shook his head; the lock of hair fell down again and he pushed it back. He seemed now to be losing patience; or confidence. 'You're wasting your time. But okay, I'll sign a release in my real name. Or what was my real name.' He looked down at his hands, stared at them, then at last looked up. Both detectives were surprised at the sadness in his eyes: 'How much are you gunna tell Lynne? About my past, my record?'

'If we find you're in the clear,' said Malone quietly, 'we'll tell her nothing. That's up to you . . . Why did you shoot him, John?'

But that didn't catch August off-balance: 'Try someone else, Inspector. It wasn't me who shot him. I've read what's been going on lately. He has enough enemies to kill him from a dozen sides.'

Malone stared at him, then looked at Gail Lee: 'Any more questions?'

'Just a couple . . . How much do you know about guns, Mr August?'

'Not much.'

'But you knew where to buy a gun? You used a gun in that job you did time for, the armed robbery one.'

'That was Melbourne. I've forgotten where I got it.'

'So a gun's an everyday item with you? You buy one and forget where?'

'It was twelve years ago, for Crissakes!' For a moment the calm demeanour was gone; then he put it on again like a mask:

'Sorry. I'll remember and let you know. Can you remember what you were doing twelve years ago?'

'I was about to start Year 10 at high school. I wasn't buying a gun.'

His look was almost admiring. Then he said, 'It's different these days, in high school, I mean.'

'Knives, Mr August, not guns. Not yet.' Then she said, 'Where do you live?'

He gave an address in Lane Cove. 'It's a flat, in Lynne's name. Why?'

'We'll get a warrant to search it. Just routine.'

The mask dropped. 'Christ, how do I explain that to Lynne?'

'Maybe you'd better tell her the truth about yourself.' Malone stood up. 'Righto, John, you can go. Detective Lee and one of my men will drive you back to Longueville. But if you want to keep your secret from Lynne, maybe you'd like to wait while Detective Lee gets the search warrant. Then we can search your flat and maybe Lynne won't need to know.'

'I'll wait. I'm not gunna hurt Lynne, if it can be avoided.'

2

'Do you think the hit was meant for one of us?' asked Aldwych.

'No,' said Jack Junior. 'All the union trouble is over. They've moved on to fight other developers.'

'I still don't trust our Chinese partners. I don't mean Les – he's one of us. Nor the Feng family – even that girl Camilla isn't gunna make waves.'

The original consortium of partners had been a mixture that at times had had Aldwych thinking he was a foreigner in his own country. Besides Leslie Chung there had been two local Chinese families; there were also Madame Tzu, representing herself, and General Wang-Te, the director from a Shanghai corporation whose connections were as murky as the Whangpoo

River. Sometimes Aldwych wondered what had happened to the White Australia policy of his youth. There were more bloody foreigners in the country now than kangaroos.

'I still wouldn't trust Madame Tzu as far as the other side of the street. As for the General –'

'You're too suspicious,' said Juliet, a foreigner.

'I thought you Roumanians loved suspicion? You and the Hungarians invented the revolving door, didn't you, so's you could watch each other's back?'

'I love you, Papa.' She knew he liked being called Papa. Once distant from each other, they were now friends. 'You'd have made a wonderful dictator.'

'Better than some you've had. That bloke Ceausescu . . . he got what he deserved. The Dutchman was a dictator, but he didn't deserve to be shot.'

They were having breakfast on the terrace of the junior Aldwychs' apartment on the tip of Point Piper. The point was almost sunk by the wealth on it; land here was valued by the cupful. Aldwych, instead of going home to his own big house at Harbord, on the northern side of the harbour, had driven out here with his son and daughter-in-law and stayed the night. He enjoyed Juliet's company and her looks, but, as with Madame Tzu, he would not have trusted her as far as the other side of the street. He had never trusted any woman but his dead wife Shirl. Beautiful women were even more suspect than others: they knew the value of their looks. Jack Junior, on the other hand, had never fallen for any but good-looking women.

The apartment was sumptuous, an estate agent could have found no other word for it; but it was not like a *House & Garden* illustration, it was *lived* in. Juliet could spend money like an IMF grantee, but Jack Junior begrudged her nothing. Aldwych Senior, sometimes to his own surprise, no longer mentally reproached Juliet for her extravagance. This apartment was a contrast to his own house, where he lived amongst Laura Ashley prints and Dresden figurines, none of which he would ever replace because they had been Shirl's choice. Shirl had died before Juliet came along and sometimes he wondered how the two women would have got along. He had had reservations about Juliet, but she had proved him wrong. The marriage was now six years old and there appeared to be no cracks in it. Juliet was extravagant, but she didn't have to be Roumanian to be that; half the country lived on credit beyond its ability to pay and half the country didn't have multi-millionaire husbands. She had proved a better wife than some of Jack Junior's other women would have been. There were no children and no talk of any, but that didn't worry Aldwych. He had little faith that the next forty or fifty years of the new millennium was going to be a cakewalk for the young. He was long past optimism.

Now, looking at a Manly ferry taking commuters to the city, he was pensive, a symptom of his ageing. 'If the hit wasn't meant for either of us –'

'Dad, keep me out of it. If it was meant for either of us, it would've been you. Some of your old mates may have wanted a last crack at you.'

'All my old mates are dead, including the ones who were not my mates. Lenny McPherson is gone, all the old mugs who had it in for me.' In his memory was a gallery of enemies. He had consorted, as the cops called it, with other crims, but he had always been his own man. Or, to a certain extent and which he would not have admitted to anyone, he had been part Shirl's man. 'Is this upsetting you, Juliet?'

'Not at all. As you said, I'm Roumanian.' Sometimes one's national bad characteristics can be indulged in.

He smiled at her approvingly. 'You'll do me, love . . .' He hadn't called anyone *love* since Shirl had died. 'Well, like I was saying – if it wasn't meant for either of us, then maybe we've got problems.'

'Don't ask,' said Jack Junior as Juliet looked puzzled.

'Of course I'm going to ask. Why will you have problems, Papa?'

'We want to build a small casino up at Coffs Harbour.'
A resort and retirement town halfway between Sydney and
Brisbane. 'Hans Vanderberg was in favour of it. He wasn't a
gambler, but anything that brought in more taxes was right up
his street. The Pope would bless gambling if it brought in more
revenue –'

Juliet blessed herself. She never went near a church except at
Christmas, but the nuns from her old school still whispered in
her ear.

Aldwych smiled at the gesture, but went on: 'We dunno about
Billy Eustace, if he takes over – he says he's anti-gambling, but
they all say that till Treasury talks to 'em. If the Coalition wins
the election, we dunno about them, either. They've got some
wowsers amongst them, especially if they're from the bush.'

'Wowsers?' Juliet had been only a child when she had come to
Australia, but she still had difficulty with some of the language,
especially slang that was older even than her father-in-law.

'Killjoys,' said Jack Junior. 'Gambling is a social evil.'

She had been a gambler all her life, but rarely a loser. 'How
quaint.'

She had a touch of larceny to her that Aldwych liked. Shirl
had never had it. She had known of his trade, but as long as he
never brought it into her home, her retreat, she had said nothing.
He was not given to fantasy, but once or twice he had thought of
her as an angel married to a demon. He had taken to reading late
in life, but he really would have to give up reading some of the
books on the shelves in the Harbord house.

'We'll have to start smoodging, leaving some money lying
around.'

'We'll have to be careful,' said Jack Junior. He was a plotter,
like his father, but in business, not bank robbery, and therefore
more skilled. 'Too many of them are more moral these days.'

'How quaint,' said Juliet.

Out on the harbour two youths on jet skis cut across the bow of
a small yacht. The yacht had to tack abruptly, its sails quivering

58

with indignation. Aldwych watched it, came as close to a snarl as he got these days: 'He should of run 'em down.'

'Who?'

Aldwych turned his head from watching the harbour. 'The Dutchman should of got them before they got him.'

He knew all about survival.

3

'Do you think he's the one?' asked Clements.

'I dunno. Who else have we got? He's the only one on that Sewing Bee list who's got a record. We just keep tabs on him. We'll get the task force to put him under 24-hour surveillance – we don't want him shooting through, changing his name again. The one good thing I could say for him – he's going to protect Mrs Masson, the woman he's living with.'

'Unless –'

'Unless she knows what he did – if he did do it.' Malone shook his head. 'No, I don't think so . . . Now you and I are going down to Sussex Street, but first we're going to look in on Roger Ladbroke. He knows more about who works what and how in the Labor Party than anyone except his late boss.'

'You vote Labor, don't you?' Despite their long association they had never admitted how each of them had voted. There is a majority amongst the natives whose vote is as secret as whether they believe or not in God.

'You vote the Coalition, don't you?'

'Okay –' Clements grinned – 'we're apolitical on this one.'

'We'd better be or the media will heap shit on us.'

Malone had checked that Ladbroke was in his office at Parliament House. They drove into the city and round the back of the government complex. As they swung into the garage they saw the group under a tree in the Domain, the city common; someone, too distant to be recognized, was holding a press conference, cameras

59

aimed at him like bazookas. Then they were in the garage and the security guard was holding them up.

Clements, who was driving, produced his badge. 'You'll be seeing a lot of us in the next few days.'

'Terrible business,' said the guard, a burly man young enough to have been Hans Vanderberg's grandson. 'He could be a cranky old bastard, but we all liked him and respected him. Good luck. Get the shits who killed him.'

'You notice?' said Malone as they got out of the car. 'He used the plural – the shits who killed him. Nobody's going to believe this was a one-man job.'

The two women secretaries in the Premier's outer office still looked stunned, as if their boss' murder had occurred only an hour ago. One was drying her eyes as the two detectives came in and asked for Ladbroke. Without rising she pointed to the inner door, as if she and her colleague no longer had anything to protect.

Ladbroke was packing files into cartons. He was jacketless and tieless; he seemed even to have shed his urbanity. He looked up irritably as Malone and Clements came, then took a deep breath and made an effort to gather himself together.

'Billy Eustace wants to move in this afternoon as Acting Premier. The king is dead, long live the king.' He still wore his old cynicism; it was like a second skin. 'You come up with anything yet?'

'We've got a few things to work on,' said Malone. 'We're on our way down to Sussex Street. We'd like some background on what's been going on the past few weeks.'

Ladbroke looked at a file in his hand, then tapped one of the cartons. 'A good deal of it is in here, but I can't let you see it. It's stuff that was leaked to the Old Man from down there.'

'We could get a warrant. Those aren't Cabinet papers, Roger.'

Ladbroke drew another deep breath, then put the file in a carton and pushed the box along the Premier's big desk.

'Okay, but read it here. There are three files – the red-tabbed ones.'

Malone pushed the carton towards Clements. 'You're the speed-reader.'

Clements took the three red-tabbed files and retired to a chair by the window. Malone sat down and looked across the desk at Ladbroke, who had slumped down in what had been his boss' chair. 'What are you going to do now?'

'I'm organizing a State funeral for him. After that—' He shrugged.

'A State funeral? When?'

'Friday. Gert insisted on it. Eleven o'clock Friday morning at St Mary's Cathedral.'

'He was a Catholic?'

'No, she is. He was everything the voters were on a particular day. If the Mormons or the Holy Rollers could swing the vote in an electorate, he was out there nodding his head to polygamy or clapping his hands and singing "Down by the Riverside".'

'Do the Mormons still practise polygamy?'

Ladbroke shrugged again; Malone had never seen him so listless. 'I don't know. Anyhow, he's a Catholic for Friday. St Mary's jumped at the idea when Gert said she wanted a State funeral. St Andrew's has had the last three, they've all been Anglicans. Friday at St Mary's they'll be tossing the incense around like smoke bombs. They might even canonize him.' For the first time since they had entered the office he smiled. 'He'd enjoy that.'

Clements came across from his seat by the window, handed the files back to Ladbroke. 'Like you said the other night – he had more enemies than Saddam Hussein. But none of that is from Party headquarters or the Labour Council – it's all from Trades Congress.'

'Party headquarters and the Labor Council are sitting on the fence. But Congress –' He pursed his lips as if he were about to spit. 'A real nest of vipers –'

61

'Why is Labor always so vicious towards each other?'

'Come on, Russ. You think the Coalition doesn't have its backstabbers? Politics in this country has never been a happy brotherhood. They'll tell you themselves, politics is the Devil's playground. Why do you think I've spent twenty-two years in it and never been bored?'

'Are you staying on?'

'Till the election, anyway. Billy Eustace wants me to hold his hand.' He stood up, went back to his packing. 'Good luck down in Sussex Street. They're a feral lot down there.'

Malone and Clements drove down to Sussex Street through a morning where the air was almost heavy enough to be seen. Sweat-shiny groups stood at traffic-lights, listless as detainees; a courier cyclist pedalled in slow motion through the traffic, urgent delivery ignored. The whole city seemed to have slowed, though it was impossible to tell whether it was because of the weather or the shock of the Premier's assassination. The voters had come to have little regard for politicians; but assassination? That was what *foreigners* did.

Sussex Street runs north and south along the bottom of the slight slope down from the narrow plateau on which the central business district is built. For most of its length it is one-way, a tribute to the policies of the two political buildings at its southern end. The Labor Council's headquarters is a ten-level building that looks like a stack of concrete pancakes. The council, an organization of trade unions, was the birthplace of the Labor Party; party headquarters, though now independent, is housed in the building. Behind the mundane exterior there has been more intrigue, more skulbuggery, as the late Premier used to call it, than in the combined halls of Versailles, Tammany, the Kremlin, the Diet and latterday Rome.

The Trades Congress building, directly across the street, was a tribute to modern design, as if its owners had been determined to show what real craftsmen could do. The Congress was a breakaway body of unions whose members were no better than their journeymen rivals; they had just had more money to spend, though no one was sure where it came from. It was too new, yet, to be a monument.

Malone and Clements rode up to the fifth floor. As they entered an outer office there was shouting from an inner office, voices raised in fierce argument. Then a door was wrenched open and Maureen, face flushed, came running out. She almost cannoned into Malone, side-stepped him, looked up at him in surprise, then was gone, shouting back at him, 'He's all yours, the bastard!'

A man stood in the open doorway, equally flushed: 'Get outa here – you fucking vultures – Hullo, who are you?'

Malone gestured at the secretary sitting at a desk to one side of the doorway. 'We were going to ask the young lady here to introduce us.'

The man looked hard at both detectives; then jerked his head up and down as if to say, *Bloody (or perhaps fucking) cops!* 'I should've recognized you. Come in. I'm not thinking too straight this morning . . . And that bloody girl from Channel 15 coming in here – where do they breed 'em?'

'Out at Randwick,' said Malone. 'She's my daughter.'

'Oh. Sorry.'

'Don't let it worry you, Mr Clizbe. I have the same opinion of the media as you do.'

Norman Clizbe was a small man in his early forties, a bantam who fought above his weight: had to, to survive in the Labor Party and its affiliates. He had quick eyes, quick mouth, quick movements; those who worked with him turned their eyes away, just for rest. He was scarred, he had seen more battles than a battalion of Ghurkas, but somehow he had kept his sense of humour. Dry, yes, but that survives longer than exuberance.

'Is Mr Balmoral around?' Malone asked. 'We'd like to talk to the two of you.'

'Sure, sure.' He went back to the doorway, spoke to the secretary, then came back and sat down behind a desk that appeared to grow paper like a wild garden. 'He'll be in in a moment. I'm not surprised to see you,' he said, looking at each of them in turn. 'But I'll get in early. We're in the dark as much as you are.'

'What makes you think we're in the dark?' said Clements.

Then Balmoral came in, closing the door behind him. He was in his late twenties or early thirties, tall, handsome, a dresser. He was in his shirtsleeves, the sleeves rolled up, the roll-ups as neat as starched cuffs. He wore a brightly patterned blue tie, an expensive item that would not have been out of place on a banker's chest. He was the New Labor, the ones who had come out of university straight into the organization, bringing theories instead of experience, bringing ambition as much as dedication. The sort that Con Malone, Scobie's father, the old battler from the barricades, would never vote for.

He shook hands with Malone and Clements, then sat down to the left of Clizbe. They were on the other side of the desk from the two detectives. The line in the sand had been drawn.

'You're not in the dark?' said Clizbe. 'You've already got a lead?'

'Just a glimmer.' Malone had been briefed by Clements on the way down as to what was in the red-tabbed files. 'Why have you been actively encouraging the stacking of certain branches, branches that you knew were antagonistic to the Premier?'

'What branches might they be?' Balmoral had a pleasant voice, one that sounded as if the spin doctors had already worked on it for the future. He would never be accused of saying *guv'mint* or claim that he was *Austrayan*, like so many of those who were in *guv'mint* and true-blue *Austrayans*.

'Harding, for one. It's being stacked by Mr Kelzo, who wants to win pre-selection against the sitting member. Who has always been a strong supporter of the Premier.'

Clizbe's quick eyes were remarkably still. 'Are you suggesting someone in the party shot The Dutchman?'

Malone looked at Clements in surprise; then back at the two

men on the other side of the desk. 'That's a thought, though we hadn't thought of it.'

Clizbe suddenly laughed; he had a quick laugh, too, one that didn't last very long. 'Let's cut out the bullshit, Inspector. Okay, there's been some branch stacking, but that happens. It's not the first time, it won't be the last time. The Coalition do it –'

'We don't think the Coalition are involved in this case,' said Clements. 'They'll profit, maybe win the election, if you don't get your act together in time. But we don't think they had any hand in killing Mr Vanderberg.'

'And you think we did?' Balmoral had hardly moved since sitting down; one could see him years ahead, a rock on the front bench, impervious to accusations of any sort. He was Prime Minister material and he knew it, was training for it.

'I didn't say that. We always begin our enquiries at home base and this is the Labor Party's home base, isn't it?' He knew that it wasn't, but a little ignorance is often a trap for the other side.

'No, it isn't. The Labor Party is across the street, that's the base. Maybe you should be talking to them. They control pre-selection.'

'No, I think we'd rather be talking to you.' *Yours are the names in the red-tabbed files.* 'We'd just like you to tell us what you know that will help us.'

The expressions on their faces said they weren't going to tell much.

'Of course,' said Clizbe and his mouth shut like a trap.

'Does Mr Eustace have any rivals for his position?' asked Malone.

The quick eyes were still again. 'Every politician has rivals.'

'True. It's part of the game.'

'We don't see it as a game,' said Balmoral and you knew he never would.

No one was more experienced at parrying questions than Clizbe; you knew that soon Balmoral would be just as good. It was against the grain to be open and frank; Frank, so the joke

65

went, was the bloke who would never learn. Malone guessed that it was like this world-wide, ever had been. Julius Caesar would have been at home in Sussex Street.

Malone took up the attack. He sometimes saw himself (though he would never admit it) as the police equivalent of the old fast bowling combination of Lillee and Thomson. He was Lillee, moving the ball both ways through the air and off the seam, bowling the occasional slower ball. 'So there may be some contenders for Mr Eustace's position? How will that go down with the voters? Factional warfare two months before the election? Vanderberg would never have allowed that.'

'Neither will we,' said Clizbe, forgetting for the moment that this was not home base.

Malone moved the ball a little wider. 'What can you tell us about Mr Kelzo?'

'He's a loyal, hard-working party member.'

'We understand Vanderberg didn't think so. Loyal, that is.'

'The Premier didn't always have his finger on the pulse,' said Balmoral.

'I think that would surprise a lot of people. He was Police Minister as well as Premier – there wasn't anything he didn't know about the Service. And you're telling me he was out of touch with his party?' Then he bowled a beamer, right at the head: 'Do you have a loyal member on your books named John June?'

'The name doesn't ring a bell. But we have thousands of members. Look –' Clizbe sat back, his elbows on the arms of his chair, his fingers interlocked; he could have been explaining the birds and the bees to the kids at the Happy Hours Child-Care Centre: 'In this business there are always rumours and counter-rumours, lies and counter-lies, misunderstandings, back-stabbing – metaphorical, that is –'

'I'm surprised anyone survives. Aren't you, Russ?' Malone stood up. 'We'll be back, Mr Clizbe. We're only just starting –'

'We'll help all we can,' said Clizbe, who hadn't helped at all. Both he and Balmoral were now on their feet, ready to sweep

66

the police out of the office, get on with cleaning up the business. 'This is the worst thing that's ever happened to the party. Ever And in Olympic year. But if there's any light at the end of the tunnel, we'll let you know.'

'Do that. But too often the light at the end of the tunnel is the track gang clearing up the wreckage. I think the party's come off the rails. You'll be flat out getting it back on them before the election.'

'You're a Coalition voter?' said Balmoral.

Malone grinned. 'My dad would shoot me if I were. He was fighting for the Left before you two were born. They used cricket bats and sling-hooks and pieces of four-by-two. They didn't use snipers with a night-'scope. It was brutal, but it had a certain honesty about it. Whoever ordered the hit on The Dutchman didn't show any of that. Good-day.'

Then Clements, the other bowler, took up the ball: 'We understand there was some discussion at one of the branches as to whether a political assassination was a Federal or State police matter. You hear anything about that?'

Clizbe looked at Balmoral, who said, 'Yes, we'd heard about it. Your other daughter told you, did she?'

Clizbe's eyes galloped. 'His other daughter?'

'Yes, she works for Iverson and Gower, who are supposed to be working for *us*.'

Clizbe looked at Malone. 'Your daughter brings home clients' confidential information?'

'No, she doesn't.' Malone could be haughty; he had learned it from Lisa. 'Mr Balmoral had a casual conversation with her. Right?' Balmoral hesitated, then nodded. 'Working for the Labor Party's law advisers she's naturally interested in finding out who killed the Premier. Where was the meeting where the discussion came up?'

Clizbe couldn't have been quicker; he was answering before Malone had finished the question: 'That'd be branch business. We can't help you there.'

Malone just looked at the two of them, then smiled, nodded and led Clements out of the office. Behind them another argument had started, in whispers, but the argument this time was not with an outsider.

Down in the street Clements said, 'You almost blew your top in there.'

'They got up my nose.' He got into the car, got out again, took the parking fine slip from under the wiper, tore it up, dropped it in the gutter and got back into the car again. 'Those buggers couldn't care less that The Dutchman was murdered. All they're thinking about is the succession.'

'When was it ever different?' said Clements. 'Except for the killing. Where to now?'

'We're going out to talk to Mr Kelzo.'

'What makes you think we'll find him at his branch?'

'This morning, mate, every branch in the State – Labor, Coalition, the Greenies, the lot – they're all going to be at their branch offices. The election is only two months away and it's wide open. The Olympics are less than nine months away and everybody wants to be up there in the eighteen-hundred-dollar seats as the Melbourne Cup winner comes galloping into the stadium with the torch between its teeth.'

'They're gunna have a horse do the last lap?'

'It'll save a fight between the swimmers and the track and field.'

'Boy, you do have shit on the liver this morning.' Then as they drew away from the kerb Clements said, 'What was Maureen doing there?'

'Channel 15 have been doing an investigative piece on Labor's faction fighting.'

'It could get dangerous. You're gunna let her keep shoving her nose in? If my daughter ever gets into investigative jour-nalism –'

'Your daughter is three years old. By the time she's Maureen's age they won't be leaving home to do any investigation. They'll do it on the Internet or whatever it's called by then. Maybe the Prynet.'

'Wouldn't it be nice if we could work that way?'

They drove west, over the beautiful Anzac Bridge with its suspension cables a fragile contrast to the heavy steel arch of the Harbour Bridge further downstream. The Harding electorate covered three suburbs on the Parramatta River, the harbour's main tributary. It was a mixture of Federation houses, smaller houses from the twenties and thirties and one or two new developments that appeared to make the Federation houses rear back as if affronted by upstarts. From certain streets one could see the Olympic complex, genuflected to by some as a cathedral.

'Maybe they should have The Dutchman's State funeral from here,' said Clements.

The local Labor Party's branch was above a row of lock-up shops in a small shopping centre; from its windows there would be a good view of the Olympic stadium. Malone and Clements climbed the narrow stairs and found only three men in the long narrow hall. Malone had expected a crowd. He had been wrong: a lot of voters were still on summer holiday and there would have been difficulty in getting a crowd for Judgement Day. The voters knew their priorities and politics was not amongst them.

They walked down the hall to a dais where Peter Kelzo sat behind a large table. The other two men were standing on the floor just below him. They turned as the two strangers walked in.

'Sorry, mates – you from the press?'

'No,' said Malone. 'From the police.'

'Oh.' All three men looked at each other as if two hold-up men had come in.

Then Kelzo got up from behind the table and stepped down to the floor of the hall. He was almost six inches shorter than either of the two detectives, but you knew he would never be afraid of big men. He put out his hand, the left hand raised as if to pat the head of any passing child; his smile was wider than that of a game show host. I'll bet he kisses babies, Malone thought.

'Anything we can do to help? This is George Gandolfo. This is Joe St Louis.'

Gandolfo was a thin fidgety man in his middle forties, hair worn thin by his speed through life. You knew he would run up escalators, saving 7.3 seconds in 30 metres, a saving that, if asked, he wouldn't have known what to do with. At school he would have tried to shorten long division, to no avail. Over the past year, according to the red-tabbed files, he had tried to hasten the Premier's retirement, also to no avail.

'Pleased to meetcha.' He put out a hand, gave the sort of handshake that said he was everybody's friend, so long as everybody voted the right way.

Clements recognized Joe St Louis. 'G'day, Joe. When did you get into politics?'

'This year, mate. It ain't much different to the ring.'

Joe St Louis was a pale-skinned Aborigine in his late thirties. He had been fighting for almost two decades, beginning in side-show tents, moving on to eight-rounders in clubs, once fighting for the middleweight title. He was good-looking in a battered way, his eyes wary under scarred brows, like beetles under chipped rocks. He had form, besides his ring record, as a stand-over man.

'I'm Greek, like you know.' Kelzo sounded as if he were reading from the branch brochure. 'George is Eye-talian. And Joe, he's fair dinkum Austrayan. We try to be as multicultural as we can, basically. Very Austrayan.'

'Lebanese, too?' asked Malone. 'We believe you've got a lot of new members, mostly Lebanese.'

'We got no prejudices here. We even got some Turks. That's something, ain't it? Greeks and Turks in the same club. We welcome all sorts.'

'Even the Irish?'

'Ah, you don't catch me like that. Inspector *Malone*? Of course the Irish.' He beamed at Gandolfo and St Louis as if St Patrick himself had just walked in. 'Who better to have in politics than the Irish? Some of the great names in Labor – Cahill, Dolan, Crean, McMullan –'

'Saints, every one of them. Could we sit down, Mr Kelzo? Maybe a cup of coffee? We want to be sociable. That's what this is called, isn't it?' He had seen the sign above the downstairs door. 'The Labor Social Club?'

'Of course. Where's me manners? Joe, get some coffee, would you?' Joe St Louis, it was evident, was the gofer. Malone wondered what other errands he did. 'Milk, sugar? There's some biscuits in a tin, Joe. Iced Vo-Vos. Very Austrayan.' He pulled some chairs into a circle. He and Gandolfo sat together, a team. 'Okay, fire away.'

'Wrong phrase,' said Malone with a grin.

Kelzo returned the grin with a wide smile; he was unabashed. 'Sure, sure. We gotta pay our respects to a Great Man.' You could read the capitals in his voice. 'He'll be missed.'

'Very much. We understand you are standing for pre-selection here?'

Kelzo nodded. 'I'm told I'm what you call a shoo-in.'

The Harding electorate had been named after an American president by a cynical electoral commissioner who knew a corrupt administration when he heard of it. The commissioner was long dead, but he had been more prescient than he knew. Kelzo ran this branch like a grace-and-favour estate.

'After the branch-stacking?' said Clements.

Kelzo saw he had made a mistake; he was saved for the moment by the arrival of the instant coffee and the Iced Vo-Vos. 'Where did you hear that?'

Clements changed tack: 'Amongst your new members, do you have a man named June? John June?'

'No,' said Gandolfo.

'Hundreds of members and you know 'em all? Including the new ones?'

'He has a photographic memory,' said Kelzo.

'And after you're elected,' said Malone, 'you'll be a strong

71

supporter of the new Premier, whoever he might be. Assuming, of course, that Labor is returned.'

Joe St Louis had sat down beside his two colleagues; they looked a formidable trio. One could not imagine that in the Harding branch there would be much give-and-take discussion with the members. 'I been around the traps. We're gunna be re-elected.'

'Basically,' said Kelzo, 'We can't lose.'

'And who'll be the Premier? Billy Eustace?'

'Who else?' said Gandolfo, but didn't sound as if it mattered.

Sure, who else? thought Malone. Eustace was a rubber doll; he would be manipulated. At present he was the Minister of Transport and Communications, known in the trade as the Ministry for Mates. He had more mates than a discount hooker.

'What about the Minister for the Olympics, Mr Agaroff? He's suddenly become ambitious, we're told.'

'Where do you get all your information?' asked Kelzo, looking a little worried, though still smiling.

'Sergeant Clements' daughter is on the Internet. All sorts of information comes up there, she tells us.'

Clements didn't deny that his three-year-old daughter was an Internet fan. 'You remember all the Clinton stuff that came up on Internet?'

'Terrible, terrible,' said Kelzo. 'Nothing's private any more.'

'Would you back Agaroff?' asked Malone. 'Do you have any Russians on your multicultural list? His parents were Russian.'

'No Russians,' said Gandolfo, starting to fidget, looking for an escalator to get them out of this questioning.

'Do you know anyone who would want to kill Hans Vanderberg?' said Clements bluntly.

Moments are expandable, small balloons of time. This moment was stretched; one could almost hear an echo of Clements' question. The three men did not look at each other, but just stared at the two detectives. The three monkeys, thought Malone; then Kelzo said, 'He had enemies, but nobody we knew.'

'Nobody,' said Gandolfo, all at once very still.

Clements looked at St Louis. 'Joe? You've been around the traps, like you say.'

St Louis shook his head. 'Nobody.'

Malone put down his coffee cup. 'We'd like a list of all your members, new ones as well as old.'

'They're confidential –' said Kelzo. One could almost see him putting up shutters, running the barricades into place, thumbing through the Freedom of Information Act. He was abruptly non-cooperative.

'No, they're not, Mr Kelzo. Explain to him, Joe, what we can do with a search warrant.'

'You have no right –' said Gandolfo, racing to his place at the barricades.

'Mr Gandolfo,' said Malone patiently, 'you don't seem to have much idea what powers the police have.'

'Of course, of course.' Kelzo beat a retreat as quickly as he had put up the shutters. He offered the plate of Iced Vo-Vos: 'Another biscuit? We'll fax the list to you this afternoon –'

'No,' said Malone. 'We want it *now*.'

Again there was the stretched moment; then Kelzo said, 'Of course, of course. George will have to go to the bank to get it –'

'The *bank*? You keep your membership list in a *bank*?'

'You gotta be careful –'

'Why?' said Clements. 'Because of the branch-stacking?'

'Well –' But Kelzo wasn't going to divulge too many secrets. The in-fighting in the Party was the Party's business. 'You just gotta, that's all. George will be back in ten minutes –'

'No,' said Malone, rising. 'We'll go with you, George. Just in case you're waylaid.'

'Waylaid?' said Gandolfo.

'He means done over,' said Joe St Louis and grinned at the two detectives. 'It happens, don't it?'

'All the time, Joe,' said Malone. *You'd know, Joe.* 'It happened last night.'

Suddenly all the fidget went out of Gandolfo. 'You mean someone might shoot *us*?'

'You never know, George,' said Malone, piling it on. 'Let's go. Which bank?'

Chapter Three

1

'I remember once, you said trying to get information out of the Chinese was like banging your head against the Great Wall of China. Mr Kelzo and his mates could be Chinese.'

'Russ, the Great Wall of China is going to run for bloody miles in this case. Get ready for a bruised forehead.'

They had collected the membership list from a safety deposit box at the local bank, had got one of the bank staff to copy it – 'We'll have to charge you, sir.'

'I'm asking you as a police officer –'

'It's not me, sir. The bank charges for everything these days – you must of read all the complaints.' The young bank clerk had lowered his voice. 'It's a dollar a page.'

'Six pages. Send the bill to Police Headquarters, the Commissioner will send you a cheque. Then you'll charge a fee on the cheque, right?'

'It's the system, sir.'

'Send the bill to us,' said Gandolfo, fidgeting.

They had driven him back to the branch headquarters, dropping him there, and now were on their way back to Strawberry Hills under a sky in which huge clouds stumbled, growing darker as they clashed and merged. The air-conditioning in the car was working only intermittently and Clements had opened his own and the passenger's window. One could taste the thick bitter air.

'Did you notice what was in that deposit box?' said Clements.

'Money, four stacks of it. It could've been a thousand bucks or ten thousand – the top notes were all hundred-dollars. Is that what they call petty cash? Or was it welfare for the branch-stacking? There was also something wrapped in a hand-towel that George didn't want us to see. A gun?'

'Could of been. I left it to you to ask him what it was.'

'I passed. We might need another excuse to come back to them.'

'Would Kelzo employ a hitman?'

'I dunno. He employs Joe St Louis. A hitman is only one step up from a stand-over man.'

In the Homicide office Gail Lee was waiting for them. They came in sweating; she looked cool and unrumpled, as if she had spent the whole morning in the air-conditioned office. But she hadn't: 'I've been to Mr June's bank. He has three thousand eight hundred dollars and twenty-four cents in his account. No big deposit in the last six months. The Happy Hours Day-Care Centre also has its account there. The manager wouldn't tell me anything about it, but he let slip we weren't the first to enquire about it. I got on to a friend in Children's Services –'

Malone nodded appreciatively. Friends were better than clues.

'– Happy Hours isn't so happy. It looks as if it may have to close – it's up to its eyes in debt. It never recovered after the Federal government cut back on child-care subsidy –'

'How much in debt? Did your friend know?'

'She got back to me. Sixty thousand.'

'Thank your friend. Send her a police tie.'

'Just what she needs.'

He grinned at her; his mood had suddenly improved. He looked at Clements. 'Would someone pay sixty thousand to have the Premier knocked off?'

'They'd want more than that, unless they did it for political idealism.'

'Is there such a thing in this state? No, if August or June, whatever we call him, did the deed he asked for money. The only idealism would be that he might've done it to get his partner

76

and the Happy Hours out of a hole. Has the task force got a tail on him?'

'Yes,' said Gail. 'But he knows it. Two of the guys watching him called in to Police Centre. Said he came across to them and said, "Don't you know a watched pot never boils? I'll let you know when and where I'm going, if I'm going, so's you can't lose me."'

'He's too smart,' said Malone, all at once feeling more certain about August. 'Why isn't he blowing Christ out of us for harassing him? Upsetting his partner? He's not angry enough for an innocent man. What's the report from Ballistics?'

Gail looked at the sheet in her hand; she always seemed to have everything to hand. 'One bullet, a .308. The gun could have been a Winchester or a Tikka – there are half a dozen with the same rifling characteristics. There was no shell casing at the scene of the crime.'

'Righto, try all the gun shops – see if anything like that has been bought in the past month. Unless he belonged to a gun club?'

'I'll check that, too,' said Gail Lee.

'How did the search of his flat go?'

'Andy Graham and Sheryl did that. No gun, nothing, not even a penknife.'

Malone went on into his own office and rang Channel 15.

'Channel 15. Darlene-Charlene speaking.'

Nobody had surnames any more. He wouldn't look forward to the day when Wombat Rose answered the phone. 'Maureen Malone.'

'Who shall I say is calling?'

'Homicide.'

'Putting you through.' As if Homicide called every day.

Maureen came on the line. 'That you, Dad? Sorry I had to blow past you like that this morning –'

'Get over here. *Now.*'

'I can't, Dad. We've got a meeting on in half an hour –'

'*Now.* Or I'll send two uniformed cops to bring you in and I'll let Channels 7, 9 and 10 know, *and* the ABC, if they've got a spare camera, and they can run it tonight and your bosses won't like that –'

'I can get our own guys to film it –'

'*Now*! Don't fartarse with me, Mo, I'm serious –'

He hung up, surprised at the sudden anger that had welled up in him. He went out to Clements' desk. 'Maureen is on her way over here. I want you in my office when she comes in. I don't want her to get the idea that this is a father-daughter discussion.'

'What am I supposed to play? Uncle Russ?'

'No, you're the Supervisor, backing up the Boss. With capital letters.'

Clements looked up at him, sat back in his chair: playing Uncle Russ. 'Simmer down, mate.'

Malone took a deep breath, tried to relax. 'I know. I don't want her to have anything to do with the case. But how can I tell her to get lost? All she's doing is her job. But –'

'Yeah. But. It was bound to happen sooner or later, coming up against her. The media are like taxes, a pain in the arse – but they're always with us. You're just unlucky your daughter has joined the enemy. Just keep saying your prayers that some day you don't finish up in court with your other daughter defending some crim you've picked up.'

'Why do I ask you to tell me my fortune?'

When Maureen arrived Malone and Clements were waiting for her in Malone's office. She had never been to Homicide before and those on the staff who had never met her studied her as if she were a candidate from the Most Wanted gallery. She was power-dressed, evidently ready for the camera. Beige suit, black shirt with the collar spread out, hair styled, discreet ear-rings: and wearing ambition. Malone, looking at her through the window of his office, saw it full-on for the first time.

She came in, flushed and angry, ready to jump hurdles or knock 'em over. She'll never be a loser, Malone thought, even when she's lost.

'My producer is bloody wound up about this –'

'Sit down, Mo.' Malone was calm; his own anger had gone. 'Sergeant Clements and I want to ask you a few questions –'

'*Sergeant Clements*?' She turned a fierce eye on Clements. 'Are you in on this, Uncle Russ? This is abuse of freedom of the press –'

'Bullshit,' said Clements. Maureen's head went back as if she had never heard the word before, certainly not from him. 'Shut up, Mo, and listen to your father.'

'Inspector Malone,' said her father.

All at once the anger drained out of her; she flopped back in her chair and laughed. 'You two should be on TV – I'll let my producer know. Okay, Inspector Malone, waddia wanna know? Is that how crims talk?'

Malone shook his head. 'Stay behind the camera, Mo. You're a bloody awful actress. Now let's cut out the play-acting and get down to business. What were you doing at Sussex Street this morning? What was that fight with Clizbe all about?'

'He didn't tell you?'

'I wouldn't have wasted my time sending for you if he had. Come on, quit stalling.'

She looked sideways at Clements, suddenly looking like her mother; Lisa had a trick of looking out of the corners of her eyes, a sceptic's glance. Clements said, 'It's serious, Mo.'

'Okay.' But she took her time. She fiddled with one of the ear-rings, then took it off and rolled it in her fingers like a gambler with a coin. Malone had seen the trick before and recognized it now for what it was, a time-waster. At last she said, 'Jerry Balmoral is going for pre-selection in Mr Vanderberg's electorate. Against the wishes of Mrs Vanderberg.'

'She's got no clout in the Party. She doesn't hold any position.'

'She doesn't need to. Everyone in the Boolagong electorate knows her. She's Mother Teresa, Princess Di and Golda Meir all rolled into one.'

'All dead,' said Malone. 'So's their influence.'

'Not hers. If she says no Mr Balmoral, there'll be no Mr Balmoral.'

'Why the shouting match with Clizbe?'

'I said we'd announce Balmoral's go for pre-selection on tonight's news. And I asked who would be financing his campaign, if Mrs Vanderberg opposed it. He went ape in a big way.'

'Why wouldn't he? When did union organizations ever tell you that their business was the media's business? You've still got a lot to learn.'

Clements picked up the ball: 'Mo, you're getting into dangerous territory. Someone paid to have the Premier bumped off. They're not gunna have any second thoughts about an interfering TV researcher and reporter. The price on you would be about a dollar ninety-five.'

She gave him the sceptic's look again. 'Russ –' proving she was grown-up now – 'you don't really think Clizbe or Balmoral is going to come gunning for me.'

'Not them, no. But there's someone wants to change the whole set-up of the Labor Party. The Vanderberg reign is over. They're going back to the in-fighting of the eighties. Your dad and I saw that, as young cops, and it was dirty.'

'Was anyone shot in those days?' Fifteen, twenty years ago was ancient history, which the young no longer studied.

'No, but there were bashings. Serious ones. We don't want that to happen to you. Do we, Dad?'

Dad asked, 'Have you got anything on the Harding electorate? Mr Kelzo and company?'

'What's all this information worth?'

'You've got the wrong end of the stick, Miss Malone,' said Inspector Malone. 'The Police Service doesn't go in for chequebook journalism.'

'I'm not waving a cheque book. But I'm doing your job for you –'

His stare might have burnt holes in a stranger; it certainly scorched her. Clements shifted uncomfortably on the couch, the vinyl gasping like flatulence. Out in the big main room there was a sudden silence, as if the half a dozen detectives there had heard Maureen and were waiting for Malone to explode.

Maureen must have heard the silence; or her father's stare told her the Malone tongue had got away from her. She retreated: 'Sorry –'

Malone still said nothing, but outside there was movement and the soft clacking of keys. Clements, pouring a little burning oil on family waters, said, 'Mo, we're striking no bargains on this. If you withhold information, I'll take the matter out of your dad's hands and I'll put you in for twenty-four hours –' He was bluffing, the law wouldn't allow him to do that.

Somehow she wasn't surprised. 'You would, too, wouldn't you?'

Clements nodded. Malone sat silent.

'Jesus!' Suddenly she was defeated. She rolled the ear-ring between her fingers, then put it back on her ear. Then she sighed and Malone recognized his own sound. 'You can't blame me for trying – God, I've worked really hard on this investigation! All of a sudden it's bigger than I ever dreamed – I could make my name –'

'On a headstone,' said Clements.

Malone broke his silence: 'Simmer down, Mo – that's what Russ is always telling me –'

'For a different reason,' said Clements.

'This case has got serious, Mo. You could make your name – dead or beaten up. When the Premier was shot, it was no longer your investigation of branch-stacking – it was our case of homicide. Now tell us – have you got anything on the Harding branch office?'

She hesitated, then nodded. 'I don't know how much it's worth. I went out there asking questions a week ago and a guy named Joe St Louis, a real bruiser, ran me out of the place. Literally. Grabbed me by the back of my shirt and ran me out. He almost threw me down the stairs that go up to their office.'

'You didn't mention that at home.'

'You'd have had some cops out there next morning, wouldn't you? No thanks. Anyhow, I did learn the branch is loaded with money –'

'How'd you learn that?'

'I asked Mr Kelzo, the boss. That was when I got the bum's rush. Mr Kelzo has put the arm on local people, but he also got a big whack from Sussex Street. I don't know whether it was from the Labor Council or the Trades Congress . . . I also learned something else that had nothing to do with Mr Kelzo. Someone donated two hundred and fifty thousand dollars to the Premier's campaign in the Boolagong electorate.'

Malone looked at Clements. 'What would we do without the help of a concerned public?'

Clements looked at the concerned public: 'Is that money still in the kitty?'

'I don't know. But if it is, it will be interesting to see if Mrs Vanderberg lets Jerry Balmoral get his hands on it.'

'How'd you get all this information?' asked Malone.

'You'd be surprised how confidential some men can get when I lean close to them wearing some of Mum's Arpège.'

Her father looked at Clements. 'I've sired a media harlot.'

'I think I'll raise Amanda to be a nun.'

Maureen grinned. 'I could kiss you both.'

'Not in front of the help,' said Clements, nodding towards the main room. 'Okay, Mo, you've been helpful. But take our advice – tread carefully. This is more than just a few political hopefuls trying to push each other out of the way.'

'Our producer is jumping up and down over the story and what we've dug up –'

'Then send him out on it,' said Malone. 'Let him shove his neck out. You take care of yours.'

She considered this for a moment, then she said, 'Will you two give me the full story when it's all over?'

'You and the rest of the media,' said Malone. 'We're playing no favourites.'

One could see the rebellion stirring in her; but she kept it in check. 'Okay, fair enough. But if I keep on prodding and I come up with something you miss, we'll run it on our show.'

'Do that,' said her father, still bluffing, 'and Sergeant Clements will hold you for twenty-four hours. Let you go, then bring you in for another twenty-four hours. And so on – it could be quite a serial. Thank you for coming in, Miss Malone.'

'Not at all my pleasure, Inspector.'

She gave them a smile that might have worked on younger, unrelated men. Clements said, 'Pull your head in, Mo. That's advice from Uncle Russ.'

When she had gone, giving everyone in the main room the same wide smile, Clements said, 'At least she didn't give us the middle finger.'

'She's going to. She's her grandfather's granddaughter. I can see Con in every other inch of her.'

He sat on in his office, staring out the window, while Clements went back to his own desk. He was troubled; sad, too. Maureen, headstrong as ever, was endangering herself; she was also distancing herself from him. The net that was the family was fraying; soon there would be gaping holes in it. He had never been, nor wanted to be, a demanding parent; neither, he knew, had Lisa. But, unspoken though it had been, they had always hoped their embrace would not be pushed aside. Maybe they had been lucky the embrace had lasted as long as it had; maybe because it had never been suffocating. Love, affection, care are only progress payments; a good parent never owned his children. Not that he wanted to. But it would have been a comfort if the payments could have gone on a little longer.

2

The strike force made little progress over the next two days. The paperwork multiplied, the computer screens were constantly alight; but Nemesis was a thwarted goddess and jokes were made about her being menopausal. The better-educated cops began to ask if there were any gods or goddesses who personified Doubt or Frustration.

John August was kept under surveillance, something that didn't appear to disturb him; he went about his job as a handyman, mowing lawns, fixing gutterings, mending broken gates. The Trades Congress and the suspect branches of the Labor Party put up invisible shutters; officers and members sneaked in and out as if visiting brothels. The Coalition, on the other hand, all at once became an Open House; the media were as welcome as corporation donors. In two months' time the sun, the political sun, might rise again. Bevan Bigelow took up jogging, getting into shape for the Olympics.

On the morning of the funeral, God, being a Catholic, as the staff at St Mary's knew He was, did the right thing by the cathedral and the State funeral. He turned off the heat and brought in a mild day. The cathedral was packed, though not with devotion. All the Catholics from both sides of politics, State and Federal, were there; likewise the Catholics from the Big End of town. But there were Protestants and Jews and Muslims and atheists and agnostics. It was not a festive occasion, but there were more smiles than tears; after all, it was a politician they were burying. God, at times, must have trouble not being cynical.

Cardinal O'Flanagan, known as Cement Crotch because of his habit of sitting on the fence on controversial matters, was uncharacteristically eloquent. He had not had a congregation as large as this since the last visit of a Pope. He praised Hans Vanderberg to the point where those in the front pews thought there was movement in the coffin, not from embarrassment but from self-satisfaction. The Dutchman had been moved up the ranks to just below St Augustine. The Coalition MPs in the congregation looked askance at each other, knowing the Catholic vote had just gone out the window. Gertrude Vanderberg, resplendent in self-made black, wiped her eyes and wondered whom they were burying.

Lord Mayor Rupert Amberton's wife had pleaded a convenient migraine; she was a Jehovah's Witness, though Jehovah didn't see much of her. Amberton had dragooned Lisa into accompanying him, but once inside the cathedral he had not missed her when she went and sat beside Malone in a side pew.

'Why are you here?' she whispered.

'Scanning suspects. Scores of them.'

'When did the Premier find religion?'

'I dunno. But when he did, God must have been worried.'

When they came out of the cathedral after the Mass Malone saw the TV crews lined up on either side of the steps. Maureen was with the Channel 15 crew; she had been promoted, though she had made no mention of it at home. Over the past two days she had been cool, but not rudely so; he had made no comment, waiting for her to thaw. Which would happen: she was too mercurial to remain cold. He waved to her and she flipped a hand that was almost dismissive.

'What's the matter between you and Mo?' asked Lisa.

'We're on opposing teams. You may have to be referee.'

'If you act like fools, I'll send both of you off.'

He kissed her, restrained himself from patting her on her rump. 'Take care.'

Lisa looked around at the crowd still spilling out of the cathedral. Old friends, old enemies, were meeting again. The dead man was forgotten: you look great, Joe, thank Christ we're still in the land of the living. Weddings are for introductions; funerals are for reunions. Handshakes clashed like swords.

'Your murderer is amongst this lot?' she said quietly.

85

'No,' he said. 'Just whoever paid him.'

Then his pager beeped. He crossed the road to where his car was parked in a No Loading zone, removed the usual ticket from the wiper, dropped it in the gutter and got into the car. He picked up the phone, pressed the buttons for Homicide. 'Russ?'

'It's on again, mate. Not a homicide, but a bashing. The secretary of The Dutchman's electoral office. You probably didn't notice he wasn't at the cathedral.'

'Russ, there's everyone and his missus here. It's like grand final day. Who did him over?'

'It happened last night, on his way home. He never saw who hit him, they got him in the dark as he got out of his car. It looks like an iron bar job – that's the Rockdale police's guess.'

'Will he live?'

'They say so. The Rockdale guys are by his bedside, but so far they haven't been able to question him. Greg Random wants us to talk to him. I'll meet you at St George's hospital.'

The Boolagong electorate covered the western and southern shores of Botany Bay. This was the harbour, some miles south of Sydney Harbour, into which Captain Cook had sailed 230 years before, where the natives were unfriendly, though they attempted no bashings. Cook thought them inferior in every way to the natives he had met in New Zealand, an opinion still held by New Zealanders towards the present natives. It is a wide bay, surrounded by flat land, much of it sandy. Kingsford Smith airport and port facilities are on its northern shore, an oil depot on its southern and round its western rim lie Rockdale, Brighton-le-Sands and Sans Souci. The French influence is non-existent, though there are still some houses that are called Mon Repos. On its northern headland there is a memorial to the Comte de la Pérouse, a Frenchman who wasn't too impressed and sailed on. The Dutch, who explored other parts of the continent, never bothered with this part of the eastern seaboard. Hans Vanderberg had laid claim to it just as James Cook had all those years ago. The natives had revered him, but only on election day. The rest of the term they called him That Old Bastard, which, in the natives' dialect, is still pretty close to reverence.

Clements was waiting for Malone outside the hospital, his unmarked car parked in a space reserved for doctors. Malone drew in beside him and at once a security guard appeared like a genie that had been rubbed the wrong way.

'You can't park there – that's for doctors!'

Clements flashed his badge. 'We're specialists.'

The two detectives went on into the hospital and the guard threw up his hands at the arrogance of cops. The hospital, like most public hospitals, had the shop-worn look of a health system short of funds. Malone had remarked that no politician of any party, large or small, or any so-called independent Independent ever pointed out to the voters that the public spent more on booze, smokes and gambling than it did on its health. There were no votes in telling the voters taxes were going to be raised for their own good. So the voters wrote Letters to the Editor complaining about the run-down hospitals, then went down to the pub and over half a dozen beers told their mates what they'd written to the Editor. And the mates raised their glasses and said, 'I'll drink to that, mate.'

Malone and Clements rode up to the intensive care ward, where the victim of last night's assault was in a private cubicle guarded by two young uniformed officers and what looked like the victim's extended family to the ninth cousin.

'They're Italians, sir,' one of the officers told Malone.

The family crowded round the man in the bed, who was bandaged so that he looked more like a mummy than a living human being. Heads turned as the two detectives spoke to the uniformed men. Their stares were as pointed as guns: *Get out of here*!

Then a voice behind Malone said, 'Who are you?'

He was short and square and plain as a fridge door; he could not have been colder in his attitude. 'I'm Barry Rix, secretary of the local Labor branch. Who are you?'

87

Malone introduced himself and Clements. 'You're the secretary? Then who is –?' He nodded back over his shoulder. 'We were told the secretary had been bashed.'

Rix jerked his head and led them out of the ward and into a corridor. Gurneys trundled by, laden with surgical cases, coming and going to the operating theatres: hospital traffic. Rix looked up and down the busy corridor, then opened a door and led them into a linen room. It was a small room, little more than a closet, and the three men crowded it.

'They got it wrong,' said Rix. He had a husky voice, as if he had spent his life shouting at a world that paid him no heed. 'That's Marco Crespi, poor bugger. He was the honorary *assistant* secretary. I'd left my car outside our office, Mrs Vanderberg had picked me up in her car, she wanted to talk to me. Marco was working back and said he'd drop it off at my place. They thought he was me. That bashing was meant for me.' He shuddered as if he felt the blows. 'Christ!'

'You any idea why?' asked Clements.

Then the door was pushed open and Clements, with his back to it, had to stand aside. A young nurse pushed her way in. 'What are you three doing in here?'

'Consorting,' said Malone.

The nurse started taking bed linen from the shelves. 'The matron finds out, she'll shoot the lot of you.'

She went out with an armful of linen. Clements closed the door after her and stood with his back to it again. 'Why you, Barry?'

Rix looked up at the two big men, so close to him they might have been threatening him. He was the perpetual ranker, the corporal or sergeant in every organization; he held the ranks together, changed the linen, read the wind. He was salt of the earth, Con Malone would have said, a man for the barricades. But he was scared by what had happened to Marco Crespi last night.

'I've been secretary for fifteen years, I ran the electorate for the Old Man. I never had any ambition, just to serve him and the party.' Somehow he did not sound as if he expected violins to be playing. 'Then Mrs Vanderberg came to me yesterday morning and said she wanted me to take Hans' place, to stand for pre-selection. I thought it over and said Yes.'

'Did you make any announcement?' asked Malone.

'Not to the media, no. But Mrs Vanderberg let head office and the rest of 'em down in Sussex Street know.'

'How'd they take it?'

'Head office didn't like it. They claim they run pre-selection. Gert – Mrs Vanderberg – told 'em to try their luck. I think they're gunna find out she's tougher than Mrs Thatcher ever was. Then the next thing –' He gestured at the closed door, at the man in the coma down the corridor. 'Poor bloody Marco.'

'Have you any idea who bashed him?'

Rix looked at them, dubious; or perhaps frightened. 'I don't wanna put anyone in the gun –'

'Barry,' said Malone patiently, 'we're investigating the murder of your boss. Your Old Man. Why would anyone want to bash you? Or kill you?'

Rix shuddered again at the word *kill*; he took his time: 'Well . . . Certain people in Sussex Street don't think I'm the guy for the job.'

'Which people? At party headquarters?'

'Yeah, one or two there. But mostly at Trades Congress. There's a bloke named Jerry Balmoral –'

'We've met him.'

'You know him? Looks like a million dollars, but it's all credit card. They're backing him, some of the trade union guys. Then I heard this morning one of the other party branches is gunna run a starter –'

'Would it be the Harding branch?'

Rix looked surprised, but made no comment. He hesitated, then nodded. 'There's a guy there named Joe St Louis –'

'We know him.'

89

'There's been talk about him – he's a mean bastard, he's threatened a coupla guys, to knee-cap 'em – he uses a tire lever –'

'You ever report any of this to the police?'

'You guys know the rules. You mind your own business, you keep your troubles to yourself . . . How many wives report their husbands for wife-beating? It's the same in politics, in the unions – you work it out between yourselves.'

'If you live . . . Has it been worked out with Joe St Louis?'

Rix shook his head. 'You don't work anything out with the Harding branch, they go their own way. That guy Kelzo, he's gunna be the biggest power broker in the State some day. That's his aim.'

Then the door was pushed open and an older nurse, all authority and starched indignation, stood in the doorway. 'What's going on in here – oh, it's you, Mr Rix! What's this – a cell meeting?'

'This is Matron Plymouth. She votes for the other side.'

'Out!' She stood aside. 'You two are police, right?'

'How'd you know?' said Clements.

'I can smell you like a dirty sheet. No offence.' She stood aside as the three men moved out of the tiny room. 'If you're here about Mr Crespi, he's regained consciousness but you can't talk to him. Not for another day at least.'

'No problem,' said Malone. 'Mr Rix has given us all we need.'

'Have I?' said Rix and looked even more worried.

There is something defeating about seeing another man's fear. It tells everyone but the fool that he himself is vulnerable. Fear is a cousin to anger and sometimes can, working against the grain, make a man heroic. But Malone knew that Barry Rix would never be heroic. He was not, after all, a man for the barricades. The death of the Premier, his general, had knocked the stuffing out of him.

'Do we ask for our money back?' said Madame Tzu, drawing on gloves for battle.

'Easier said than done,' said Jack Junior. 'Do political bosses in Shanghai give back donations?'

Everyone looked at General Wang-Te. He was an ex-general, if there is such a thing. Generals are like cardinals: unless executed for treason or heresy, they retain their rank, like a late birthmark. Wang-Te had been the financial comptroller of China's southern command; though an honest man he had experience of how money came and went in the army. It was an army of entrepreneurs as well as the military trade. When he had left the army to join Madame Tzu and the Bund Corporation all he had to do to adapt was to change from a uniform to mufti. He now wore a Zegna suit, but it was a uniform in which he was still not comfortable. He still wore the hair-shirt of his wife's mission upbringing. She had taught him the meaning of sin if not an understanding of it.

'Of course they don't,' said Jack Aldwych. 'That would be like preaching the meek shall inherit the earth to a congregation of stockbrokers. They'd bust a gut laughing.'

'So our money goes to waste?' Madame Tzu hated the thought. Charity should not begin at home, it shouldn't even leave home. And giving money to politicians was charity unless they gave something in return. She never understood why corruption was looked upon as sinful, whatever that was.

'Not necessarily,' said Leslie Chung.

The directors of Olympic Tower were in Chung's offices on the forty-ninth floor of the tower. The offices were a converted apartment and took up one corner of the huge block. From its windows there was a magnificent view of the city stretching north and east. The light in the distance to the east was oddly clearer than close to the city, as if the sea kept it washed; the silvertail eastern suburbs basked on the hills like seals sunning themselves. Northwards one could see the Harbour Bridge vaulting the water towards the silvertail suburbs of the North Shore. There was no view to the south or west, where there was less money. Les Chung took the long view, which is to the pot of gold at the end of the rainbow. It was his considered meteorological opinion that all rainbows ended either in the east or the north.

'So what do we do?' Camilla Feng was the youngest director, but her youth did not make her naive. 'If Jerry Balmoral gets the pre-selection, do we let him use the money?'

'Who told you this – Mr Balmoral? – is going for pre-selection? Who is he? Do you know him?' Madame Tzu was opening a file in her mind: another name would be added.

'I know him,' said Chung. 'The Trades Congress offices are only a block from Chinatown. He comes occasionally to the Golden Gate –' a restaurant owned by him and Aldwych – 'he's a very ambitious young man. Clever, too. In ten years' time he will be a very good minister. In twenty years' time a very good Prime Minister.'

'But we don't want him now,' said Aldwych. 'So how do we get rid of him?'

'Perhaps I can help there.' Camilla Feng was at ease amongst her fellow directors. Like Balmoral she had the look of someone whose future was assured. 'I've been out with him a couple of times. He was with me at the dinner the other night.'

'I saw you,' said Leslie Chung. 'I didn't realize he was your partner.'

'Perhaps because he was working everyone else at the table. He never misses an opportunity.'

Everyone had leaned forward, even Madame Tzu. They were never rude to her, but she was *young*; they were waiting for her years to catch up with theirs. Even Jack Junior, who was only ten years older than she, had been perfunctorily polite when discussing business. She was beautiful and decorative, with a cool elegance; but she was *young*. Now, suddenly, she might be taken seriously, an apprentice with the spanner that might work.

'Is it serious?' Aldwych liked to get to the point. 'Between you and him?'

She had the sort of smile that some women have from nine to ninety; men can never read it. 'It could be for him. For me?' She shook her head; the short black hair caught the light. 'Whoever marries him will only be baggage. Some men are like that.'

'How true,' said Madame Tzu, who had discarded baggage of her own, but male.

'So how do you get rid of him?' Aldwych was practised at practical questions. He had once held a gun at the head of a man for twenty-two minutes till the man, crap-sodden, had finally told Aldwych what he wanted to know. 'We're not gunna pay money to someone who won't listen to us. Mrs Vanderberg wants the branch secretary, some bloke named Rix, she wants him to get the pre-selection. Jack here has looked into him –'

'I met him when I gave him the cheque,' said Jack Junior. 'That was before The Dutchman was shot. He looked to me like a guy who wouldn't make waves – he doesn't want to be Prime Minister. Or even Premier. He'd be satisfied with his eighty-one thousand dollars plus electoral allowance plus perks and superannuation –'

Madame Tzu wondered how the near-poor could be satisfied so easily.

'—but he'd run Boolagong the way Mrs Vanderberg would want it run.'

'And how's that?' asked Camilla.

'To look after the people in the electorate, the voters. All she's interested in is the grass-roots.'

'Then what's the point of leaving our money there?' Madame Tzu didn't believe in watering weeds.

'The point is,' said Les Chung, 'we don't leave our money

there, we take it out. But if Balmoral and the guys handling him get their hands on it –'

'We could shoot him,' said Aldwych, being practical though smiling.

'He's only kidding,' said Jack Junior hastily.

Wang-Te rarely asked a leading question, but he tried one now: 'Does this Mr Balmoral have any dirty secrets we could use against him?'

'A good idea.' Madame Tzu clapped her hands as if a rock were about to be turned over.

'Maybe he has no secrets,' said Jack Junior.

'A man who has no secrets has no intelligence.'

'Confucius?' asked Aldwych with a grin.

'No,' she said, 'Madame Tzu.'

'Leave Mr Balmoral to me,' said Camilla and it seemed that she, too, drew on gloves.

'Good luck,' said Aldwych solicitously.

She looked at him in surprise, got up, passed behind him, kissed him on top of his thick head of hair and went out.

Aldwych looked at the others. 'I think I might start being a ladies' man.'

'Too late,' said Madame Tzu, as practical and blunt as he.

4

Lisa, being foreign and a gourmet cook, looked on barbecues as something for cannibals and *auto-da-fé* enthusiasts. Occasionally, however, she relented, so long as the children did the cooking and she was allowed to sit as far as possible from the smell of grilling steak and sausages. She did provide the desserts, though even there she felt she was slumming, cooking *American*: upside-down cake and lime pie. She had one strong rule: the wine had to be out of bottles, preferably at least three years old and not out of cardboard casks that, she said, had been sealed yesterday. She was a culinary snob and unashamed of it.

She had invited two women from Town Hall, who came with their husbands, both of whom showed the plump sleekness of double-income living. Malone had invited Phil Truach and his wife, a jolly woman who smoked as much as her husband and was racked by coughing every time she laughed. Russ and Romy Clements were there with young Amanda. Tom had brought his Girl of the Week, a lanky pretty girl who, she told Lisa, was studying medicine and men and finding them equally easy. Maureen brought a student director from the North Ryde film school who, so Claire said, believed in shooting through venetian blinds, crossover dialogue so that the audience had to pay attention and thought Spielberg was too sentimental but was learning. Claire herself had come with Jason Rockne, her live-in partner.

Jason's mother was doing life for, with her lesbian lover, killing Jason's father. He and Claire had been on-again-off-again sweethearts as teenagers, then they had drifted apart for two or three years. Now, six-feet-four and lean, a junior engineer with a major construction company, he was back with Claire, his life apparently adjusted, his love for Claire very apparent.

'You never worked on Olympic Tower, did you?' asked Malone.

'No, thank God. They tell me it was nothing but headaches. Still is – for you, I mean.'

'It's political now. You interested in politics?'

'Not really. Is it worth it? Being interested, I mean. They all go their own way, they're not really caring a damn about what the voters are trying to tell them.'

'Is it like that with youngsters your age?'

'Mostly.'

'It was different in my day,' said Con Malone, coming feet first as usual into the conversation. He had just arrived with Brigid, Scobie's mother. Malone, glancing at him, remarked how old his father looked lately; the years of struggle were coming out of him like leprosy. 'In my day the pollies listened or we got rid of 'em, no mucking about. Those days they come out into the open, on soap-boxes, the backs of trucks. None of this stuff like today, hiding away in TV studios. You didn't like what they said, you pulled 'em down off the soap-box and did 'em. They listened then, all right.'

'The good old days,' Malone told Jason with a grin.

'It might've been better. Now –' Jason flicked the switch on an imaginary remote control. 'You can just turn 'em off.'

'We turned 'em off in the old days,' said Con and put up a fist bigger than any remote control. 'Still, the next few weeks are gunna be innaresting. You're gunna see more in-fighting than in a yard fulla roosters.' His rheumy old eyes suddenly looked younger with relish. 'They'll be fighting each other to get on the *7.30 Report*, you watch.'

'What about *Wanted for Questioning*?' said Jason, grinning.

'That's my territory,' said Malone and left them.

He passed the student director telling a small group, 'Antonioni was the greatest director the screen's ever seen. He made the audience *think*.'

'He directed the Marx Brothers, didn't he?' said Clements and gasped as Maureen hit him in the ribs. Mrs Truach started a laugh that turned into a hacking cough and the student director looked pained at the dumb taste of the middle-aged.

Lisa and Romy were sitting in deck-chairs on the far side of the pool from the barbecue; Romy, even though German, had better taste than sauerkraut and dumplings. Amanda was seated on her mother's lap. She was a chubby little girl, the hint of her mother in her broad-cheeked face, of her father in her build. She gave Malone a hug and transferred herself to his lap as he sat down and took the glass of Hunter semillon Lisa poured for him.

'How's my girl?'

'I just one of your girls,' said the three-year-old.

He looked at her mother. 'Are you teaching her to count or be suspicious of men?'

'Both,' said Romy, and Lisa nodded appreciatively.

'That's you Europeans.'

'Women have gone further in Europe than we ever have out here. Catherine the Great, Isabella of Spain –'

'Nymphos –'

Both women laughed, then Romy said, 'Changing the subject – did you know Janis Eden has been released from prison?'

'No. When?'

Janis Eden had been holding a large briefcase full of hundred-dollar notes, drug money, when Romy's father Peter Keller, a serial killer, had plunged a poisoned syringe into his own arm and committed suicide rather than be arrested by Malone and Clements. It had happened just over nine years ago, had brought Romy and Clements together, but it was a shadow that would never go away. Malone stole a glance at Amanda and hoped she would never be told the truth about her grandfather. She saw his glance, smirked at him and gave him the two-eyed wink that Wombat Rose had given him. He hugged her, as much for protection as for affection.

'Four months ago. She got out of Mulawa, time off for good behaviour. While she was in there she counselled a lot of the women who had drug problems.'

'That was what she was before she went in, a professional drug counsellor. She was also a drug seller. She had a nice set-up. Her patients didn't know it, but they were her customers as well as her patients. She might still be going if she hadn't got greedy.'

'Well, she's out now.' Romy sounded cautious, as if a door had suddenly opened again.

'Where is she?'

'I don't know. I don't want to know,' she said and looked at Amanda as if protection was already necessary.

Malone held the little girl for a moment, looking over her head at her mother. Lisa sat quiet, but there was a warning in her eyes:

Don't say anything. Then he kissed Amanda, gave her back to Romy, got up and went along to where Clements had just joined Phil Truach. The latter put out his third cigarette since arriving; Malone didn't like the smell of cigarette smoke. Truach smoked two packs a day and boasted that his doctor said he had lungs that could work a steel forge.

'Janis Eden is out,' said Malone. 'Did you know?'

'Romy told me this morning.' Clements was sipping a beer, his pre- as well as his after-lunch drink. He drank wine and had a good cellar, but the habits of youth still clung. 'I think she's known for a week or more, but didn't want to talk about it. Janis is history.'

'Janis Eden?' said Truach. 'Wasn't she involved with Jack Aldwych's son? I did some work on that one with you two. You had me and Andy Graham tailing Jack Junior at one stage.'

'We were never able to hang anything on him. Jack Senior got to him and pulled him out of it before we could land him. He's been squeaky clean ever since. And happily married.'

'While Janis did nine years?' Truach automatically took out another cigarette, remembered whose company he was in and put it back in its pack. 'I wonder if she hired a hitman and he got The Dutchman by mistake?'

Chapter Four

1

Monday morning there was a strike force conference at Police Centre, presided over by Chief Superintendent Random. Laconic as ever, he still managed to have an edge to his voice, a drawl that was a slow cut across the throat:

'Every editorial writer, every talk-back host, every columnist is on our back about this case. Five days have gone by and they can't understand why we haven't got the hitman, tried him and hung him by now. We have a suspect, as you know, but so far we haven't enough evidence to convict him of even a traffic offence. We know of the throat-cutting going on in the Labor Party – is that door shut?' He looked towards the back of the big room and was assured that, yes, the door was shut. But everyone in the room knew that shut doors do not stop leaks. 'We're walking on eggshells here, both parties will knock us arse-over-head, for different reasons, if we put a foot wrong. So we tread carefully. At the same time we'd better get a move on. Now, has anything new come up?'

Malone hesitated, then spoke up: 'I've something we still have to look into –' he was aware of every eye in the room on him, like a battery of laser beams – 'there is a possibility that the bullet that got the Premier wasn't meant for him –'

He paused. Everyone in the room was abruptly still. Even Greg Random, as relaxed as a bolster, seemed to stiffen.

'It could have been meant for one of the Aldwyches, father or son, who were on either side of him when he was shot.'

'Shit!' said someone and a wave, like a bad smell, stirred the audience. Complications were never welcomed; they bred like rabbits. To have lost a Premier and Police Minister was bad enough; to have lost him by accident, even if someone else's accident, was disaster compounded.

Then someone else said, 'Well, that takes the heat off the Labor Party,' and there was a second flutter, of relief.

'Not necessarily,' said Random. 'Not till we've eliminated the Premier as the intended victim. We say nothing to the media about this new development – it may lead us to nothing. We give them the usual release – investigations are proceeding and we are hopeful of an early arrest, blah, blah. In the meantime –' He looked at Malone.

'In the meantime,' said Malone, 'we look for a woman named Janis Eden. She was released from Mulawa four months ago.' He gave a brief summary of why she had been put away. 'She's dropped out of sight, maybe gone interstate, maybe gone overseas. Or maybe she's still around, under another name. We want to question her. *I* want to question her – she's my pigeon.'

'Why you, sir?' said someone from the back of the room.

'Because he said so,' said Random, the edge to his voice even sharper.

'It's personal,' said Clements.

'Sorry,' said the someone and sank down out of sight.

There was another question from the floor: 'What about our suspect? August, June, whatever we call him?'

'We call him August on our sheets,' said Malone. 'Russ Clements and I are going out to talk to him now.'

When the meeting broke up Random gestured to Malone and Clements to wait behind. When they were alone he said, 'Do you think this Janis Eden could be involved?'

'Greg, we don't know. Christ, the last thing we wanted was a complication like this. Unless we find her, the only way we're going to find out is by leaning on August.'

'Does he respond to being leant on?'

'I think you could run over him with a tank and he wouldn't tell you a thing.'

100

'Neither would I,' said Random and a thin gully appeared round the corner of his mouth. 'Good luck.'

Outside in their car Malone called the two surveillance officers tailing August. 'Where is he now?'

'At the Clontarf Gardens nursing home in Clontarf. We're in the parking lot, we can see him working on the verandah.'

'We're on our way. Don't tell him.'

They drove through the city, over the bridge, out through Cremorne and Mosman, silvertail suburbs that the dead Premier had never bothered to visit; Labor voters there were as scarce as Christian voters in Iran. The unmarked police car went down the long curving slope to the Spit bridge, where they joined a long queue held up by the opening of the bridge to let three small yachts through into Middle Harbour. The bridge had been built by an American firm three or four decades ago; they had told the government of the day that a drawbridge was going to be a major hindrance to the increasing traffic of the future, but the government had known best. The long view is not a national habit, especially amongst politicians. The next election is the horizon.

At last the bridge was down, traffic started to move and they climbed the opposite hill to the ridge where Clontarf looked back over the outer reaches of the main harbour. It is a pleasant suburb, with solid houses surrounding the wide block on which the nursing home stood.

Two young officers in plainclothes got out of an unmarked car as Malone and Clements drove into the parking lot. They introduced themselves: 'Sutcliffe and Crivic, sir. He's over there, entertaining the old ducks.'

'Has he shown any narkiness with you and the other fellers tailing him?'

'None at all, sir. He brought us morning coffee and biscuits. He got the old ducks to wave to us.'

'He's told them you're cops?' said Clements.

Sutcliffe was a beefy young man with close-cropped blond hair, a broad snub-nosed face with a long upper lip and light blue eyes that squinted in the bright sun. He put back on the sunglasses he had taken off. 'I don't think so. He's a smartarse, but I don't think he's a dumb smartarse.'

'He's not worried.' Crivic was lean and dark, Sutcliffe's thin shadow. He was not squinting, his dark eyes wide open as if daring the sun to dazzle him. 'If he did the hit, sir, he's not gunna help us bring him in.'

'We'll see,' said Malone.

He and Clements left the two young officers and crossed the hot lake of the parking lot and went through a small garden to where August was repairing the railing that ran across the verandah fronting the wide building. Half a dozen elderly women sat in wheelchairs watching him like a covey of charge-hands.

'Mr Malone and Mr Clements!' August put down his tools and smiled at the two detectives; then he turned to the old ladies: 'Two gentlemen from Meals on Wheels. They help me deliver.'

Two of the old women smiled at Malone and Clements; the others sat staring at nothing. They don't even know we're here, thought Malone. They had neither the long view nor the short view, they were trapped in the blindness of Alzheimer's. All at once Malone wished he and Clements had not come. Murder and politics were another world from this last oasis.

As they moved away from the verandah Malone said, 'You travel the gamut, don't you? From the kids at Happy Hours to *this*.'

'It's a living.' August was affable, didn't seem to resent their coming. 'I don't mind the old ones. We'll be like that ourselves one day. I just hope I go, though, before I finish up a vegetable in a wheelchair.'

'John,' said Clements, 'how can you be a hitman and be so considerate of those old ladies?'

'Easy. I'm not a hitman.'

There were three timber garden chairs under a large camphor laurel. August sat down and waved to the two detectives to join him. It was all very informal, an interrogation amongst the flowers and shrubs. The two old women with sight watched them from the verandah; the others just stared at nothing. A kookaburra dropped down out of nowhere and sat on the verandah railing, not laughing.

'You're wasting your time.'

'I don't think so,' said Malone. 'Do you know a woman named Janis Eden?'

August frowned. 'Who's she?'

'We thought she might have approached you to do the hit.'

'Oh, really?' As if she had approached him for a quote on mowing a lawn. 'What does she do?'

'She's just done time. Nine years.'

'And she had a grudge against Hans Vanderberg?'

'No, not him. But she does have a grudge against two men named Aldwych, father and son. They were with Vanderberg that night, we think you might've meant to hit one of them and you got the Premier by mistake.'

August laughed: naturally, not at all forced. 'You buggers beat the band, you know? First, you accuse me of being a hitman, now you accuse me of hitting the wrong guy. What else are you gunna dream up?'

'John,' said Clements, 'you needed the money.'

He shook his head. 'You saw my bank account. That, incidentally, embarrassed me with my bank manager. I hadda tell him it was a case of mistaken identity and you'd apologized.' He smiled; he could not have been friendlier. 'Okay, I'm not rolling in it, but there's enough to pay the bills.'

Clements took his time, turned his head as over on the verandah railing the kookaburra gave a short laugh, like a snort of contempt. Then he looked back at August: 'Mrs Masson doesn't have enough to pay the bills. The Happy Hours is up to its neck in debt. You could of done the job to help out your partner.'

The change in August was sudden. The round face hardened, darkened; another man stepped out of the skin of the good-natured deliverer of Meals on Wheels. 'You bastards!'

'We have to be, sometimes,' said Malone.

'I told you to stay away from her! Jesus Christ, I should—' He choked.

'What, John?' said Clements. 'Take a hit at us?'

Then Malone, taking over the bowling, said quietly, 'We haven't been near Mrs Masson, John. We got that information through the proper channels.' Even if illicitly.

'What fucking proper channels?'

He had raised his voice. All six women on the verandah lifted their heads; one woman put a hand to her ear. The kookaburra abruptly took off, as if it had been offended by August's language.

'We have our sources.'

August glared at both of them. He was still red-faced; a strand of hair had fallen down over his brow. Then with an obvious effort, like a cripple arranging his limbs, he relaxed, sat back against the hard wood of his chair.

'Why me? Why the fuck are you picking on me?'

'John –' Malone kept his voice casual. Neither he nor Clements had shifted their positions in their chairs; they were as relaxed, even more so, as August. They could have been discussing tomorrow's delivery of Meals on Wheels. 'You were the only one on the list of customers at the Sewing Bee who had a record. You went to the window, we were told, and looked across at the entrance to Olympic Tower. Not once, but twice. You told the woman who runs the place you were interested because you were once an architect. John, we looked up your CV. You never even got close to designing a garden shed or an outdoor loo.'

'Well –' He waved a hand, looked unexpectedly embarrassed. 'You know how it is. You bullshit –'

'Of course. We all do it – occasionally. But not now, John. We're not bullshitting you now. Do you know Janis Eden?'

'No.' He was climbing back into the skin of the man at ease. 'Describe her.'

That, Malone suddenly knew, was where he and Clements

had made their mistake. It was nine years since they had last seen Janis Eden; she was a faded image, viewed through the astigmatic eye of memory. Both men had sat opposite her in a Bondi café while Romy's father had held the poisoned syringe against her wrist; it was the only time that Malone had taken out his gun and threatened to shoot a man in cold blood. It was Peter Keller's image that was burned in their brain, not hers. They had attended her trial for only one day, to give evidence in the witness box. In the dock she had changed her appearance, done something with her hair, but Malone couldn't remember how. She would be thirty-five or thirty-six now and he knew that women could be more chameleon-like than men.

'Dark-haired. Attractive.'

'No,' said Clements. 'Auburn-haired. You know, sorta dark red.'

'Dark-haired, auburn-haired, attractive – that could be a helluva lot of women.' August shook his head in amusement. 'If she's one-legged, it'll help.'

Malone had to admire him. 'Do you ever lose your sense of humour?'

'Occasionally.' No longer amused. 'When you keep pestering my partner.'

'It's regrettable, John, but we may have to keep doing it.'

'No,' he said. 'You don't have to. I'm no hitman and my partner's problems are her own.'

'And yours, too, John.'

He stared at them a long moment, then he nodded. 'You two married? Happily married?' It was their turn to nod. 'So you understand?'

'Yes.' Malone stood up. He knew now they were going to achieve nothing with August by beating him into the ground. He would never crack that way. 'We'll keep in touch.'

'You're not gunna leave me alone? Get off my back?' He had not risen, sat looking up at the two big men.

'Afraid not. It's what we call Chinese water torture. We're good at it.'

'I'll bet.'

They left him there under the camphor laurel; the sun had moved and he looked a little vaguer in its shade. They waved to the old ladies on the verandah and the two with sight waved back. Malone paused for a moment and looked at the long verandah. The six figures sat there like a frieze of statues, waiting for the last door to open and welcome them. Then the six figures shrank into four; four familiar faces stared at him. His father and mother, Lisa's father and mother: he turned away and headed for the parking lot. We too often close books we don't want to finish reading.

2

Gertrude Vanderberg, unlike her late husband, was a monarchist. That is, she saw herself as queenly; it was her only vanity and self-delusion. Never in front of The Dutchman, always behind him, she had, nevertheless, reviewed the troops with an eye as searching as his. She knew the domain of Boolagong better than he, she had spent more time in it. Attending fêtes, to which she always donated her home-baked pumpkin pavlovas; visiting sick voters, sometimes even if they were not Labor; housekeeping, such as checking the branch's accounts. The rest of the State she left to Hans. Queens have better recognition in small domains; empresses are acknowledged only on coins. Everyone in Boolagong knew Gert Vanderberg.

'You're from *where*?' She made it sound like Antarctica.

'Channel 15,' said Maureen.

Mrs Vanderberg was not in good temper. She was still feeling not only the death of Hans but the manner in which he had died. She had always recognized that politics was a dirty business; but murder was a horror she could not come to terms with. She knew the pain of losing someone; her and Hans' only child had died of breast cancer ten years ago; she was not new to grief. She was here in the Boolagong branch office in the main street of Rockdale because she had found the house, hers and Hans', too lonely. She had sat there in the rooms for the whole weekend, still hearing the sounds of him, feeling his presence like a visible ghost. The grief and loneliness had been too much for her and she regretted that she and Hans had never had more children. Friends and relatives came and sat with her, but they didn't fill the space that had been left. Today, escaping the loneliness, she had come here to the office to comfort Barry Rix, who was still shaken by his own narrow escape. And now here was a damned TV reporter intruding.

'What do you want?'

Maureen was not yet case-hardened; she knew she was intruding. But her producer, a man isolated by the distance of his office from any door that had to be knocked on, who saw the world at one and sometimes two removes, had insisted she come out this morning and follow up the branch-stacking story. The maw of television is the black hole of entertainment and infotainment: reporting cancer cure as a divertissement. That was enough excuse, the producer had told Maureen, for any intrusion.

'We are preparing a story on branch-stacking –'

'Not here,' said Mrs Vanderberg and looked at Rix. 'Not here, Barry?'

'No,' said Rix and made coffee for the three of them. If he won pre-selection he might need all the media help he could get. He brought biscuits. 'Home-made. By Mrs Vanderberg.'

'Very nice,' said Maureen and bit into a sweet pumpkin cookie.

This branch office was not a social hall; it was two medium-sized rooms. The Dutchman, coming here once a month, had seen the advantages of having voters waiting for him out on the pavement; there is no public value in having all your supporters packed together out of sight. Mrs Vanderberg, Rix and Maureen were in the inner room, its walls plastered with old posters from the days before TV commercials. Maureen had looked around at them with the curiosity of the young looking at old campaign recruiting posters; indeed, she would not have been surprised to find The Dutchman glaring at her from a poster, finger pointed: YOUR COUNTRY NEEDS YOU! In the outer room there were half a dozen people, two volunteer workers and four supplicants. One never calls voters beggars.

'No,' said Rix, 'we've never had any stacking here. The Boss would never have stood for anything like that.' Nor would he have needed it.

'No,' said Maureen, 'not here. Not yet, I'm told.'

'Not ever,' said Mrs Vanderberg. She was not wearing widow's weeds, which might have been more flattering; she was in an orange blouse and a green skirt. 'We don't go in for that sort of thing here. Mr Rix –'

'We understand Mr Rix is going to have opposition for pre-selection –'

'You're young, Miss –?'

'Malone. Maureen Malone.'

Mrs Vanderberg gave her an acute look. Like her husband she had a memory for names: they are the blood cells of politics. 'Mr Rix told me an Inspector Malone is handling the investigation into my husband's murder –'

'My father,' said Maureen and wished her name was Lewdinsky or McTavish. 'He doesn't know I'm here – I have my own job to do –'

'Of course,' said Mrs Vanderberg and made it sound as if there were far better jobs than being a TV reporter. 'You're young, Miss Malone, and you will find out that rumours are like the whipped cream on my pavlovas – they go off after a week.' The aphorism was one of her husband's, but she didn't mangle it as he had. Then she looked past Maureen: 'Why, here comes a rumour himself!'

Jerome Balmoral stood in the doorway. One knew that when

he got into parliament he would be Jerome and not Jerry; Labor was the Old Mates party, but it would not be Jerry, mate, when he became Prime Minister. He looked at Maureen with a very unmate-like stare.

'What's she doing here?' He sounded as if he already owned the office, that there was no need for pre-selection, he was already selected and elected.

'She's here at my invitation,' said Gert Vanderberg, not looking at Maureen.

'You're letting her go ahead with their dirty muck-raking?'

'No.' She looked sideways at Maureen; it might have been a motherly glance or a keep-your-mouth-shut look. 'She's just been taken on as my assistant. My private secretary, if you like. Or my minder, as my husband used to call them.'

'You need a minder?' Balmoral was unimpressed. Or perhaps he was impressed, meant she would never need a minder.

'Occasionally,' said Mrs Vanderberg.

Maureen was no actress; but she managed to remain blank-faced, which in television soap opera can be mistaken for acting. 'Good morning, Mr Balmoral.'

He ignored her. 'Can I see you alone, Mrs Vanderberg?'

'Of course not,' said she affably; she spread her hands to include Maureen and Rix. 'We're a team here. What do you want, Jerry?'

For a moment it looked as if Balmoral would retreat; but in the Trades Congress such tactics were never taught. 'Well, basically –'

Maureen had noted that over the past couple of years no one in the nation seemed to be able to get through a statement without using *basically*. She was waiting for a priest to remark that The Lord, basically, was God. Jerry Balmoral had no ambition to be God, but that was only because, basically, the voters didn't believe in the Eternal.

'– I came to see if we can't come to terms.' He had sat down, arranging his trouser-legs; the creases could have cut one of Gert's pavlovas. He was in a beige summer suit, a darkish blue shirt and a tie that suggested he was in favour of the Olympics but only discreetly. Maureen, against her will, admitted he was handsome, good to look at. 'I think if I get pre-selection, I can win this seat easily, keep it in the Party –'

'We think Mr Rix can win just as easily. Don't you, Miss Malone?'

'With no effort at all,' said Maureen, slipping with no effort at all into the role of minder. 'This is, basically, a blue riband seat for Labor, always has been. With no branch-stacking.'

'Barry –' Balmoral turned to Rix as if Maureen hadn't spoken. 'You'll be looked after – we can find you a job in Macquarie Street, maybe in the Upper House –'

'I've worked my arse off here,' said Rix and for a moment appeared to change character; he seemed to forget that his ex-boss' wife and Maureen were there beside him. 'I'm *owed*, Jerry. I'm not gunna roll over for some whipper-snapper from Sussex Street –' Then he remembered he was in the shadow of the boss' wife: 'Gert here wants me to run and I'm gunna do just that. No argument.'

'Barry –' Balmoral was all patience – 'the branch has a hoodoo on it. Hans has – forgive me for mentioning this, Mrs Vanderberg –' He was like an undertaker trying to excuse the delivery of the coffin. 'Hans has been shot. Your assistant secretary – what's his name?'

'Marco Crespi,' said Gert Vanderberg. 'His name was in every newspaper and on radio and TV. You must have missed it.'

'I must have,' Balmoral admitted; one could almost see him wiping sarcasm off the beige suit. 'Yes, Marco Crespi was bashed up. Someone wants to destroy the tradition of this branch. We don't know why –'

'Yes, we do,' said Gert Vanderberg.

'Why?' Balmoral had learned the trick of looking innocent, which comes in handy in an environment of skulduggery.

But she dodged that question, put one of her own with brutal force: 'Do you know who killed my husband, Jerry?'

'No, no.' He was off-balance for a moment. Then: 'Well, yes. The police are said to have a suspect – have they?' He looked at Maureen.

'My father doesn't confide police business in me. He might now,' she said. 'Now I'm Mrs Vanderberg's minder.'

'But you do know, don't you, who bashed up poor Marco Crespi?' Mrs Vanderberg wasn't going to let him off the hook. Under her dowdy queenly air there had always been an affable lady; but now there was iron in her soul, she was a widow who wanted revenge. It surprised her how revengeful she felt. 'It was that crowd from Harding, wasn't it? Kelzo and his mob.'

'I don't know –'

'If you don't know, you must be the only one in the party who doesn't. We know, don't we, Barry?'

'Yes,' said Rix, but sounded apprehensive.

'You can try your luck, Jerry, and run for pre-selection here, but you are going to be wiped like a snotty nose.' She didn't sound at all queenly now, at least not a Christian one with afternoon-tea manners and a retinue of elderly courtiers. 'Go back to Sussex Street and tell them you're as welcome out here as the plague. While you're at it, tell your mates out at Harding that if Joe St Louis comes into this electorate again, I'll have the local police lock him up.'

'What for?' Balmoral had had no experience of Gert Vanderberg at close quarters; she was giving him a crash course in a woman's power. He was a success amongst younger women, or thought he was, but this old battle-axe was another proposition altogether. He was so off-balance he repeated himself: 'What for?'

'For threatening me.'

'Has he?'

Her smile threatened to cut his throat. 'I'm Saint Gertrude around here. Nobody doubts my word. Goodbye, Jerry.'

He stood up, looked at all three of them, searched for some

warning to spit at them, found none and left. The room seemed to expand with his going, the old posters on the walls took on an added shine like old victories revived.

Gert Vanderberg, looking neither queenly nor saintly, settled back in her chair. 'You're downsized as my minder, Miss Malone. Now what was it you wanted to talk about as a TV reporter?'

Maureen took out her tape-recorder. She hoped Mrs Vanderberg, a mincer if ever she'd seen one, would not mince words.

3

Outside the Clontarf nursing home Malone picked up the car-phone and rang Jack Aldwych's home at Harbord. It was only ten minutes' drive from here and he felt like some relaxation after the frustration with August. He always enjoyed any sort of encounter with Aldwych.

'Yeah?'

'That you, Blackie? You don't sound like the butler.'

'Who's this, smartarse?'

'Scobie Malone.'

'Oh shit – sorry, Mr Malone.' Blackie Ovens had been with Aldwych for thirty years. He had been an iron-bar man, had had a reputation, had done time time and time again. Now, like his boss, he was retired, spent his days as general factotum around the Aldwych big house. 'The boss ain't here, he's over at the office with young Jack. Once a week he goes in there, plays the big businessman. Don't tell him I said that. He ain't been as good-humoured lately, not like he used to be.'

'I've never grassed in my life –'

'Neither have I, Mr Malone.' He was one of the old-style crims, always polite to senior officers if they weren't being manhandled.

'I know, Blackie, and I respect you for it. Call Mr Aldwych and tell him Sergeant Clements and I are on our way and to wait for us.'

Malone and Clements drove back into the city and to the AMP Tower where Landfall Holdings, the Aldwych family company, had its offices. There was no hint of Aldwych Senior's past in the offices; rather, they suggested a company that had come out with the original settlers and convicts, but with credentials, in 1788. The discreet gilt lettering on the double doors named seven companies, but Landfall was the umbrella. The attractive brunette on the reception desk, the granddaughter of one of Aldwych's one-time brothel-keepers, was as soft-spoken and genteel as any girl out of Jane Austen.

'Mr Aldwych is expecting you, Inspector. Shall I bring coffee?'

Malone and Clements went into the big inner office. Out beyond the large windows the harbour and the Opera House caught the eye at once; the only mote in the view was the large block of apartments that development greed and civic maladministration had allowed to be built. It sat in front of the Opera House like a huge outhouse.

'Scobie –' Aldwych didn't rise from his chair; kings let their manners be taken for granted. But his smile was genial, that of a commoner; he always met Malone on equal terms. 'Some good news?'

'Maybe, maybe not.' The two detectives sat down, looked at the two Aldwyches. 'Did you know Janis Eden is out of jail?'

The receptionist brought them coffee, strong and rich, not instant. 'No sugar, just milk for you both, right?'

'How'd you know?' asked Clements.

She gave him a smile that would have earned her grandmother's girls an extra quid or two. 'I keep a file.'

After she had left the room Malone said, 'You've trained her well, Jack.'

'Not me. Her grandmother,' said Aldwych. 'So the slut is out?'

Out of the corner of his eye Malone waited for a reaction from Jack Junior, but there was none. The younger Aldwych had lived

113

with Janis Eden for a short period; the relationship had appeared deep, at least on his part. Then his father's command and his own awakening to the totally selfish Janis had frozen the relationship. He had supplied the money that was to pay for the drugs for which she was arrested; it had been the pay-off, the cold way of saying it was all over. She had kept her mouth shut during her trial, had never attempted to contact him. He knew, however, that she would always feel that he should have gone to jail with her. Like most selfish people she never blamed herself for what had happened to her.

'Four months ago, out of Mulawa,' said Malone. 'She's dropped out of sight, hasn't been heard of. But –'

'But?' Aldwych was doing all the talking; his son sat saying nothing. 'There's always a *but* with women.' His wife Shirl would have clouted him for that, no *buts* about it. 'That's why you're here. But.'

Malone said admiringly, 'You haven't lost your touch, Jack. A bit heavy, but still there.'

Aldwych nodded, sat waiting. Malone looked at him, then turned his gaze bluntly on Jack Junior. 'Could the hit have been meant for you and not The Dutchman?'

Father and son looked at each other, then Jack Junior said, 'We've thought about it. But we didn't figure it might be Janis – we just didn't think of her –'

'You never kept track of her?' asked Clements.

'Why would I? I'm happily married –' He shook his handsome head. He was an imposing figure behind the big desk, every inch a corporation man. He and Juliet graced the better social events, but always in the background; an inheritance from his father, he had a deep aversion to being photographed. He and Juliet were never found amongst the miles of teeth on the Sunday social pages. 'Janis was history, as far as I was concerned. I got myself into a mess with her, but I got out of it. You knew and I knew you knew. But I got out before you could pin anything on me.'

'That's frank enough,' said Malone and nodded approvingly.

114

'I gave him a fatherly talk,' said Aldwych.

'With an iron bar?' said Clements with a grin.

'I'd have used it if it'd been necessary. It wasn't, he was sensible. That's all dead and gone now. History, like Jack says. But that's not to say the bitch thinks the same way. Have you picked up the hitman yet?'

'No.'

'But you've got a suspect.'

'We might have. How'd you know?'

'Scobie – Russ –' He looked at them, old friends. 'There are – what? Fourteen, fifteen thousands cops in the service? You think I don't still have contacts? I don't have any of 'em on my payroll, not any more. But I ring 'em up, they talk to me. If there's a hitman out there and you got a suspect, they're gunna let me know. A sorta civic duty.'

'You must miss the old days, when you could buy cops like that?'

'No, Scobie. The honest bastards are easier to deal with – you know where you stand. I never trusted Fred Krahe and those other shits. You were a pain in the arse at times, but I always knew you were never gunna stab me in the back.'

'Can we get back to Janis?' said Jack Junior, looking pained at his old man's revival of memories.

'Sure,' said Malone. 'If you were the target, either of you, where would she get the money to pay a hitman? We've estimated that if the target *was* Hans Vanderberg, the fee would have been anywhere between fifty and a hundred thousand. It would be less for either of you, but not much.'

Aldwych grinned. 'Thanks.'

Jack Junior said, 'You confiscated all the money she was holding when you picked her up. But she had other money coming to her – I don't know how much, but it was considerable. She had bank accounts that I knew nothing about, the money could be in them. They probably weren't in her name. If she got her lawyer to invest all that cash in shares or property or whatever, it would've been making money for her all the time she's been put away. I don't think Janis would've come out of jail stony-broke. It wouldn't have been in her nature.'

'Who was her lawyer?' asked Clements.

But Jack Junior wasn't going to get himself caught up in the net, not after all these years. 'It would be in the court records.'

'Leave us out of it,' said Aldwych. 'We can take care of ourselves.'

'With all your contacts,' said Malone, 'what happens if you find her? Will you take care of her, too?'

'That remains to be seen,' said Aldwych, and one knew once again that he might have retired but was not reformed.

4

'Why did you go out to Rockdale today? I told you to stay out of this case.'

'Are you having me tailed, for God's sake?'

'No, I'm not. But a watch is being kept on Mrs Vanderberg and Barry Rix, just in case someone tries to do them over again. Mo, stay out of it.'

'Dad –' She understood his concern for her; but she had to make her own way in life. That, unstated but recognizable, had been her aim since she was fourteen. 'My producer sent me. If I'd said no, I'd have been told to get lost and he'd have sent someone else and I'd have finished up in a back room. I'm not shoving my neck out –'

'May we get on with dinner?' said Lisa.

'Dad,' said Claire, coming in from his right, 'we're not little kids any more – you can't keep protecting us.'

'Are you butting in on the case?'

'I was in it – our firm was – before you came into it. You're getting your chronology wrong.'

116

'Chronology?' said Lisa. 'If we're going to have chronology, can we make dinner Number One?'

'Can I get in on this?' asked Tom. 'I'm the odd one out. Even Mum is in on it, indirectly.'

'Right now Mum is trying to keep the whole thing away from this table,' said Lisa. 'Now to change the subject –'

She gave them her Dutch glare and the subject was changed. It was their weekly family dinner, a ritual she tried to preserve as much as possible. Claire came home for the evening without Jason, and Maureen and Tom made no dates. Lisa prepared the meal the night before and the girls helped her to serve it. The two men waited to be waited upon, true-blue old-time Aussies. Tonight's dinner was Tasmanian salmon, cold, with a salad and new potatoes. The dessert was crème caramel, with slightly more cream than milk in the recipe and the sauce done to her own prescription. The wine was a West Australian white burgundy. They would like the meal or else. Dutch cuisine was not all cheese and schnapps, not for those Netherlanders who looked south.

'You haven't lost your touch, Mum,' said Tom, who would have said the same thing to an Eskimo over a blubber hamburger. His taste buds would never lead him to starvation.

'Changing the subject slightly,' said Claire, 'who is going to be the new Police Minister?'

'Billy Eustace, for the time being. After that –' Malone shrugged, took a sip of his wine.

'What does he know about the police?'

'He knows we're the ones who are supposed to stay out of jail. But that's about all.'

'If Labor loses the election, who gets to run the Olympics?' asked Tom.

'Ask your mother,' said Malone. 'She's the Olympic expert.'

'It will be a free-for-all,' said Lisa. 'All-in wrestling. It'll be a new event on the Olympic schedule.'

'How will they get Nick Agaroff out of the box seat?' said

117

Maureen. 'They'll have to shoot—' Then she waved an apologetic hand. 'Sorry.'

'Nobody else is going to be shot,' said Malone. 'But throats may be cut and backs stabbed. Just your usual State politics.'

Tom raised his glass. 'Here's to democracy.'

Later in bed Lisa said, 'Are you any closer to finding out who killed the Premier?'

'If I listen to my bones – yes.' Malone lay with his arm under the curve of her back; she turned, putting her leg over him. They were experienced explorers of the geography of each other, knew every port of call. 'But no Crown prosecutor would listen to my bones.'

'Is there going to be more violence? More shootings, more bashings? I hate the thought of Mo covering that sort of thing.'

'I might have a word with her producer –'

'She'd bash you if you did.' She put her hand between his legs. 'Am I being too protective?'

'Go for your life, Delilah.'

5

Peter Kelzo was at home. It was the Parthenon reduced to a suburban villa. He was, as someone said, more than one pillar of the community; there were at least a dozen holding up the roof of the house. Two fake Praxiteles copies of the female form stood on either side of the steps leading up to the front door, arms raised as if hailing the owner. The villa stood, not on the Acropolis, but on a slight rise that looked out on the Parramatta River. The Parthenon had had no resident oracle, but Peter Kelzo didn't bow the knee all the way to tradition. He gave advice, whether requested or not.

'You gotta be more careful, Joe, understand? When you do over a man, you gotta be sure it's the right guy. What you did was collateral damage.'

'No,' said George Gandolfo. 'Collateral damage is when you kill civilians with bombs meant for someone else. The Americans invented it.'

Did Socrates and Demosthenes need nit-picking advisers? 'I'm not talking to you, George.'

'Pete –' said Joe St Louis.

'Peter.'

'Peter, I done the right thing, you know what I mean? I picked a dark place, no street lights, nothing like that, the car was Barry Rix's, the guy gets out – what was I gunna do? Ask him for his driving licence before I whacked him? It was just one of them unfortunate things. Like George says, collateral damage.'

They were sitting out on the front porch of the villa, between two of the Doric pillars. It was a ritual once-a-week meeting, except in inclement weather; Kelzo didn't invite the local elements to call on him, but he liked to be seen; a family man at home with his friends. Down in the driveway Kelzo's teenage son was washing the family Lexus 400. Mrs Kelzo, a pleasant-looking woman but a wraith in the public gaze, was back in the house doing a woman's work, whatever it was. Peter Kelzo was not as chauvinistic as Euripides, but he believed the playwright had a point in putting women in their place. The world would be a better place if the Greeks still ran it.

Out in the street a waste disposal truck went by, homeward bound. Its driver tooted the horn. Kelzo had once read that the major waste disposal companies in the United States were owned by the Mafia and he had decided that if anyone knew where a profit was, it was the Mafia. He had bought two waste disposal companies and money rolled in as the garbage rolled out. The four men clinging to the back of the truck turned their heads right and saluted Kelzo, like tank captains saluting their commander. They were Maoris and hated their dago boss, but he paid their wages and turned a blind eye to their sorting the waste before it got to the dump. He thought of himself as a philanthropist, a good Greek word, but there were few who agreed with him.

119

'That's two wrong guys who've been done, Joe –'

'I had nothing to do with The Dutchman copping it.'

'I'm not saying you did, Joe. That was lucky – collateral damage?' He looked at Gandolfo.

'Yeah, in that case, yeah. But how do we know the hit was meant for Jack Aldwych?'

'We don't. Maybe it *was* meant for The Dutchman. In which case, who hired the hitman?'

The three of them sat there, faces as stony as the two statues hailing them. George Gandolfo's was the stoniest of the three. He had worked for Pete, excuse me, Peter Kelzo for fifteen years, first as a clerk in his building business, then as his general handyman in everything but mostly politics. Yet he had still not learned the *secret* Peter Kelzo, the one buried deep inside the *bonhomie* of the public man. Gandolfo had, by accident, discovered several secrets that Kelzo had never revealed and he had learned that his boss was much more ruthless than he had believed. He wondered now if Kelzo knew more about the hitman than he showed.

Then Joe St Louis, a man who had no secrets but wasn't lovable because of that, said, 'I could go and visit a few guys down the Trades Congress or at the unions. That guy Balmoral might know a thing or two. We done him a favour, like.'

'We done him nothing of the sort,' said Kelzo, wondering why these two dickheads were his closest associates. But knowing why: George Gandolfo could count in his head quicker than a calculator and Joe St Louis was the best stand-over man in the business. 'All we done is stirred up Mother Vanderberg and she's gunna be twice as tough to deal with. Hell hath no fury like a woman scorned. That's an old Greek saying.'

Neither of them contradicted him; they had little knowledge of literature and took no notice of a woman's fury or her scorn. 'We done nothing to her,' said St Louis.

'Of course we did, dickhead!' He was losing his patience, on which he had a frayed rein at the best of times. 'Joe, we let her know we're not gunna let her run Boolagong. We let her know we were gunna put our own man up for pre-selection.'

'Who?' said George Gandolfo: this was another of Peter's fucking secrets.

'Garry Fairbanks.'

'Garry –? That dummy?' Gandolfo knew a dickhead when he saw one. 'He couldn't count the runners in a three-horse race.'

'He does what he's told.'

'Pete – Peter, you ever listened to him? He says he's a lateral thinker, he doesn't know what it means.'

'What does it mean?' asked St Louis.

'His brain is wider than it's deep. He'll be a dead loss, Pete. Peter.'

'He's our man,' said Kelzo stubbornly. 'I've arranged it. I'll do his thinking for him. Laterally, right side up, arse up, whatever.'

'I hear the cops've got a suspect,' said St Louis. 'I could go looking for him.'

'And do what?' said Kelzo.

'I dunno. Talk to him, ask him who paid him, like. Do him over.' He had a simple approach to truth.

'Why would you wanna do him over?' asked Gandolfo. 'He done us a favour.'

Kelzo shook his head at the problems these two gave him. 'George, he could be looking to do us next.'

Gandolfo said nothing; then Joe St Louis said, 'We got another problem. Then Channel 15 mob, we gotta do something about them.'

'It's that girl who's been nosing around,' said Gandolfo. 'She's getting to be a real pain in the arse. Something I found out – she's that cop, Malone's daughter.'

'Then we can't touch her,' said Kelzo.

'Why not?' said Joe St Louis.

121

6

Balmoral had wanted to take Camilla Feng to the Golden Gate. It was expensive as Chinese restaurants went, but was bargain basement compared to some of the other establishments around town.

'Why?' she had asked.

'Well –' He was a ladies' man, but he was still working his way through the infinite variety of them. 'Well, I just thought you liked Chinese food. You know, national dishes . . .'

'You notice I'm Chinese, but I don't dress Chinese? No cheongsam? I do like Chinese food, but I also like French and Italian and Vietnamese.'

'Not Australian?' His smile could be quite charming.

'Some of the best chefs in the world are Australian, but they don't *cook* Australian. I'd like to go to Ampersand.' She saw his smile stiffen and she added, without her own inner smile that tickled her, 'I'll go Dutch.'

'No, no.' She heard the catch in his throat, like a missed key on a cash register. 'I'll book. The Ampersand it is.'

So here they were at Ampersand, a hundred and eighty dollars for two, plus drinks. Bargain basement compared to London, Paris and New York, but Balmoral had never had to pick up the check in those exotic places. Delegations these days do not worry about expense and he had been on two delegations overseas. Taxpayers never knew what they were paying for.

'What does ampersand mean?' she asked, though she knew. Feigning ignorance is a form of flattery, especially in male company.

'It's that curly piece, the symbol that stands for *and*.' If he had not known, he would have looked it up before coming here. He would not have been fazed by the Dead Sea Scrolls or the Book of Han Fei in the original script. He was looking at the menu, running his eyes down the prices as if reading some dreaded writing on a wall. His pocket could be fazed, Camilla thought: he's mean. 'What would you like?'

She was a swift reader of menus as well as men: 'I'll have the jelly of lobster and the rack of lamb.'

She turned to look out at Cockle Bay, a revived name dredged up from the waters of Darling Harbour. Her father, dead from a killer's bullet, one of the victims of the jinx on Olympic Tower, had told her of his arrival here in this back inlet on a rusty freighter from Shanghai. Drugs and gold had been smuggled in here as ships docked at the wharves, now gone. Though she did not know it, Jack Aldwych had been a gold smuggler and Con Malone had fought pickets and police on those wharves. Now both sides of the inlet were devoted to pleasure and entertainment: convention centres, tourist shops, an aquarium, restaurants and cafés. History was sunk beneath the murky waters.

She looked back at him. 'Are you interested in history, Jerry?'

'Political history, yes. The other sort?' He shrugged. 'The future is more interesting than the past.'

'How can you know?' She was leading him on. 'Is that because you're ambitious?'

'Yes. There's no point in being ambitious about the past, is there? It's contradictory.'

A waiter poured some wine for them, took their orders and went away. He was different, she noted, from Chinese waiters, who always gave the impression of doing you a favour by serving you.

'No, I suppose not.'

'Are you ambitious?'

'Yes,' she admitted without hesitation. 'I want to be rich and accepted.'

'Not as Chinese but as yourself?' She nodded and he went on, 'You and I would make a good pair, Camilla.'

She had not expected him to come on so soon; maybe he

wanted to get out of here before dessert and coffee. She was still smiling inwardly at him. 'In what way?'

'Would there be a better-looking couple, ever, in The Lodge in Canberra?'

Migod, he's unbelievable! 'You're going to be Prime Minister?'

'Eventually.' He took a sip of wine, smiled at his own conceit. 'You think I'm swollen-headed, right? I may be, but modesty never got you anywhere in this country. The voters like you to be up-front.'

She knew nothing of the past political history of the nation; she had heard her father speak of Ben Chifley, a modest man, but she couldn't remember whether he had been PM or Premier. He was a dim figure from another age, when maybe modesty had been an admired attribute. Jerry Balmoral was right: salesmanship was the order of today.

'Are you proposing to me, Jerry?'

Again the charming smile: she could see it on television screens in the future, women falling on their backs at the sight of it. 'We could consider it.'

'Like one considers a mortgage?' she said with her own smile. 'Ask me when you're PM.'

The waiter brought their first course and she dug her fork into the jellied lobster. He had ordered the savarin of blue swimmer crab, which, she had noted with her quick eye, was more expensive than her own order. Maybe, she decided, he had become reckless, in for a penny, in for a pound. Or perhaps he thought it was what Prime Ministers would order.

'But where do you start?' she asked.

'I've started.' He was enjoying the crab; or enjoying himself. 'I'm aiming to get the pre-selection for the Premier's old seat, Boolagong.'

'If you get it, what then?'

'Two terms, then I'll run for a Federal seat. I'll have established myself by then, be a minister in the second term.'

She wanted to shake her head at his certainty of himself; but she was not here to play superior. 'If you win Boolagong or whatever it's called, will you have any influence? Because it was Mr Vanderberg's seat?'

'Of course.'

She was still finding it hard to believe his self-assurance. 'Would you use it?'

'Yes. That's what politicians are for, to use their influence. What can I do for you?' Again the smile, round a piece of blue-eyed crab.

'You don't think Boolagong is – what do they call it? – a danger zone? That someone doesn't want a Labor member?'

He looked at her shrewdly. 'You know something about politics? I thought –'

She hurried to cover her mistake: 'Only what I've read in the newspapers, seen on TV. You won't be afraid to step in there?'

'Not at all.'

She wasn't sure whether it was bravado or confidence. 'You won't have any opposition?'

'None that can't be handled.'

She changed tack: 'If you get the pre-selection, will it cost much to run a campaign?'

'You want to contribute?'

She hesitated, then said, 'We – I might.'

'We?' He hadn't missed her slip.

She was proving to be less competent than she had expected; he was not yet in politics but he was already a politician. 'I meant our family company.'

'No.' The smile this time was less charming. 'You meant Olympic Tower.'

She waited while the waiter took away their plates; she was glad of the interruption, gave him a smile like a tip. When he was gone, she said, 'What makes you think Olympic Tower would want to give you money?'

'You gave it to Hans Vanderberg.'

'How do you know?'

'Let's just say I know. Is that why you came to dinner with me?'

She dodged that one. 'Who else knows?'

'Besides me, those on my side? Nobody. I don't think anyone in the Boolagong branch knows, outside of Mrs Vanderberg and Barry Rix. What were you buying from The Dutchman?'

She took her time, waited while the waiter came back to pour more wine.

'Your main course will be here soon.' He was a young man who obviously enjoyed serving good-looking women who smiled at him. 'We never rush our guests.'

'We like to take our time,' said Balmoral, winking at Camilla. 'Don't we?'

He was a mixture of gaucheness and smoothness. But he was not alone: she had met scores of men like him.

When the waiter had gone away again she said, 'I don't think you will ever take your time.'

'Oh, you're wrong there, Camilla. You'd be surprised at how patient I can be to get what I want. What was it you wanted from Hans Vanderberg?'

She was still re-gathering herself, though outwardly she looked at ease. 'You would have to talk to my partners about that.'

'Will I have to take all of them to dinner, too?' But he said it without malice.

'They are never dinner partners,' she said and realized for the first time that it was true.

'Do *you* know what they want?'

'Yes.' She looked at him across the table, all at once regaining her composure; sure of herself but surer of her partners. This PM-aspirant opposite her would be no match for Jack Aldwych and Madame Tzu. 'But I didn't come to talk business.'

'Why did you come?'

'You intrigue me. I've never met anyone at the bottom of

126

the political ladder, someone who hasn't yet got his foot on the bottom rung.'

He had time to recover from that. The waiter brought their main courses, the rack of lamb for her, grilled john dory for him. His, she had noted, was the higher priced; he was dining *haut prix* as well as *haute cuisine* tonight. She wondered if an expense account would be presented at Trades Congress tomorrow morning. Somehow he had found an expansion to his credit card without causing him to collapse.

At last he said, 'I think we must get to know each other better.'

'You really think I could help your career?' She was not a good flirt, but she was trying.

'You're beautiful, you're smart and from what I've read, Chinese women are the strength behind their men.'

'That depends on the woman.' She thought of Madame Tzu, who didn't need men to show her strength. 'You'll have to learn to temper your flattery. You're too – too direct.'

'That's how a politician should be. The voters suspect you if you soft-soap them with flattery. They like you to be direct, even if they dislike you. Will you marry me?'

She hoped he was joking. 'No. Is that too direct?'

He nodded appreciatively, the charm back in his smile. 'You'll be an adornment to The Lodge. We can make it multi-racial.'

'Wouldn't it be better if I were also part-Aboriginal?'

'One can't have everything,' he said, but one knew he would never settle for less.

As he looked at the bill, his face stiffening in apparent pain, he said, 'Your place or mine?'

She wanted to laugh; but said, 'Mine.'

'Where do you live?' He had picked her up at the Feng offices in Chinatown.

'Drummoyne. On the water.'

'Nice.'

He had a Mercedes, one that she guessed was at least twelve

years old. She judged him to be the sort who would always choose an imported luxury car, even one second- or third-hand, to anything local. That might have to change when he became a politician, but for the moment vanity was at the wheel.

He drove well, with flair. He really is well-rounded in everything needed to get ahead, she thought: vanity, flair, ambition. And, she was sure, buried under all that, ruthlessness.

Drummoyne is on the south bank of the Parramatta River. It is in the Harding electorate; Peter Kelzo lived two streets away, though she had never met him and had no desire to. The Mercedes drew up in the quiet dead-end street and Balmoral looked out at the large modern house between the street and the water.

'Very nice. You live here alone?'

'No,' she said and kissed him on the cheek. 'My mother always waits up for me.'

7

Next morning she told her senior partners: 'He knows about the money, but he doesn't know what it's for.'

'Could he be useful?' asked Les Chung.

'Not yet. Maybe in the future. He wants to be Prime Minister.'

Aldwych shook his head. 'He won't be any use to us there. You don't buy influence down in Canberra, unless you're looking for tax concessions. You shop for influence in Macquarie Street. That's what State governments are for.'

Les Chung smiled. Democracy had been defined.

'If he knows about the money, will he talk about it?' asked Madame Tzu.

'If he does,' said Aldwych, 'I'll get my man Blackie Ovens to talk to him. Blackie can come out of retirement for a day or two.'

'No,' said Jack Junior, second youngest and least bloodthirsty. 'How is he getting on with you, Camilla?'

128

'He wants to marry me.'

'Really?' The four men and even Madame Tzu were surprised.

'Love at first sight?' asked General Wang-Te, who was short-sighted when it came to love. His wife had been a bride of convenience, an inconvenient one when he discovered she thought sex was a sin. American missionaries were more insidious than their CIA.

'No.' She gave them the smile she had given Balmoral when she had kissed him goodnight. 'He thought I was his mirror.'

But Madame Tzu remembered the advice of the Emperor Tai-zong. If one used others as a mirror, one might learn of one's achievements and failures.

Jerry Balmoral might be brighter than they thought.

Chapter Five

1

'They've traced Janis Eden,' said Clements.

'Where'd they find her?'

'She's a blackjack dealer at the Harbour Casino. Changed her name to Joanna Everitt. They never miss, do they? Always the same initials.'

'They're the smart ones, just in case they've got something with their initials on it, something they want to keep. Have they picked her up?'

'No, they've left it to us. She was our pigeon originally, they said.'

'That was what Pilate said. Everybody washing their hands.'

'It's the system, mate. That was why God invented water.'

Malone and Clements drove over to the big casino complex just across the water from the western edge of the city. It was a huge futuristic concept, like the set for an Arnold Schwarzenegger movie. A vast arc of steps, or steppes, led up to the main entrance, an ideal stage for a massacre. Clements drove round to come in a wide entry where escalators led up to the main gaming floor.

He pulled the unmarked car in behind a Bentley turbo that was being guided into a line of expensive cars cordoned off by a long red rope. A parking valet, like the grey bombers of the parking police out on the streets, appeared out of nowhere.

'Not there, sir. You can't park there –'

'Why not?' said Clements, who knew the purpose of the exclusive area.

'That's for regular clients, sir –'

'You mean the high rollers?'

'We-ell, yeah –'

'We're high rollers,' said Malone, stepping out of the non-exclusive Holden Commodore and showing his badge. 'We roll anyone who gets in our way, that right, Sergeant?' Then he grinned at the young valet. He stepped out of the way as a Ferrari rolled in behind him, its exhaust thrumming like a gambler on heat. 'We shan't be long, son. We may be bringing someone out. The less fuss the better, isn't that what your bosses would want?'

He and Clements went into the casino and up to the main gaming floor. In the four years the casino had been operating Malone had never been in the place. He was not a gambler; when the kids had been at school they had had difficulty in persuading him to buy a raffle ticket at the school fête. His money never came out of his pocket looking for chances; if he was not guaranteed at least an equal return, forget it. He was the low roller of all rollers.

He stood for a long moment looking at the scene. The banks of poker machines stretched away in all directions, their fronts showing more expression than the faces of the humans pulling the handles. Beyond the poker machines were the gaming tables, where the players seemed capable of more expression, even the odd burst of excitement.

'You notice?' said Clements. 'Three outa five players are Asians. They come here, do their money, keep coming back. All wanting to be rich tomorrow. The land of milk and money.'

They moved on. Malone, not a man of much aesthetic perception, found himself looking at the surroundings and the decor. Long ago, on the trip to London when he had first met Lisa, he had gone to an exclusive gambling club, tracking a suspect. It had been a discreetly opulent atmosphere, good taste in every drape and every stick of furniture; but that had been years ago, before taste had gone downhill in the world. This was Las Vegas Down Under; he found it hard to believe that so much bad taste could be under one roof.

131

Perhaps it was psychological, designed to keep the gamblers on edge.

They came to the blackjack tables. Malone looked along the row of them, recognized Janis Eden at the far end. She had changed, he had to look hard and long at her. But it was she, all right: if nothing less, the old coolness was still recognizable, like a favourite dress.

'You know the game?' Clements asked.

'I know the rules of two-up and that's about it. What are your chances of winning at blackjack?'

'I'd rather bet on the horses. You take your cards from the dealer and they've gotta total 21 or less. You win if your total is higher than the dealer's. There are over 1300 different ways two cards can total the numbers from 2 to 21. There are 560, maybe a few more, two-card combinations worth 16 or more. That's all you have to remember,' he said with a grin and moved towards the end table. 'Let's go and talk to Janis.'

She looked up as they approached, gave no hint of recognition. 'You wish to play, gentlemen?'

'Not here, Janis,' said Malone. 'Could you have someone relieve you? We'd like to talk to you.'

She frowned, only slightly. She glanced around her; for a moment it seemed she might try to flee. Then she gestured to a supervisor, said something to him in a low voice, then jerked her head at Malone and Clements and led them away from the gaming tables.

'What's this all about? Are you going to make trouble for me here?'

'It's got nothing to do with all this.' Clements gestured around them. 'How'd you get the job? You been doing a blackjack course while you were in Mulawa?'

'I worked in Las Vegas eleven years ago. They were looking for an experienced dealer. I got the job.'

'Why'd you change your name?'

'It's my real name. My birth certificate, my passport – Joanna

132

Everitt. Janis Eden was the name I invented for that other game – in case I got caught, I guess. My mother was very strait-laced North Shore –' She paused a moment and Malone wondered if there was still a spark of decency in her. 'The name I went to prison under.'

'So you're clean? Joanna Everitt is okay with the Gaming Squad and the casino people? They're tough with their checks on whom they employ.'

'I'm clean.'

She was holding something back, but Malone didn't press her. Police divisions don't interfere with other divisions unless asked; one had enough troubles of one's own. If the Control Authority had cleared her he wasn't going to wise them up.

'I'm making a fresh start,' she said. 'Isn't that what we're supposed to do when we come out of prison? I'm rehabilitated. Now what's all this about?'

The cool exterior was brittle now. She was a good-looking woman who had started with a barely attractive face and built on it. Her dark auburn hair was thick and lustrous, the sort of unbelievable hair one saw in TV commercials; Malone bet that she would get more men players to her table than women. Her figure was good, suggesting sex but not easily available. Men wouldn't pass her by without looking at her. Women would pass her by, sniffing.

'Righto, Joanna. Do you know a man named John June? Or John August?'

She shook her head, eyes blank. 'What does he do? Come here to play?'

'He might. Or to talk to you. He shoots people. A hitman.'

She was not the type who would ever shriek with laughter; but she put her hand over her mouth now as if afraid that she might. She looked from one to the other. 'You're joking!'

'I don't think we are.'

'Oh, for Crissakes—' She looked as if she might walk away from them. 'Why would I know a – a *hitman*?'

133

'How do you feel about your ex-boyfriend?' asked Clements. 'Young Jack Aldwych?'

'Candidly?' She might have been telling them what she thought of the latest fashions; the composure was thickening. 'I hate him. His father, too. But what've they got to do with this – this hitman?'

There was a shout from one of the tables; someone had just won a jackpot or something. Heads turned, but nobody moved: everyone was chasing his own fortune.

'Don't you read the papers? Look at television?' said Clements. 'The Aldwyches were on either side of Premier Vanderberg when he was shot. The shot could of been meant for either of them.'

'So –' If she was acting, she was good at it. Maybe nine years in Mulawa had taught her never to show her true face. Prison is an education, one way or another. 'So you think I might have arranged it? Do me a favour, gentlemen. Get lost. You're going to lose me my job here. The security guys are watching us.'

Malone glanced towards the two big men standing ten or fifteen metres away. They had *security* written all over them, like an invisible logo; they were in suits and wore badges, but the badges were superfluous. They moved towards Joanna and the two detectives.

'Something wrong, gentlemen?'

'We're police,' said Malone. 'Miss Ed – Everitt had her home broken into and we think we've got the feller who did it. We'd like her to come with us, identify some of the stuff we took from the bloke.'

'You didn't tell us, Joanna.' They were both huge young men; side by side they could have blocked a freeway traffic lane. 'Why not?'

'Excuse me,' said Clements. 'This is police business. Are you suggesting you should of handled the case?'

The security man who had spoken backed down. 'No, of course not. We just are concerned for those who work for the casino.'

'It's okay,' said Janis Eden; or Joanna Everitt. 'I'll go and see

134

if any of my stuff has been picked up. I'll go when I finish my shift. That all right?'

'Yes,' said Malone. 'Just call me when you're coming. Good luck back at your table.'

'Do you play?' asked one of the young men.

'Only solitaire. I'm not very trusting.'

He and Clements left then, not hurrying, almost strolling past the tables and the poker machines. Every machine was fronted by a player, each of whom sat there like an animated doll, faces dead as plates. An elderly woman turned to look at them; her grey hair was in a clenched perm, the sort that Malone thought had gone out years ago; the plate of her face was cracked, her eyes dull. He recognized the type: she would have begun at bingo games years ago, seeking not fortune but just company. Now the machines had imprisoned her. He tried not to be judgemental, but the blind eye only works with sympathy. He had seen too much addiction, of all kinds, and sympathy had worn threadbare.

At the top of the escalators a young man, too slim to be a security guard, joined them and rode down with them. 'Constable Gregan, Inspector. I'm keeping tabs on Miss Everitt, we're working shifts. You're not taking her in?'

'Not yet. Get back up there and don't let her out of your sight. Bring her over to Homicide when she comes off work. Has she cottoned on to you?'

'No, sir.' He was small, barely medium height; he had blond hair and a cheerful freckled face. 'I've been playing the pokies, had a coupla games at the tables. Looking like I'm here for the fun.'

'Who's financing you? Office petty cash? You must be made of money over at Surry Hills.'

'No, my own cash, sir. I like a flutter now and again.'

'Righto, flutter back up there again and keep an eye on her. Don't get glassy-eyed in front of a poker machine.'

'No, sir,' said the young officer and looked at Clements as if to say, *Is he a Jehovah's witness?*

135

As they walked across to their car Clements said, 'You were a bit rough on him.'

'Yeah, I know. I thought I'd forgotten all about Janis, but I haven't. She still gets up my nose. That young bloke was just unlucky I got narky on him and not her.'

The parking valet dropped the red rope to let Clements take the Holden out from between the Ferrari and the Bentley. 'No luck, sir?'

'We'll be back,' said Clements. 'Keep our spot.'

2

Detective Constable Gregan and another young officer introduced as Detective Constable Styron brought Joanna Everitt to Homicide at 4.45. She came into the big room, smiled at the half a dozen detectives there as if they were casino clients and strolled into Malone's office. He asked her to sit down, then went out to the two young officers from Surry Hills.

'Go down and wait for her, but keep out of sight. I'll send her back home in one of our cars – I still want you to keep tabs on her. Where does she live?'

'She has a flat in Neutral Bay, not a cheap block,' said Gregan. 'She's renting at the moment, but she's trying to buy it.'

'You've done your homework. How much?'

'She's paying six hundred a week, furnished. The guy who owns it wants five thousand a week during the Olympics. She's either got to buy it from him or move during the Olympics.'

'How much does he want?'

'Eight-fifty thousand, the agent says.'

'Has she got that sort of money?'

'We dunno. Our ticket wasn't to look into her bank balance.'

There was just a little cheek in his answer, but Malone let it pass. His own tongue had not always trodden the straight and

136

narrow. 'Righto, keep up the surveillance on her. She thinks you were just detailed to bring her in, nothing else?'

'No, sir. I chatted her up on the way in, she thinks we were on routine stuff around the casino when we got the word to escort her in here. She's very pleasant.'

'Yeah,' said Malone.

'Is she the one, sir?' Styron was an overweight young man with a bushy black moustache and bushy hair. His voice, however, was soft, as if he would rather reason with crims than bounce them. 'Paid the hitman?'

'We're working on it. But your guess is as good as ours at the moment.' It was a concession to the two young men to state that, but they were the ones who had found her. 'We'll see what we can get out of her.'

When he went back into his own office, Clements had already joined Joanna. 'I've offered her coffee, but she says she only drinks tea. But she's like you, she won't take tea-bags.'

Malone sat down. 'You've got taste, Janis. Sorry, Joanna.'

'I always have had.'

She had changed out of her casino uniform and now wore a beige suit with a green silk shirt. Her auburn hair had been let down and contrasted well with the shirt; it also softened her face. She had tan shoes, a tan handbag and a thick gold bracelet that winked just below the cuff of the shirt like a hint of hidden wealth. She looked rich enough to be a high roller. She certainly did not look like someone who had recently spent nine years in jail. Unless it was rehabilitation taken beyond Corrective Services' aim.

'Well, Joanna –'

'Miss Everitt. I don't like strangers calling me by my first name – you sound like those familiar types on office switchboards.'

'I didn't think we were strangers.'

'You're not friends. And I'm no longer Janis. It's Joanna.'

'I like that,' said Clements.

She looked sideways at him on the couch, as if the lower orders

137

had spoken. 'Thank you, Sergeant. I don't think my mother had you in mind when she chose it.'

Both men laughed, settled back. Malone, because of the three women in his house, enjoyed an intelligent woman. Which was not to say that he wanted to enjoy Joanna Everitt for too long. 'How are you fixed for money, Miss Everitt?'

'Asking a question like that proves we're not friends. I'm comfortable.'

'You'd saved something from your drug sales before you were arrested?'

There was a pause before she answered and her eyes hardened for a moment; then, without heat, she said, 'No. My mother died while I was in Mulawa and I sold our house. I bought shares with the money and doubled it. Commonwealth Serum Laboratories. Drugs again.'

Malone looked at Clements, the stock market punter, who said, 'CSL. They've gone up six or seven hundred per cent since they were floated. Honest drugs for honestly sick people.'

'Thank you,' said Janis/Joanna.

'Would you object if we asked to look at your bank account?' said Malone.

'Yes, I would. Why do you want to look at it?'

'To see if there have been any large withdrawals lately. Say fifty to a hundred thousand dollars. Or maybe less, maybe twenty thousand. Shooting one of the Aldwyches would cost less than a hit on the Premier. Unless you're a Coalition voter?'

'Of course I am, I'm a conservative through and through. But there are other ways of getting rid of politicians than by shooting them. Voting against them, for instance. I'll admit I wouldn't have wept at all if either Jack or his father had been hit, but I didn't pay anyone to do it.'

'We can get a court order to look at your account. Or accounts.'

She considered for a long moment; she was never going to be hurried. Malone wondered if she paused as long as this

138

before she dealt the cards in blackjack. 'All right, I'll sign permission.'

'Which bank?'

'The Commonwealth, in Martin Place. Will they charge me for letting you look at it? They charge for everything else. Things were cheaper in jail.'

Malone nodded agreement. 'The Colombians are on their way here. They've heard banking is more lucrative than drug-running.'

She smiled. 'I should have gone into banking. I might've stayed out of Mulawa.'

The mood now was easier. 'The account – what name? Janis Eden or Joanna Everitt?'

'Joanna Everitt.'

'Do you have one somewhere else in the name of Janis?'

The smile had gone. 'No. Janis is dead. I've got a new life.'

'But you still remember Jack Junior?'

She was very still; even her lips didn't appear to move. 'Yes.'

'Have you been near him, gone to his office or his home?'

'No. He's married now and I have no fight with his wife. I'm not a home-wrecker.' She sounded almost prim; buttery words wouldn't melt in her mouth. Then she changed the tack of the questioning, asked one of her own: 'How did you find me?'

'I haven't checked yet. Maybe the hitman told them where you could be found, that you'd changed your name.'

She smiled again, but this time it looked an effort. 'You never give up, do you?'

'Never. You'll always be Janis with us.' He stood up. 'I'll have a car take you home or wherever you want to go.'

'New York?'

'Don't try it. Not till we've cleared you. Thanks for coming in.'

Clements escorted her out, turned her over to Gail Lee to take her home. Malone sat on in his office. An Indian mynah walked up and down the sill outside the window, chirping at its reflection in the glass like a busker telling a competitor to get lost.

Then Phil Truach came in, plumped himself down in the chair Joanna Everitt had just vacated. He looked in need of a cigarette or two. 'Are you in a good mood or have you got shit on the liver?'

'You've got bad news?'

'It could be. For you. Your two daughters are in a legal stoush. Claire has just issued a writ, on behalf of Clizbe and Balmoral at the Trades Congress, against Channel 15 and Maureen in particular. Evidently they put out something on the midday news.'

3

'You should settle out of court,' said Tom, 'if you want an economist's opinion. It's always cheaper, out of court. The lawyers don't like it –'

'Shut up, smartarse,' snapped Maureen.

'The damage is done,' said Claire. 'They have to pay for it. Plenty.'

'Pull your heads in, all of you,' said Malone. 'I –'

'Pull *your* head in,' said Lisa. 'I'm in the chair and we're going to discuss this without getting at each other's throats.'

Malone had called Claire and Maureen and told them he wanted to see them at home this evening, no matter what arrangements they had made. 'You'll come or I'll bring both of you in here to Homicide and question you as to what you know.'

'That's an empty threat and you know it,' Claire had said.

'Try me.'

Now they were sitting in the living room at Randwick, surrounded by home; but the atmosphere was anything but homelike. Dinner had been eaten in threadbare silence, Lisa vetoing any discussion or argument while they were eating. True to form, she insisted the girls clear the table and stack the dishwasher.

Dutch order was being forced on the evening. Malone had no idea how Dutch parliaments were run, but he knew they would not be of the order, or disorder, of Italian, Japanese and New South Wales parliaments.

Lisa went on, 'Why did you have to do that midday piece, Mo?'

'It was what we came up with. Balmoral, backed by Clizbe and the Allied Trades union and two or three other unions, is flat out to take over Boolagong. They're holding a gun at Labor Party headquarters on the pre-selection issue.'

'That's where you made your first mistake,' said Malone. 'Using that phrase – holding a gun at their heads.'

'I got carried away – it wasn't in the script –' She had inherited the Malone tongue that slipped its leash too often.

'If it wasn't in the script, then you'll be carrying the can,' said Tom. 'Channel 15 will just wash its hands of you.'

'Oh shit!' Maureen was all at once deflated, slumped in her chair.

'Who's the lawyer here?' asked Claire. 'The piece was filmed at 11.45, it went out at 12.05. The editors could have cut it if they'd wanted to. We're suing the channel, not Mo. She has no money.'

'Now you're talking like an economic rationalist,' said Tom admiringly.

'Shut up,' said his mother. 'What we have to discuss is if it goes to court. Once the Malone name is bandied about it could mean Dad being taken off the case.'

'No complaints,' said Malone, but they all looked at him, telling him they didn't believe him.

'It'll go to court,' said Claire. 'Balmoral and Clizbe have already asked us to hire senior counsel. My boss says he'll handle it as instructing solicitor. I'm to be the dogsbody, so maybe I shan't be noticed.'

'Not much,' said Tom. 'Can you get out of it, Mo? Let Channel 15 carry the can.'

'No, she can't,' said Claire. 'I'm sorry, Mo. I'm only doing my job.'

'So was I.' But Maureen was still low, still angry with herself. 'If I hadn't shot my mouth off . . . Why did I inherit your tongue, Dad?'

'Ask Grandpa. He gave it to me.'

'Would they have sued if I hadn't said the bit about holding the gun at the Labor Party?'

'Yes,' said Claire. 'The complaint is against the general statement. The inference is that Balmoral – and Clizbe, too – have gone to any lengths to take over Boolagong. Even to getting rid of the Premier –'

'Oh, come *on!*' Maureen sat up. 'There was nothing like that in our piece –'

'Mo –' Lisa put her hand gently on her daughter's arm – 'when you were doing Communications at university, they should have taught you to read between and write between the lines. I've learned that at Town Hall, writing press releases. There are a dozen different ways of reading anything you see in the press or hear on radio and television. That's why politicians are always ambiguous, even when wishing the voters Merry Christmas. They know there are going to be a dozen different ways of its being interpreted. Your producer should have double-checked what you were going to say, even before you shoved in your own little piece. Litigation is a way of life these days. Ask any doctor.'

Tom opened his mouth and Malone said, 'Shut it! We're getting nowhere right now. The case will go ahead?' Claire nodded. 'Righto, it'll be in the lists. It'll be 2002 before it'll be heard, maybe longer. By then I'll be long off the case, we'll have found out who shot the Premier and you two will probably be in other jobs elsewhere. Crowded court lists have their advantages. But for the time being, Mo – watch yourself. There are some nasty bastards in this whole set-up and you're too young and pretty to be bashed up. Or worse.'

142

They all looked at him; then Lisa said, 'Your father's right. You too, Claire, be careful.'

'Maybe I should say some Hail Marys that nasty bastards don't beat up economists,' said Tom.

'Your turn will come, the way you're buggering up the country,' said his father. 'One other thing. If Channel 15 follows up our investigation of who killed the Premier – which they will, they're not going to stand back and let the others have it – tell your producer you are not to ask me questions or come on camera while I'm there.'

'You don't know him,' said Maureen. 'He should've been an opera director. If I told him what you just suggested, he'd have me on camera twenty-four hours a day. I'm working for a *news* producer, not *Sesame Street*. What you've just suggested is news. Police intimidation.'

Malone looked at Lisa. 'Why couldn't she have been a nun?'

'Then the Church would've been sueing us,' said Tom. 'I think your only out of this, Mo, is for Labor to lose the election. Then it won't matter what you or Channel 15 said, especially if Mr Balmoral doesn't make it into parliament.'

'He's right,' said Lisa. 'There's nothing so boring as old politics. Especially the politics of a party that's out of power.'

Malone stroked her arm. 'You've had an education none of us has had. Two years at that school outside Lausanne – where the IOC lives and had to have explained to it what corruption is. Then two years at the High Commissioner's office in London, eighteen months at Town Hall – none of us will ever be as cynical as you.'

'I'm not cynical,' she said. 'Just disillusioned.'

'Same thing, different label.' Then he looked at his daughters. 'I'm not fooling when I say there are some nasty bastards in this set-up. Both of you take care.'

It was police advice, not fatherly advice, which is rarely taken seriously by the young, especially young girls. They nodded, but there was no way of knowing if they agreed with him.

The Premier was dead; long live the Premier. The Acting Premier, the media called him; and that hurt. He would have sued them if he could have got Legal Aid to finance the suit. Take no notice of them, Ladbroke, the real if dead Premier's minder, had told him. Don't start small fights with the media when the Big One is coming up:

'We'll have a battle to win the election,' said Ladbroke, who no longer cared but hid his feelings. 'Keep all side issues out of the way.'

'What do you think, Bill?' Billy Eustace looked at Police Commissioner Zanuch.

'With all due respect, Mr Premier, the police have only one issue. Finding who killed the – Hans Vanderberg.'

Billy Eustace nodded. He had been in politics twenty-three years, had been a union organizer for ten years before that. He was bald and thin, with close-set eyes, a wide mouth and a tendency towards volubility, his only profligacy. He was not unintelligent, but his brain and his personality were always at odds. He had risen to be Deputy Premier because everyone else, thinking Hans Vanderberg would last forever, had not wanted the job. Standing in the shade is not a favoured location in politics. Only over the last couple of months had the Party's members woken up that there were people in the Party who wanted to get rid of The Dutchman.

'Of course. It would help, Bill, if you could nail the culprit soon.' Say a month before the election. 'It would look good for the Service.' And Us, he added under his breath.

Something's happened to him, thought Ladbroke: he's become almost cryptic. He said, 'It won't look good for us if the hitman, or whoever hired him, turns out to be someone in the Party.'

Both he and Eustace looked at Zanuch, as if expecting him to produce the hitman there and then. The Commissioner was in uniform, silver-braided like a five-star doorman; it was his first visit to Eustace in the latter's role as Premier. Or Acting Premier. Or Police Minister. Or Acting Police Minister. Billy Eustace was like a man in a clothing warehouse sale, trying to find a suit to fit him.

'Do the police think someone in the Party organized the shooting?' Eustace sounded as if the question was choking him.

'What's happened over the last couple of days hasn't helped.' Zanuch was even more reserved than usual. This man on the other side of the big desk might not be there in a few weeks' time. Yet again, he might be. Sometimes the Commissioner yearned for the comfort of a police state. 'The bashing in the – in Hans Vanderberg's electorate. Then the stupid writ yesterday from those two at the Trades Congress.'

'Oh yes, yes – Christ, that was just incredible!' For a moment Eustace looked as if he might be his old voluble self; then caution fell on him like a sack: 'But we can't say anything. How do I not say anything, Roger?'

A good question. 'Leave it to me. Look busy elsewhere.'

'Good idea,' said Eustace and looked as if he wondered if *elsewhere* would be far enough. For years he had always been available for a statement, at great length, and now he was being advised to keep his mouth shut. 'Give me a list of things to do. Make me busy.'

'In the meantime,' said Zanuch, 'I am taking thirty men off the Olympic security detail and adding them to Task Force Nemesis.'

'You can't do that!' Eustace looked on the point of being voluble again. 'Nick Agaroff will drop his bundle – he's had enough trouble with SOCOG.'

In his three years as Minister for the Olympics Agaroff had had more trouble and dissension than the gods on Olympus.

'Get your extra police from the bush – get them from anywhere! The bush are going to vote against us anyway on the law and order bullshit.'

145

The Commissioner for law and order remained impassive. 'Now that you are Acting—' he seemed to emphasize the word – 'Police Minister, you should be well aware that we are almost two thousand men short of what is agreed the necessary establishment. Country stations are already short of personnel. The only place where I can draw experienced men is from the Olympics security detail. This is the first political assassination in this country and it happened in my bailiwick. I'm going to clear it up as soon as possible with the maximum number of men at my disposal.'

Eustace backed down; he was lost for words, a vacuum he didn't believe could exist. 'Well, of course –'

Ladbroke stepped in; he still had a certain loyalty to the Party, despite his cynicism. 'I'll get on to Nick Agaroff, explain the situation, Commissioner. We'll keep the transfer quiet, make no press release.'

'Good.' Zanuch stood up. He had the look of a man who had just won a gold medal, broken a world record and not raised a sweat. 'We'll find out who organized the killing of the Premier. Let's hope it's none of your friends.'

'Oh God,' said the Acting Premier, finding a couple of words.

In another office on Level 10 in the parliamentary complex the Leader of the Opposition and his Deputy Leader were fencing with each other. Up till last week the polls had shown that the Coalition was a certain loser in the coming elections. Now all at once darkest night had faded, the sun had risen, bands were playing, heavenly choirs singing. It was heady stuff, especially to two men as light on intellect as Bevan Bigelow and Byron Lavenham. No one had wanted the top job while the party looked as if it would be in Opposition forever; Bevan and Byron had floated to the top, like tiddlers in a stagnant pool. Now, with the sun risen and the bands playing, both men saw competition coming from the back benches, big trout rising to the bait.

'There's a whisper going around,' said Lavenham, 'that we might have arranged to shoot The Dutchman.'

'We? You mean your mob?'

'No!' Angrily. '*Us*. The Party. We've got some hotheads from the bush. They're still fighting the gun laws.'

'Byron –' sometimes Bigelow could be avuncular, though nephews shied away from him – 'we fight dirty, like every party, but we don't go around shooting our opponents. We're Australians, for Crissake!' He stole a glance out the window of his office, but there were no flags to salute. If re-elected, he would have a flagpole erected right outside the window. 'I'm from the bush originally, I know the blokes out there. They want their guns, sure, but only to shoot foxes and kangaroos.'

'And Greenies,' said Lavenham. 'They're always at war with someone.'

'Not me, mate.' He had other wars, much closer. Right opposite him, in fact.

Laveham sat back, contemplated the future. He and Bigelow had swapped the Opposition leadership several times; the voters had hardly noticed. He was a handsome man in a vacuous way; he looked good on television, but his image faded as quickly as the switch to the next item of news. He had no vision of the future, but since the nation was myopic when it came to the long view, the voters did not hold that against him. He was an agreeable man, always agreeing with the last three persons he had spoken to, but now something was happening to him. Inside, a new Byron Lavenham was beginning to stir, jelly was turning to steel. He saw himself standing on the official dais at the Olympics in eight months' time, exposed to a billion TV viewers around the world. Celebrity makes human balloons.

First, however, he had to topple the man sitting opposite him.

Chapter Six

1

The country had never known such police co-operation. The State Premiers, even the Prime Minister, suddenly were aware that back-stabbing could be lethal. Certainly they were a wild bunch in New South Wales, always had been, and no one should be surprised at what went on there. But *assassination*? The other police services had been told there was a suspect under surveillance and they had told their political bosses. They were also told there was no evidence against the suspect and that he was not a known political ratbag and, as far as could be ascertained, had no connection with any subversive group. The Premiers and the Prime Minister breathed no more easily, because they knew that, now an example had been set, copies could follow. For the first time in a hundred years the nation's leaders felt as if they were family.

'The bugger hasn't given us a thing to go on,' said Malone. 'He's going about his handiwork as if we didn't exist. He asked the fellers watching him last Friday if he could give them something from Meals on Wheels.'

Clements was at work at his own desk, fumble-fingering his way through a bibble-babble of papers; true to bureaucracy's rule, nothing should be said briefly that could be said at length. Homicides hadn't stopped with the shooting of Hans Vanderberg; there had been seven murders in the past seven days. Clements had the look of a man who had fallen into a quicksand, one he knew but which he had been unable to avoid.

'Don't come to me with your troubles –'

Malone was sitting on the edge of Clements' desk, his bum

a paperweight on a sheaf of reports. 'Who's got shit on the liver now?'

'I have.' Clements pushed the papers away from him and sat back. 'Scobie, I've got enough problems. There's one here –' He searched amongst the papers, held up a report, 'Some couple murdered their two-year-old son and skedaddled – they're druggies. Bondi wants us to handle it because the guy, the father, is the son of a local alderman. They don't want to shit on their own carpet. I'm turning it back to them – I haven't got enough personnel to handle what we've got. So you go chasing Mr August or Mr June of whatever he calls himself and I'll go back to all this crap and ask myself why I still have some respect for human nature.'

'Join the club,' said Malone and left him as he heard the phone ring in his own office.

It was from a member of the task force: 'Inspector Malone? This is Detective Constable Heston. We've been looking into Peter Kelzo and the guys with him, Gandolfo and Joe St Louis. We've come up with something. John June did some finishing work for Kelzo's building firm – he'd be brought in after all the major work was done. I thought you'd like to know,' he added with the satisfaction of someone who knew he had come up with a nugget that might turn into gold. 'You want us to bring in Mr June?'

Malone thought a moment; then: 'No, let him run around a while longer. We've got tabs on him. We'll talk to Mr Kelzo first. You any idea where he is at the moment?'

'He's out at Homebush. One of his bigger companies is working on a project in the Olympic complex. We're keeping an eye on him right now.'

'I'll be there. Don't lose him.'

He went back out to Clements. 'Righto, we're going out to Homebush to talk to Mr Kelzo.'

'I told you I can't –' Clements gestured at the papers on his desk.

'Who's got the rank around here? Get your coat, give all that to one of the girls.'

'Chauvinist,' said one of the girls behind him.

He grinned at Sheryl Dallen. 'All the time, Sheryl. Do a coupla old men a favour and see if you can get some system into that mess Russ calls his desk.'

She was a plain girl who looked attractive because she was so healthy; she kept trim only because of regular work-outs at gym. She handled men as well as she did dumbbells and sometimes wondered where the difference lay.

'No worries,' she said and implied the mess would be cleaned up five minutes after they had gone out the door.

Malone was in good humour; light was glimmering at the end of the tunnel, even if it was only a firefly. They drove out to Homebush through a stampede of traffic that didn't augur well for when the Olympics arrived. When they came to the huge complex Malone looked out at it while Clements sought directions. He was an opponent of the Games, because of their cost to taxpayers, but he had to admire the job that had been done in building this vast showplace. Most of the many sections of the complex were already working, but the real test was still to come when the hordes, competitors, officials, media and spectators, came swarming in. Malone, a careful man when it came to money, his own or anyone else's, hoped that taxpayers would not be left holding too many bundles.

Kelzo's men were working on a small building on the edge of the complex. Hard-hatted, he came towards Malone and Clements as they got out of their unmarked car. 'Oh!' He slowed down, came to a halt some distance from them. 'I thought you were building inspectors – I'm expecting 'em today –'

'We are inspectors, in a way,' said Malone. 'We've been inspecting someone you employed. John June.'

Kelzo took off the hard-hat, held it by its strap as if he might throw it in some Olympic event. 'June? Oh yeah, yeah.

150

He did some finishing work for me. He in trouble or something?'

'We brought up his name last week, when we asked if he was on your branch membership list. Mr Gandolfo said he wasn't. You didn't contradict him.'

'That's right. He don't live in our electorate, he couldn't be a member.'

'You weren't interested in why we were asking after him?'

Kelzo put on dark glasses, as if the glare from the yellow earth was blinding him. It was hot out here in the open, but he wasn't going to invite them into the shade of the bulding behind him. All around them the huge structures of the complex stood like monuments to the future. Silent as monuments can be: everyone seemed to be at lunch. Even the workers on Kelzo's project had disappeared.

'I never ask the police why they want anyone – it ain't none of my business. I'm in a tough game, Inspector, there are a lotta tough guys in the building trade. You mind your own business and things go along nicely. But yeah, I know John June. A good worker, no complaints.'

'He ever do anything else for you, outside of the building trade?'

Even the dark glasses didn't hide the narrowed eyes; they seemed to pinch in from the outside. 'I'm not with you, Inspector –'

'The sort of job Joe St Louis does, only more lethal.'

'Ah!' He lifted his head, the sun caught on the dark glasses, like a flash of understanding. 'We're talking something serious here, ain't we? I could sue you, Inspector, making accusations like that.'

'I haven't heard any accusations from Inspector Malone,' said Clements.

'You guys stick together –'

'Just like you do in the building trade. Or the Labor Party. Sometimes, that is, in the latter case.' Clements put on his own

151

dark glasses. 'All Inspector Malone is doing is asking questions. Like do you employ Mr June to do other things, we mean besides fixing up shoddy work?'

Kelzo didn't ask what that meant; he knew. 'You're just shooting arrows inna the air.' He was Greek, though he couldn't quote any Greek poets. He wasn't really attracted to poets, they would never have been tough enough to get far in the world in which he lived and fought. 'You ain't gunna hit any targets like that.'

'You'd be surprised,' said Malone. 'We may be off-target sometimes, but most times we're more accurate than the hitman was.'

Kelzo looked blank; or the dark glasses did.

'You see,' said Malone, letting out a little fishing line, 'we're not sure that Mr Vanderberg was the target.'

'Who was then?'

'Oh, we can't divulge that. We might be sued.'

'Is Joe St Louis a friend of Mr June?' said Clements.

'Not that I know.' He put the hard-hat back on. 'Look, you ain't got nothing to say I had anything to do with the shooting of Hans Vanderberg. That's what we're talking about, right? Bullshit, that's all I gotta say. Now I gotta get back to work, so piss off.'

He turned and went unhurriedly back to the small building. Graffiti had already been scrawled on its unpainted walls: FUCK THE GAMES! Under which someone had scrawled: *You're easily satisfied*!

Clements called after Kelzo: 'What's the building gunna be?'

Kelzo shouted back over his shoulder: 'First Aid post.'

'He might need it,' Clements said to Malone.

2

'G'day, Janis,' said Jack Aldwych.

He had waited for two or three minutes before ringing the

152

doorbell. The climb up the stairs to this third-floor apartment had sucked the wind out of him and he had always made sure he was never caught at a disadvantage. This was an old-style three-storey building and evidently back in the twenties, when it was built, lifts had been too expensive or tenants and their visitors had been younger and healthier. He wanted to take Janis Eden's breath away, not his own.

He wore a Herbert Johnson panama hat, a Dunhill navy blazer, grey Daks, Church black brogues and a club tie (I Zingari, Taverners, Woop Woop Nondescripts? He hadn't a clue). A real gentleman caller, neighbours would have said if they suspected Janis of earning a bit on the side or any other position.

Janis' breath was taken away, but she didn't gasp; he had to admire her control. 'How did you find me?'

'I come in? I might look like a customer, you keep me out here.'

'You still know how to insult someone, don't you?'

'It's a gift.'

She opened the door wider, stood aside as he entered. Then, stiff and silent, she led him along a short hallway and into a large living room. An old-fashioned picture window, not the modern sort that went right to the floor, looked out on to tiny Neutral Bay. Aldwych was not an expert on furnishings, but he knew this room had not been furnished by Harvey Norman or K-Mart. The Church brogues felt as if they were walking on carpet two inches thick.

He took a chair without being invited, sat down with his panama on his knees; he might have been a bishop, a worldly Renaissance one, holding his mitre. He had a judgemental look. 'You've changed. Not much, but you've changed.'

'What did you expect, after nine years?'

She sat down in a deep chair opposite him, crossed her good-looking legs. She was in a navy blue shirt and white shorts and had bare feet. Her hair was down and she looked as if she had been enjoying a relaxed hour or two; a book was open on the small table beside her chair. She was not relaxed now, despite the attempt at it.

'How did you find me?'

He gave her his grandfatherly smile, though he had no grand-children. 'Janis, I was thirty, forty years in my business. You work that long in the game, you make contacts both sides of the fence. I heard you were outa jail, so I asked around. It was only a matter of time.'

'You know where I work?'

'Of course. I know you've changed your name, too. Good luck to you. I thought of changing mine once. Glad I didn't. I like being Jack Aldwych. It still scares the shit outa some people.'

He stared at her, eyes smiling, but she didn't take the bait. 'I've kept an eye out for you at the casino. I thought you might've been a high roller.'

He shook his head. 'I never gambled. Except when I was doing a bank or running a brothel – I knew the odds. Nobody would run a casino if he thought he was gunna be a loser. When you worked in Las Vegas, you think the Mafia guys who ran it were in it as a gamble?'

'You knew I worked in Vegas?'

'Janis, I know what size shoes you wore at school. Did you hire someone to shoot me or Jack Junior?'

He hadn't raised his voice or quickened his words. She half-turned her head, as if the last words had come from outside the apartment. Then she looked back at him, her breath quickening. 'Why would I do that?'

'Come on, Janis . . . Are you gunna offer me a drink? It's almost midday. A gin and tonic is what I like.'

She struggled for rebellion: 'You've got a hide –'

'I always had it, girlie. I didn't get to where I did, being a shrinking violet. Have a drink with me.'

She got up abruptly and went out to the kitchen. He stood up and walked to the big window. Down beyond a canopy of camphor laurels the small bay was a splintered blue mirror under a southerly breeze that had sprung up. Out on the harbour a large yacht sliced an arc through the water, its blue-and-gold sails gorging themselves on the rising breeze. He picked up the book Janis had been reading; it was a Patricia Cornwell crime novel. He never read crime fiction, only the real thing. He always felt a malicious pleasure when the criminal figures, especially those in business, got their come-uppance. It increased his pleasure at how successful he had been. He turned back as Janis brought in the drinks.

'Since I've retired I've read up on the history of Sydney.' Which he had robbed blind for years. 'Back in the early days Governor Phillip made all foreign ships drop anchor down there in Neutral Bay. He was afraid the lags, the convicts, would piss off if they got half a chance to board a foreign ship. You thinking of pissing off anywhere?'

'Have you been talking to Inspector Malone?' She sat down again, more relaxed now, sipped her drink.

'Why?' He took a mouthful of his gin and tonic, nodded his appreciation of the drink. He had been a beer man up till his retirement, but Jack Junior had altered his taste, though it had not been easy. 'You know how to mix a drink. They teach you that in Mulawa? I hear they're dead keen on rehabilitation courses. You rehabilitated? Why would I of been talking to Scobie?'

'He asked me – no, he told me. Not to piss off, as you put it.'

'Were you thinking of doing that? If you did, Janis, I'd think you had something to hide. Like hiring a hitman who shot the wrong bloke.'

She was still not fully relaxed, but she was more composed now. She had never been uncomfortable with men, even as a schoolgirl; they just got more difficult, more varied, as she and they grew older. Aldwych was rare in her experience: he was *old* and he was criminally ruthless.

'You're wrong, Jack. I admit, when I was in Mulawa I used to dream about what I'd do to you and Jack when I got out.

When you're locked up, you do a lot of day-dreaming. You must remember that?'

'They locked me up only twice, girlie. I didn't day-dream. I *planned*. The first time I come out, I did a bank two days later. The plan worked. It wasn't any day-dream.'

'And the second time? The plan didn't work?'

He sipped his drink again. 'No, it worked. I broke the knee-caps of the bloke who grassed on me.'

She considered this; then ran a hand over a bare knee-cap. 'Okay. Early in the piece, yes, I *planned* what I'd do to both of you. Jack left me holding the can –'

'No, Janis. You were always on your own. Jack was just your ball-boy. I saw that right from the first time I met you. He set you up with seed-money –' He looked around him, gestured with the hand that held his drink. 'Where'd you get the cash for all of this?'

'It's rented.'

'I know that, girlie.' He smiled, as he might at a naughty child; though he would have belted a naughty child. Jack Junior had only been protected by his mother. 'I know *all* about you. The money you had when you were picked up, the police took all of that, it's in State revenue or whatever they call it. I hadda buy someone off to hide the fact Jack had given you all that cash. You milked him for it, but you had other cash stashed away somewhere. Right?'

'Look, I don't have to put up with this –'

'Siddown, Janis.' He hadn't moved, but the menace was unmistakeable. 'Don't try tricks with me, girlie. I've been retired for, I dunno, eight, ten years, and I've become a model citizen, almost. I was hoping they would of named me a National Treasure, like all them other names on that list. But a week ago I was standing two feet away from the Premier when someone put a bullet inna his neck.' The old rough slur was coming back into the voice. 'Jack was two feet on the other side of him. The bloke with the gun was a coupla hundred feet away on the other

156

side of the street. He could of been off-target, he could of shot the wrong man. If you've got the money to pay for a flat like this – and I hear you might *buy* it – if you've got that sorta cash stashed away somewhere, you'd have the cash to buy a hitman.'

She looked at her drink; then took a swift gulp at it, as if it were bitter. She ran her tongue round her lips, but not with relish. Then she said, her voice steady, 'I've got money, yes. I never bring anyone from the casino here – they'd think I was cheating at the tables.'

'That wouldn't be easy. They've got almost a thousand cameras watching you and the punters.'

She looked at him shrewdly. 'I thought you didn't gamble?'

'I took a stroll through the casino once. Just curiosity.' He didn't tell her about their plans for the casino at Coffs Harbour.

'Well, like I said, I've got some money. But I never hired anyone to shoot you or Jack – I'm not that stupid –'

He studied her in silence. He wasn't looking at her as a woman, but as an enemy. She was attractive, sexually desirable; but he saw past that, saw the cold calculation inside her. He wouldn't trust her as far as he could get Blackie Ovens to throw her. He wondered if a belting would get anything out of her that words couldn't. At last he put down his glass.

'I'm not finished with you, Janis. Or Joanna, whatever you call yourself these days. Till the cops find out who killed Hans Vanderberg, find out who paid him, I'll be keeping an eye on you.'

'You'll be wasting your time, Jack.'

'Not my time, girlie. A little money, maybe. You'll be watched day and night, wherever you are. Till we know for sure who paid the hitman.'

'Tell whoever you've got watching me, not to make themselves too obvious at the casino. I don't want to lose my job.'

'How'd you get past all the checking they do on casino workers?'

'There are ways, Jack. You know someone who knows some-one who'll take a little gift . . . The way you used to work.'

He stood up and she, too, rose. 'Money talks, doesn't it? How'd you explain your nine years when you were outa circulation?'

'I was overseas, working in France and Italy. I'm passable at French and Italian – in Mulawa there wasn't much to do, so I studied. I spent six months in France before I met Jack. There was an old boyfriend there – a little word –' She smiled. 'He came good with a reference, said I'd worked for him as his secretary, he's in computers. Like I said, you know someone . . .'

'What about your passport?'

'Jesus, Jack, you should've been a cop!'

'I know how thorough they can be. Unless you knew someone there who didn't ask for your passport and the visas?'

She relaxed again, smiled: one crim to another. 'You know how it is, Jack . . .'

'I could let the casino people know.'

They stared at each other. She hated this old crim, wished him dead. 'You'd grass on me?'

He smiled. 'Relax, girlie. You've hit my one soft spot – I've never grassed. You're not working today?'

She led him to the front door, opened it. 'I go on at four o'clock. I'm waiting for a man to come and fix some kitchen cabinets. Goodbye, Jack.'

'Look after yourself, Janis. I'd hate anyone to do you some harm before I can.'

She said nothing in reply to that, but gave him a stare that should have chilled him. He was, however, unchillable and she should have known that.

He fitted the panama carefully on his head and went down the stairs, breathing easily, looking like a gentleman caller who'd just had a pleasurable visit to a willing girl. It pleased him that, at his age, he could still frighten the shit out of someone. The feeling was almost sexual.

Outside in the narrow street Blackie Ovens waited for him in the midnight blue Daimler. 'How'd it go, boss?'

'We just have to wait and see, Blackie. If she's the one she's gunna slip up sooner or later.'

'They always do. Women, I mean.'

'True, Blackie. That's why we fellers still run the world.'

The Daimler purred away from the kerb, like an echo of their self-satisfaction.

3

'Scobie, I hear you've got a suspect.'

'Just the usual suspects, Jack. Like in *Casablanca*.'

'Not one of my favourite fillums. All that honourable sacrifice bullshit. And I never understood what Ingrid Bergman saw in Humphrey Bogart.'

'That's because you're not a woman, Jack. That's what my wife and daughters tell me.'

'I can find this bloke you're suspecting.'

'Don't threaten me, Jack. Not if we're still friends. When I'm sure we have the right bloke, I'll let you know. But stay out of my paddock. I don't want to have to run you in.'

'What for?'

Malone laughed. 'With you, Jack, do you think I'd have to look for offences? I could dig up something from twenty years ago, just to hold you and keep you out of mischief. And out of my hair.'

'Have I ever been in your hair?'

'You were today, Jack. You paid a call on Janis Eden.'

'You've got a tail on her? I was just seeing if she needed any help. The poor girl's just come outa jail.'

'When did you join the Salvation Army? Stay away from her. We're keeping tabs on her, she won't disappear. Take care, Jack.'

'I always have, Scobie.'

Malone hung up, reached for his jacket and hat. He wore the hat, a pork-pie model, against sun cancers, but it was starting to look a bit old and limp. Much like he felt. He came out of his office into the big room as Phil Truach came in the main security door. Truach looked satisfied, as if he had just smoked two cigarettes at leisure.

'They're fighting amongst themselves now.'

'Who?'

'The guys at the Trades Congress and Kelzo's mob over in Harding. Seems Clizbe and Balmoral went out there to complain about someone – meaning Joe St Louis – bashing up Mr Crespi. Sussex Street sees Boolagong as their turf. St Louis didn't like Clizbe's attitude and decked him. He has a broken nose.'

'Whatever happened to law'n'order?'

'I dunno. In cases like that, I aint gunna enquire. You don't want to do anything about it, do you?'

'No. But tomorrow morning I think we may pay another call on Sussex Street. See if we can put Mr Clizbe's nose back in shape.'

He drove home through a bottleneck of road rage. The day's heat had flattened everything, including motorists' tolerance. Blue was his favourite colour, but this evening's sky was pitiless. He never turned on the radio in the Fairlane, so that he didn't hear the drive-time jockeys telling the world it would be even hotter tomorrow. He never listened to radio news, it never told the full story. And he had learned long ago that, until you heard the full story, there was no point in having an opinion or getting excited.

A woman in a Honda Prelude screamed abuse at him as he prevented her from cutting in. He gave her a Humphrey Bogart smile, a baring of the teeth, but she wasn't Ingrid Bergman and yelled at him again, blasting her horn as she fell in behind him. He drove on, exaggeratedly turning up his collar against the blaring of her horn and her abuse.

160

He pulled the car into his driveway, waited while the garage door swung up, then drove in. He sat a moment, like a sailor who had come safely into home port through a rough sea. He knew that in many places home was not the safest haven, but this house, this ambience, was the best end to a day.

'What sort of day did you have?' asked Lisa as she stood in the front garden hosing the gardenias and camellias.

'Don't ask. You?'

'Don't ask.' She turned off the tap, coiled the hose.

'If ever the house burns down, you'll do that. Coil the hose afterwards.'

'Waiting for the next fire.' She kissed him. 'I'm becoming pessimistic.'

'Let's sell up and retire.'

'Where to?'

'Tibooburra.' Where the sun fell off the end of the world and crime was a diversion and not a pain in the head. He pinched her behind. 'You have a lovely arse. The best one I know.'

'Don't try getting to know a better one.'

He followed her into the coolness of the house, stopped in the hallway at the door to Maureen's room. She was sitting at her computer, motionless, staring at the half-finished line on the screen.

'More Mills and Boon? Has Clothilde or whatever her name was lost her boobs again?'

She turned round as if glad of the interruption. 'I found out something else today. I was out at St George's hospital. Mr Crespi talked to me – there was no one else there and I think he was glad of any visitor. His face is all dressings, but I held his hand and gave him a whiff of the Arpège.'

'You're worse than Clothilde.'

'I kept my shirt buttoned up. He told me that your friend, Jack Aldwych, gave two hundred and fifty thousand dollars to the Boolagong election kitty. Mr Balmoral heard about it and that's one of the reasons he wants the Boolagong pre-selection. With all that money to spend, following in the footsteps of someone like Hans Vanderberg, he can't lose.'

'Why did Jack Aldwych part with so much money? I've never heard of him being charitable.'

'Mr Crespi didn't know. It was something between Aldwych and Vanderberg. *Mrs* Vanderberg knows about it and she's hanging on to it as if it's her housekeeping money.'

'Why did he tell you all this?'

'I told him I was Jerry Balmoral's deadliest enemy. And that we were gunning for Joe St Louis.'

He sat down on her bed and patted her knee. 'Mo, don't get too involved in this. There's been another bashing – well, not exactly a bashing, but a brawl. Joe St Louis broke Mr Clizbe's nose. They're fighting amongst themselves now. If some outsider like you gets in the way, they're not going to pull a punch. You'll cop it for just being there.'

'This is a *big*, serious story, Dad –'

'I know that, Mo. That's why they're going to be very serious about keeping it to themselves. I don't want Romy calling me up, telling me there's someone I know lying on a slab in the morgue –'

'Oh, come on, Dad –'

He hadn't meant to be so melodramatic, but having said it, he meant it.

She saw that he did. She bit her lip. 'You're really worried for me?'

He nodded, afraid of words.

She put her hand on his cheek, the most affectionate gesture she had made in ages towards him. 'I'll take care, Dad. I promise.'

He turned her hand over, kissed her palm, got up and went out of the room. Out in the hallway he blinked away the tears that suddenly blinded him. Then he was aware of Lisa watching him from their bedroom doorway.

'You're learning,' she said, touched his arm and went past him on her way to the kitchen.

Then at the back of the house he heard Tom say, 'What's for dinner?'

It was as good a way as any to resume normal transmission.

4

'What's Mr Balmoral like?' asked Gertrude Vanderberg.

'Politically, he's gunna be brilliant.' But then Barry Rix wrinkled his nose. 'As a bloke, he's the sort toasts your health with an empty glass.'

'He should do well in politics then.' Illusions, like virginity, were gone forever. She had never regretted losing her virginity, though it had not been to Hans, but she did regret that her illusions had gone. Because she had loved him, she had never blamed Hans for that.

They were sitting on a park bench at Brighton-le-Sands looking out at Botany Bay. Mrs Vanderberg was in a summer dress that looked like a fireworks explosion; she sat beneath a sunshade of green-and-yellow stripes. Beside her Rix was a monotone of pale grey. In the late afternoon passers-by stopped or slowed their step to greet Gert and she smiled at every one of them as if they were her extended family. Hans had had the political smile, than which there is nothing more false, but hers was genuine and everyone knew it.

'We have to keep him out, Barry. We can't let him succeed Hans, not here in Boolagong. Mr Balmoral isn't interested in Boolagong or even New South Wales – they are only stepping stones for him. Hans, for all his skulbuggery, as he called it, really loved this State. He lived for it. We're not going to let Mr Balmoral have it.'

'He's using a lotta pressure, Gert. He wants that money we've got in the kitty.' He looked out at the wide bay turning dull as the sun dropped behind them. A laden tanker was coming in the heads, low in the water, dark and menacing against the horizon.

163

He said casually, 'You know why Jack Aldwych and his mates gave us the money, don't you?'

'No, I don't, Barry. Should I know?' She smiled at another passer-by, another voter, and bobbed her sunshade up and down like a reverse plunger.

'I dunno, Gert.'

She waited. She knew Hans had always seen honesty in politics as an elastic band, to be stretched as far as the situation called for. She knew of the skulbuggery (she loved the word, but never told him so) that wove State politics together like a scatter-rug designed by travelling salesmen not sure if their next sale would be their last. She had loved The Dutchman (though she had never called him that and never allowed anyone to use the nickname in her presence) and, as the young would say, she owed him. Even if she had to protect more skulbuggery.

At last, still staring out at the bay, Rix said, 'Hans was gunna put through a bill authorizing a casino up at Coffs Harbour. Just a small one, to cater for the tourists and the retired people up there.'

'How small?'

'I dunno, I never saw any plans. Smaller than Harbour City, bigger than the Panthers Club up at Penrith. I don't think Aldwych and his mates wanna turn Coffs Harbour into Las Vegas.'

'If we get you elected, will you promote a casino bill?'

He was still gazing out at the bay, as if waiting for Captain Cook to come in and rescue him. 'I dunno, Gert. I'll be just a backbencher. Ordinary members' bills don't get much of a run.'

'What about Billy Eustace? If it was his bill?'

'Billy would want his share of the 250,000 bucks. He wouldn't promote the Second Coming unless he was paid.'

She thought a while, nodding almost mechanically at another voter as he went by. Then she said, 'I think we should talk to Mr Aldwych.'

'He's got partners. Four Chinese. Two of 'em are women. I hear Chinese women are tougher than their men.'

'We'll see.' Gert Vanderberg brought down her sunshade. 'Arrange it, Barry. Somewhere discreet. I don't want it to be conspicuous.'

Wear black, he told her silently. But he helped her to her feet and they walked back to his car, he pale as a winter shadow beside the aurora borealis of her dress.

Chapter Seven

1

Task Force Nemesis was on a not-so-merry-go-round. John August was still under surveillance, but he went about his handiwork as if he hadn't a care in the world. Surveillance was also kept on Joanna Everitt, who appeared calm and untroubled most of the time, though once or twice she gave the middle finger to her watchers, but in a ladylike, almost regal way. An eye was also now being kept on Joe St Louis, but his arrogance was a challenge to them to do what they liked, they hadn't anything on him. Discreet enquiries were made to trace hidden bank accounts, if any, but nothing was uncovered. The media blared criticism and Bev Bigelow and other Opposition shadow ministers demanded to know if New South Wales was on its way to becoming the New Russia. There were clarion calls for Lorne Order to come riding into town again. Civilization was falling apart and what, for Crissakes, was that going to do to the Olympics? Things had to be kept in perspective.

Malone and Phil Truach went down to Sussex Street to talk to Norman Clizbe. Despite the forecast, the weather heat, if not the political and media heat, had eased; the air had a sparkle to it, there was a spring in pedestrians' step. Road rage was still fermenting, but one couldn't ask for everything. They parked the car in a Loading Zone and went up to the tenth floor of the Trades Congress building.

Norman Clizbe squinted at them from either side of his barricaded nose. 'I'm making no charges –'

Malone held up a hand. 'It wasn't attempted murder, was it,

Mr Clizbe? We're interested only in those sort of things. A little stoush between friends – Is Joe St Louis a friend?'

Clizbe hadn't lost his sense of humour; he grinned, but it seemed to hurt as his nostrils stretched. 'I wouldn't call him that. He just forgot himself.' He touched his nose. 'I was in the way.'

'It happens,' said Phil Truach, who had told Malone on the way down that he had known Clizbe for years. 'Relax, Norm. We just came to talk about the general situation.'

But Clizbe wasn't comfortable. His desk looked like a rubbish tip of papers; whether it was his usual filing system or just today's, he looked as if he was floundering. One hand shuffled papers, but it was just a nervous gesture, not an attempt at putting his desk into some sort of order.

'Why aren't you across the road talking to Party head office?'

'We've been there, Norm.' Truach lay back in his chair, legs crossed, as if he came here to this office every day. 'Inspector Malone has had me over there twice. They're as pure as the driven slush, as someone once said. You wouldn't see more clean hands in an operating theatre.'

Clizbe thought about that for a while; then nodded. 'So we're the bunnies.'

'Looks like it.'

'Norm –' Malone felt that Clizbe, if not exactly rushing to be co-operative, was not antagonistic – 'we know that you here in this office were looking at ways of getting The Dutchman to call it a day. Or am I putting it too mildly?'

'No.' Clizbe's eyes had started to quicken. 'You're putting it exactly.'

'Then why are you sueing Channel 15 for stating the obvious?'

Clizbe looked at Truach, the old friend; or anyway acquaint-ance. 'Is that what this is? To get us to lay off his daugh-ter?'

'I wouldn't even think that if I were you, Norm,' said Truach.

'He might be even more dangerous than Joe St Louis. He's a heavyweight, Joe's only a middleweight at the most.'

Clizbe looked back at Malone. 'Sorry –'

'That's okay, Norm. We're not here about Channel 15 or my daughter – that just slipped out . . . Were you out at the Harding electorate office trying to persuade Mr Kelzo to keep out of the Boolagong pre-selection?'

'Why would I be doing that?'

'We've heard a rumour that Mr Balmoral wants that seat.'

'Where did you get all this garbage?' He sounded suddenly irritable.

'Moles, Norm. They're everywhere.'

'Your daughter, wasn't it? Is she undercover for you?'

'Careful, Norm,' said Truach, still relaxed in his chair. 'You increased union members' fees recently. That would of added up to quite a sizeable amount. What were you gunna do with it, Norm?'

Clizbe's hand roamed like a rat over the rubbish tip of papers.

'Mr Kelzo has his own pet nominee for Boolagong,' said Malone. 'A Garry Fairbanks. You know him?'

'He's assistant-secretary of Allied Trades. He'd be Kelzo's puppet, a real dickhead.' Then he looked up as his office door opened. 'Not now, Jerry –'

But Jerome Balmoral wasn't going to be excluded. As sartorially neat as ever, like a model out of the fashion pages of a men's magazine, he came in and sat down in the spare chair at the end of Clizbe's desk. He looked at the clutter with distaste; one knew his own desk would be as clean as an ice rink. He glanced at the two detectives, then sideways at Clizbe.

'Maybe you need some back-up, Norman.'

This bloke has talent, thought Malone. Or ego, gall, whatever you want to call it. He's telling his boss what Norm needs. 'Maybe you *can* help, Mr Balmoral. You're hoping to get the Boolagong pre-selection?'

Balmoral looked at Clizbe, who hesitated, then said, 'His daughter told him.'

'Watch it, Norm,' said Malone. 'Is it true, Mr Balmoral?'

'Yes.' As if the result were a foregone conclusion.

'Is Joe St Louis an acquaintance of yours?'

'After what he did to Norman?' His indignation was perfect.

'I said an acquaintance, not a friend.'

'Yeah, well, yes, we know him. In Labor circles, *everyone* knows him.'

'You know, of course, that he's the main suspect in what happened to Marco Crespi out at Rockdale? He just did the wrong man. If he'd scared off Barry Rix, the way would be open for you in Boolagong, wouldn't it?'

'Are you suggesting we might have hired Joe to beat up Barry Rix?'

'Leave me out of this,' said Clizbe and seemed to retreat behind the dressing on his nose.

'I'm not suggesting anything, I'm just asking questions. Like politicians do, what I guess you're hoping to do when you get to Macquarie Street. In the meantime, before then, how were you going to finance your pre-selection campaign and then, if you got it, your chances in the election? We understand Mrs Vanderberg holds the purse-strings out at Boolagong.'

'Have you been talking to Mother Gert?' asked Clizbe.

'Not me personally. We've been talking to *everybody*, Norm. You have no idea the number of people we've talked to.'

'And you still haven't come up with who killed The Dutchman,' said Balmoral.

'Touché, Jerry. But someone like you, hoping to get into parliament, shouldn't be surprised at how many dead ends there are in the world. We'll get there eventually.'

'Not talking to us, you won't,' said Clizbe.

'Oh, we never give up. You might know more than you think you know. For instance, do you know a man named John August?'

There was nothing apparent to suggest that the name meant anything to either Clizbe or Balmoral. There was no frown, no narrowing of the eyes, not even that frozen reaction that is a silent lie. Yet in their very calm, their momentary silence, they had given themselves away. They had failed to recognize an interrogator who had been reading silences for twenty-five years.

'No,' said Clizbe after a silence that could not have been more than three seconds but seemed like thirty to Malone. 'Who's he?'

'He's a member of Allied Trades. Under his other name of John June.'

Clizbe's recovery was quick: 'You asked about him the other day. I don't know him.'

'Do you, Jerry?'

'No.' His recovery now was perfect; he could have been asked if he knew John the Inuit from Greenland. 'What does he do?'

'He's a handyman. He does everything . . . Well, good luck out at Boolagong. Watch out for Mother Gert.'

Out in the street Phil Truach, forty minutes without a cigarette and looking ready to expire, took the parking ticket from behind the windscreen wiper and stuffed it in his pocket. 'They know August?'

'I'd say so. Wouldn't you? In this mess everyone seems to know everyone else. What is it they say about six degrees of separation? Someone sooner or later is going to prove there's no separation at all. You want a smoke? Go ahead, but stay out of the car. I'll make a phone call.'

He called Clements: 'Get someone from the task force – keep us out of it – to get a warrant to look at any withdrawals from the accounts of Clizbe and Balmoral.'

Clements' surprise was like a puff against the ear. 'You think they might of had something to do with August?'

'I don't know. But they *know* him.'

'It figures. In the Labor Party everyone knows who carries the knives. Or guns.'

170

'And it's not like that in the Coalition?'

'Of course. They just never let the blood show.'

'Righto, get on with the bank search, but keep us out of it. I want to keep going back to 'em.'

'Jesus –' He could almost hear Clements shaking his head. 'We've got more starters in this than in the City to Surf marathon.'

'You wouldn't want it otherwise. I've gotta go. Phil is ready to start on another cigarette. I've got to save him from lung cancer.'

'He won't thank you.'

Malone hung up, waited while Truach butted his cigarette and got back into the car. He popped some gum into his mouth, looked at Malone. 'Where to now?'

'Let's go out and talk to Mother Gert.'

'How much separates her from everybody else in this mess?'

'The width of Botany Bay, I'd say.'

2

But Gertrude Vanderberg wasn't at home. Wearing a grey outfit with flounces that made her look like a giant dove ruffling its feathers but also made her as inconspicuous as she would ever get, she was having lunch in a private room at the Golden Gate restaurant in Chinatown. With her were Jack Aldwych and Leslie Chung, the two owners of the restaurant; Madame Tzu and Camilla Feng; and General Wang-Te. And Barry Rix, who sat quiet and ignored, like an afterthought.

'We were great admirers of your husband,' said Les Chung as they sat down.

'So was I,' said Mrs Vanderberg.

That left a little silence into which Madame Tzu finally put her foot: 'He was a pragmatic man.'

Gert Vanderberg gave her a smile like an aid worker in a

171

foreign country. She would teach Madame Tzu how aid worked. 'Oh, he was that all right. So am I. A pragmatic woman.'

Aldwych had never had much time for the pragmatism of women, though he conceded that Madame Tzu could link cause and effect more effectively than any man he had met. Except himself, of course. He just hadn't expected Gert Vanderberg, the Mother Teresa of Boolagong, to be like this.

'That's what makes the world go round,' he said. 'Idealistic bull – baloney, it never moves anything. You must of learned that, all the time you were married to Hans.'

Gert Vanderberg was the sort who thought everyone at a table should have a say: 'What do you think, General?'

'In my country idealism died when the Great Leap Forward fell on its face.' He waited to be struck dead for such heresy, but here in the Golden Gate heresy was frequently part of the menu. Still, he hedged: 'Basically, that is.'

Barry Rix waited to be asked his opinion, but Mrs Vanderberg had passed on: 'We're talking – pragmatically and basically, that is – about the two hundred and fifty thousand dollars you put into my husband's election fund? Am I right?'

'You put your finger right on it,' said Aldwych.

She toyed with her prawns, looked at Rix, bringing him in from the edge of the world: 'Was Hans going to bring in a casino bill, Barry? He never spoke to me about it.'

Rix had been brought in from the edge of the world, but he was still out on a limb; The Dutchman had had the same habit. 'I think he liked the idea, Gert. Coffs Harbour has always been a dicey seat. With all the retired people up there, nothing to do but look at each other, play golf and bowls, things like that, he thought they'd welcome a casino. Be something else to do.'

'For the tourists, too,' said Les Chung. 'People like to gamble. It's an Australian thing.'

'And a Chinese thing, too, I've heard,' said Gert Vanderberg. She ate a prawn. 'Are you a gambler, Madame Tzu?'

172

'Not in casinos,' said Madame Tzu and sounded almost pious, a thought that brought on mild vertigo.

'What about you, Miss Feng?'

'Occasionally.' On men: but she didn't say that. She had been sitting quietly, comparing Mrs Vanderberg and Madame Tzu, wondering which one would prevail in the deal that lay ahead. They were as dissimilar as two women could be. The one sleek, elegant, as cold as a Sinkiang wind, the other bluff, over-dressed, as warm as a westerly breeze: she wouldn't bet on who would win. But she saw more in Mrs Vanderberg than the three men at the table did.

'I'm not a gambler,' said Gert Vanderberg. 'People have come to me telling me how it's ruined their lives.'

'You can't change human nature,' said Aldwych, who had never tried unless he held a gun.

'It wouldn't be built in time for the Olympics,' said Rix, desperately holding his place in the conversation.

'No, no,' said Les Chung. 'It would be the end of the year at least before we could start. The plans have been drawn –'

'You were pretty confident?' Mrs Vanderberg finished her prawns and wiped her fingers delicately on a napkin.

'No,' said Madame Tzu. 'Well prepared.'

'That would always be your motto, Madame Tzu?' said Mother Gert.

'Always.' Madame Tzu recognized a worthy opponent.

Camilla Feng sat silent, learning from watching these two older women. She wished Jerry Balmoral were here, to learn how out-matched he would be if and when he ran up against them.

'I'd hate to see the Olympics spoiled by bad publicity,' said Gert Vanderberg. 'That we are turning into a nation of gamblers.'

You're two hundred years behind the times, thought Aldwych. And what did she think last year's Olympic corruption scandal had been but a gamble? A gamble against being found out. He was always amused at the naivety of women.

Then she said, 'Of course there was that corruption business last year. They should have all been shot. But we don't want anything more to give our Olympics a bad name. Hans' Olympics,' she added and for a moment Barry Rix thought she was going to bow her head.

'We'd hate to see it, too,' said Aldwych. 'We're all right behind the Olympics.'

'What's your favourite sport?'

'Oh, the synchronized swimming.' Aldwych looked for amusement in all sport; it was the only way he could take sport seriously, except cricket. He was amazed at times at how unAustralian he was. 'It's the funniest act since Wilson, Keppel and Betty.'

'Wilson, Keppel and Betty?' said Rix, coming in from Ultima Thule. 'Lawyers?'

'No, a Pommy music-hall act. They did a cartoon sand dance, dressed up as a couple Gyppos and their dancing tart. I used to fall over laughing.'

'I like synchronized swimming,' said Mrs Vanderberg.

'Well, there you go,' said Aldwych, unabashed.

'When we get Barry elected, he won't be able to do much to push through a bill for the casino. He'll be just a very ordinary member.'

Rix tried not to look like a limp penis.

'We'll have to talk to Billy Eustace,' said Gert Vanderberg. 'He won't be a pushover, Barry tells me.'

'What if Jerry Balmoral upsets the apple-cart and wins pre-selection?' asked Camilla Feng.

Gert looked hard at her. 'Do you know something Barry and I don't?'

'I've been out with him a couple of times. He's so sure of himself.'

The stare hardened even more. 'You're his girlfriend?'

Camilla laughed softly. 'Let's say he thinks I might be his girlfriend. He's wrong, but I'm not telling him yet. We want to find out a bit more about him. He's so damned ambitious, I

174

wouldn't write him off getting pre-selection. He's not going to go away just because you ask him to.'

'I know that. But my husband must be spinning in his grave—' Abruptly she stopped. It was the first hint that grief was still gripping her like a virus. Aldwych, watching her, all at once felt sympathy for her: I'm getting old and soft, he thought. Then Gert Vanderberg went on: 'I can't let that happen. We'll stop him, won't we, Barry?'

'All the way,' said Barry Rix and for a moment looked assertive, challenging.

'If Mr Balmoral wins,' said Madame Tzu, whose eyes at times looked like the keys on a cash register, 'what happens to our money?'

Gert Vanderberg looked at Rix. 'Did you declare it to Party head office?'

Rix looked as if he had been asked if he had declared it to the Taxation Office. Though he admired her, he sometimes thought Gert was too honest for her own good; or anyway the party's good. 'No, it's in a private account. Hans said he would give it back if he couldn't get the casino bill through.'

Like hell he would, thought Aldwych. He never blamed another robber for being *pragmatic*.

'We wouldn't want it to get into the wrong hands,' said Les Chung. 'As a matter of principle.'

Aldwych was debating what to do with the money they had donated; he had no doubt that someone could be bought with it. Over the past few years the national opinion of politicians had gone downhill. He shared the cynicism of a majority of voters in the State that honest politicians were as rare as celibate rabbits.

'Leave it where it is for the time being,' he said at last. 'Is it in an interest-bearing account?'

'Of course,' Rix sounded offended, as if he had been accused of not being able to handle money.

'If we take the money back, you can keep the interest.' At

four per cent for three months that would pay for stamps. His idea of charity was no more liberal than Madame Tzu's.

'Thanks,' said Rix and sounded as if he had passed wind.

Then Madame Tzu said bluntly, 'Who do you think killed your husband?'

Camilla Feng looked shocked; even Aldwych and Chung raised their heads at the question. General Wang-Te sat impassive and Barry Rix, for the first time ever, put a hand over Gert Vanderberg's.

But if she flinched, it was inwardly; no one saw it. 'If I knew, do you think I'd be sitting here?'

'No,' said Aldwych, shutting out Madame Tzu before she could deliver another hammer blow. 'And neither would we.'

Then General Wang-Te, who had been silent most of the meal, tried to save China's reputation. These bloody women, as the Australians would say: they had been the ruin of China. The empresses; the Soong sisters; Chiang Ch'ing; his wife . . . 'Should we employ security to look after Mrs Vanderberg and Mr Rix?'

'A good idea,' said Les Chung, and Aldwych and Camilla Feng nodded. Madame Tzu took her time, then she, too, nodded.

'Thank you but no,' said Gert Vanderberg. 'Hans never let a security man near him. He said they kept the voters away . . . Well, it's been a nice lunch so far. Usually I don't like Chinese food –' She gave Madame Tzu her foreign aid worker's smile again. 'But we must learn to share our tastes, mustn't we?'

'One does one's best,' said Madame Tzu in tones she had learned at Oxford years ago. 'It's just a pity Western cooking has so much catching-up to do.'

Later, driving back to her home in Brighton-le-Sands, Gert Vanderberg said, 'Do you think we fooled them, Barry?'

'I think so, Gert.'

'They took us for naive. Shows how much they've all learned, even Jack Aldwych, about Labor politics.'

'What will you do with the money?'

176

'We'll use some of it to win you pre-selection and then the election. After that I think St Vincent de Paul and the Salvation Army are going to get a windfall. I'll get them to send a thank-you card to Madame Tzu.'

'What about the casino bill?'

'Forget it.'

'Hans would of been proud of you, Gert.'

'I know that. I was thinking of him all the time we were there at lunch.' She turned her head and looked out of the car. The surroundings went by, blurred as if by water.

3

When Malone and Truach got back to Strawberry Hills Gail Lee followed Malone into his office: 'Good news. They've just been on to us from Surry Hills. The boys over there have traced a credit union account for Janis Eden out at Sutherland.' The southernmost shire of Sydney. 'They got a warrant and had a look at it. One hundred and forty-four thousand dollars. She drew out fifteen thousand a month ago.'

'Janis or Joanna?'

'Joanna – actually, that's the name on the account. She seems to have dumped Janis Eden as a name . . . Fifteen thousand wouldn't have hired the hitman, but it could have been a down payment. She drew it in cash.'

Was it chauvinistic or genderless malice that he felt? Whatever, there was a certain satisfaction that the finger was now pointing, no matter how waveringly, at the cold and callous Janis. 'I think we should go and have a talk with her. Where is she now – at work?'

'I've checked –'

Of course; why would I have expected otherwise?

'– she's at home, she's still being watched.'

Malone went out to tell Clements where he was going. The big

177

man was reading from his computer screen: 'It says here that leading figures in the community are questioning the competency of the New South Wales Police Service . . . Are you competent?'

'Point out to me one of those leading figures in the community and I'll belt him in the ear.'

'The proper response. So you're going over to see Janis? Gail told me what's been dug up. Good luck. Be competent.'

'Up yours.'

He and Gail Lee drove over to Neutral Bay; or Gail drove and he sat in the passenger seat with his toes clenched in his shoes. Though it was a working day it was still the summer holiday season; they drove amongst traffic where so many looked pleasure-bound. Murder, unemployment, drug addiction were problems on another planet. The hunt for the Premier's killer was already on the inner pages, was a secondary item on television and radio news. Australia had lost 4 wickets for 56 yesterday evening and things couldn't get much worse. Despite what leading figures might say . . .

Gail Lee saw the two men in the car parked across the street from Joanna Everitt's apartment. She drew in behind the car and Malone got out and walked along to the two men. They were Detectives Gregan and Styron.

'She's inside, sir.' Both men got out of the car.

'She had any visitors?'

'Only Jack Aldwych. But –'

Another *but*: Malone waited.

'About an hour ago that suspect John June, or August, whatever his name is, he drove down here. He slowed when he drove past, but he didn't stop. We didn't know who he was till we recognized the two guys from the task force, the ones tailing him.'

'It was sorta crowded,' said Styron with a grin.

Gregan went on: 'He drove right on down to the end of the street, turned round and come back, driving slow like he was looking for a number. Then he drove off and the two guys went after him.'

'Righto, call up Surry Hills and tell 'em to send two blokes over here to knock on all the doors in this street, ask if anyone had booked a handyman to come and do a job for them. You two just sit tight, keep tabs on our girl if she comes out. Constable Lee and I are going in to have a chat with her.'

'She knows we're tailing her, sir.'

'I'd be surprised if she didn't. Not your fault – she's just so damned smart.'

'Women usually are, aren't they?' Gregan flashed a smile at Gail Lee.

'There's no competition,' she said.

Crossing the road Malone said, 'Are you a feminist?'

'No more than most women. I just get tired of the obvious Don Juan.'

Malone made no reply, never having considered himself a Don Juan. He had had success with women before Lisa, but he couldn't remember if his approach had been obvious. Possibly, even probable: fast bowlers had never been noted for subtlety.

They climbed the stairs to Joanna Everitt's apartment. 'They don't build them like this any more,' said Gail. 'I think that's real marble in those steps. And look at all that woodwork. That's quality timber.'

Malone was out of breath; he would have to increase his sets at Saturday tennis, do more laps in the backyard pool. 'I thought she'd go for more glitz than this. This would've been conservative even back in the twenties.'

Joanna was waiting with the door open. 'I saw you down there with those two dummies who've been following me. I keep an eye on them occasionally out of the window. I don't want the neighbours complaining. What do you want this time?'

'Invite us in, Joanna. You haven't met Detective Constable Lee, have you?'

Joanna looked her up and down, then nodded. 'How do they employ you? As a housekeeper?'

179

'Occasionally,' said Gail, not looking at Malone. 'May we come in?'

Joanna led them into the apartment. She was wearing a pale pink skirt with a black shirt; Gail, who had an eye for such things, remarked that she was wearing expensive shoes, possibly Ferragamo. Her own outfit was stylish, but her shoes were comfortable, not costly. Italian shoes were not meant for chasing crims, not even Mafia.

Gail took her eyes off the shoes and, without moving her head, quickly looked around her. The furnishings also were not cheap items.

'Don't do sums in your head, Constable Lee,' said Joanna, sitting down and waving them to chairs. 'I can afford what you're looking at.'

'I'm sure you can,' said Gail, voice almost demure. 'With the money you have in the Co-Operative Credit Union at Sutherland.'

Joanna stiffened. 'You've got a bloody hide!'

'They also had a warrant,' said Malone. 'It wasn't us who did the prying, Janis –'

'Joanna.'

'Joanna. Why did you withdraw fifteen thousand in cash?'

'Is it any business of yours?'

'Maybe. We could add fifteen thousand to other amounts we don't so far know about and it could all add up to what you paid the hitman.'

'What hitman?' But she said it as if to herself. She looked from Malone to Gail Lee, then back at Malone: 'It was a pay-off. Someone was blackmailing me.'

'Why?'

She hesitated, but not as if looking for words; she was still in control of herself if not of the situation. 'Someone found out I had a jail record. If the casino knew that, they'd sack me. I'm Joanna Everitt there, spotless as a nun.'

'And you worked in Las Vegas? Some nun. Who's the person blackmailing you, Joanna?'

'It's none of your business.' She was adamant, one could see the concrete setting around her.

'I'm afraid it is. Otherwise we'll disbelieve you and reckon you gave the cash to the hitman. Jack Aldwych has been to see you – if we told him about the money, he might think the same as us –'

That cracked the concrete a little: 'You'd turn me over to him?'

'No, Joanna, You're ours. But Jack Aldwych hasn't reformed – he'll tell you that any time you ask him . . . We'll be keeping an eye on you, but we're not going to waste men keeping an eye on whatever Jack does . . .'

It was a cheap threat and he was aware that Gail Lee was suddenly very still in her chair. But most threats are cheap and that is why they are used openly; expensive threats are kept secret, for fear they may cost even more. He would explain that to Gail later. She was half-Catholic as well as half-Chinese, so she would know the uses of threat. The Vatican thought of it as a virtue.

Janis/Joanna was weighing up the value of what he was saying, like a dealer before turning over the last card. Then she said, 'There was a girl who was in Mulawa with me. She told her sister about me and the sister found out I was working at the casino.'

'Name? Where can we find her?'

'Ruby Griatz.' She spelled the last name. 'I don't know where she lives. I met her in town, in Wynyard Park, and gave her the money.'

'Has she troubled you again, after the first bite?'

'Not so far.'

'You think she will?'

'I don't know. If she does –' She left it unfinished.

'Would you kill her?' asked Gail gently.

Her stare should have stunned Gail, if not killed her. Then she looked at Malone: 'Are you going to try and find her?'

'Of course,' said Malone. 'Have you any idea what she does?'

181

'I think she's a hooker. Her sister, the one in Mulawa, was. She was in for rolling men – the sister.'

'We'll pick her up. Let's hope she backs your story.'

'Look, if you pick her up, will you charge her? It'll all come out if it gets to court – bang goes my job –' She was looking worried now, the concrete turning to sand.

'Joanna, if you can afford this –' He waved a hand around him. 'If you've got money stashed away, why is the job at the casino so important to you? You're not making a fortune there unless you're milking the kitty.'

She smiled at that, but without humour. 'We're under more surveillance there than you cops could ever mount. I want the job and the experience – I've got my eye on something else –'

'What?'

'A job as a supervisor or even a manager at a casino they're trying for up at Coffs Harbour.'

'Who?'

'I don't know. I heard about it at work. Casinos don't like competition – even as far away as Coffs Harbour. It won't happen for at least twelve months or more, probably longer, but by then I'll have had the experience and worked my way up from the blackjack tables to the high rollers.'

'There's been nothing about it in the papers. Well, good luck, Joanna.' Malone stood up. 'We'll find Ruby Griatz, let you know what she tells us. Her story had better check with yours. Any questions, Gail?'

'Yes,' said Gail, leaning forward as if at last coming into the scene. 'Where else do you have money stashed away, Joanna?'

'I've already told Inspector Malone that. There's an account at the Commonwealth Bank in Martin Place.'

'We've looked into that. The balance on Monday was twelve thousand and a bit. That and a hundred and forty thousand in the credit union and your salary – we know that, too. Unless you're eating into capital, that doesn't add up to what you're paying for this apartment or if you hope to buy it. Where's the money you told Inspector Malone you got from the sale of your mother's house and that you invested? We checked on what you got for the house – seven hundred and ninety thousand.'

Malone tried not to look admiringly at Gail. She had read the computer print-outs through a magnifying glass.

'How do you pay your rent of six hundred dollars a week? We can go to the agents, ask them, cash or by cheque?'

Janis/Joanna took her time; then: 'Okay, I have another account with the National, in George Street. I pay my rent from there.'

'Why all the accounts? What are you trying to hide and who from?'

'The tax man.'

That stopped Gail for a moment: it was odd to see her without a word. Then Malone stepped in: 'Righto, Joanna, so long as we don't let the tax man know, you won't mind if we look at the National account? We'll need an authorization. You don't have half a dozen accounts somewhere else?'

'No.' She stood up, moved no further for a long moment, then crossed to a sideboard. She took a pad out of a drawer and wrote on it. She came back and handed the note to Malone. 'If the bank manager wants to verify that, tell him to call me. Now I have to go to work.'

'We'll let you know when we've got in touch with Ruby Griatz.'

'Don't bother. I hope I've heard the last of her. Goodbye, Constable Lee. You must come to the casino and try your luck. You sound as if you have a grasp of how money works. Is that the Chinese in you?'

Malone remarked again how much sharper women were at insults than men.

'It could be,' said Gail. 'But you seem to know how it works, too. What's that in you?'

'Experience.' She opened the front door for them. 'Tell the dummies downstairs I'll be going out in a few minutes, to the casino.'

'Somehow I don't think you'll ever make that casino up at Coffs Harbour,' said Malone. 'Take care, Joanna.'

Out in the street Malone said, 'What d'you think?'

'She's told us only half the truth.'

'Is that Chinese intuition?'

'No, it's feminine intuition.'

'I'll gamble on that,' he said, but only because he wouldn't have to lay out any money. He crossed the road to the surveillance car, motioned to Gregan and Styron to remain in it. 'If Miss Everitt visits a bank, let me know. We know two of her banks and a credit union.' He named them. 'We think there's more. You might fake losing her for a while, give her some rein, see if she goes to another bank. But if you lose her completely, you're for Tibooburra.'

Gregan and Styron looked at each other. 'I think the inspector is fair dinkum,' said Gregan.

'Oh, I am,' said Malone. 'She's my pigeon and she's not going to get away.'

In the car going back to Strawberry Hills Gail Lee said, 'Do you think she hired the hitman?'

He was silent for a couple of hundred metres, then he said, 'I think so. One or other of the Aldwyches was the target, but the Premier was the unlucky one.'

4

'What do the polls show today?' asked Billy Eustace.

'Not good.' Ladbroke tried to keep the satisfaction out of his voice. A week as Eustace's minder had been a wounding reminder of how much he had enjoyed the previous twenty-two years. Working for the Acting Premier was like working in watery dough; no matter how much you tried to shape him, he fell apart. Each time he appeared on television he seemed to be asking directions of the interviewer, like a traveller on a street corner in a strange city. He was suddenly blinded by limelight. 'The Coalition and us are even-stephen, thirty per cent.'

'Thirty per cent?' The dough sat up straight, but looked bruised. 'Who's got the rest?'

'A couple of Independents have got two per cent each and that's it. Thirty-six per cent are undecided.'

'Unbelievable! Incredible!' Eustace wobbled his head, then stopped, as if afraid it might fall off before the voters got to it. 'What's the poll as preferred Premier? Me and whoever gets it for the Coalition.'

'Twenty-four per cent each.' Ladbroke swallowed his satisfaction; it tasted sweet. 'Undecided, twelve per cent. Couldn't care less –'

'*Couldn't care less*?'

'That's what the pollsters say. Couldn't care less, forty per cent.' Ladbroke closed his file. 'Basically, Billy, it looks like the end of the day.'

Eustace sat slumped in his chair. It was a leather, high-backed chair and even after a week in it he still didn't look comfortable. He gave the impression of someone waiting at a bus stop for a bus to take him somewhere else: the stranger in the strange city again. Or perhaps, thought Ladbroke, it was the ghost under the buttocks goosing him. The Dutchman was still in the corners of this big room, still prowling. Ladbroke himself still felt the presence.

'Jesus, Jesus –' Eustace wasn't praying; he was an atheist, though he didn't work at it. Atheism never won one enough votes to get one elected. 'What are we gunna do, Roger? We can't let those other bastards into government – not with the Olympics coming up –'

'If the police could come up with Hans' killer –'

'Yes, yes, that's it! How's it coming?'

'I understand they have a suspect –' He wondered why Eustace, as Acting Police Minister, wasn't *au fait* with every aspect of the case; or didn't Eustace care? 'They can't pin

185

anything on him, unfortunately. They're still not sure whether the hitman meant to get Hans or Jack Aldwych.'

'It's gotta be Hans! We'll lose the sympathy vote if it was meant for that old crim Aldwych. Jesus!' For an atheist he kept hammering on the wrong door. He wobbled his head again, then ran his hand over it, as if looking to check if his baldness had increased in the past week. Then he looked up as his secretary put her head in the door. 'Yes, Wendy?'

'It's Mr Balmoral – he has an appointment –'

'Yes, yes, of course! Show him in –' He stood up, almost as if glad to escape the chair. 'Roger, give me something encouraging to say on the polls. Some convincing bullshit . . . Jerry! Come in, come in! You know Roger –'

Ladbroke went out and Eustace sank into his chair, looking back over his shoulder as if checking to see that it wasn't already occupied. Balmoral, cool and immaculate in Armani navy blue, sat down and arranged the creases in his trouser-legs. He looked around the large office as if about to make a bid for it. He had never been here before: Hans Vanderberg had had no time for minor union officials.

Then he said with something like a sigh, 'We're going to lose the election, Billy.'

Eustace managed not to reply at once. He never felt at ease with these up-and-comers. He came of the old breed of trade unionists and these kids with their polish and education had to be handled carefully. At last he said, 'Maybe, maybe not. I'll be re-elected, personally. You still have to get pre-selection. How's it going?'

'I need help, Billy.'

'I've already helped you.' At three per cent above bank rate.

'Not financial help. Political help, Party help. Clout. Gert Vanderberg thinks she owns Boolagong.'

'She does, basically. She inherited it from Hans.' He was awkward acting close-mouthed.

'That's bullshit, Billy. Nobody *inherits* an electorate. At least, not unless they're going to take up the electorate themselves. She can't act the *éminence grise*.'

Eustace had always thought that *éminences grise* were masculine. But it wasn't a term that had been used in the Party, at least not back in the old days. Nowadays with so many bloody foreigners around, you never knew what they were going to spring on you next. There was no denying, however, that Gert Vanderberg was an *éminence*, *grise* or otherwise.

'There's another thing at Boolagong,' said Balmoral; Eustace had never seen him so on edge. 'Peter Kelzo has got some guy named Fairbanks up for pre-selection.'

'Forget him. He's one of Kelzo's puppets.'

'So's Joe St Louis. A bloody puppet that goes around beating up other candidates. He would've done me if I hadn't got out of the way. Norm Clizbe copped what I was supposed to get.' For a moment he seemed to be looking for somewhere to spit. 'Maybe I should've joined the Coalition. I'm good-looking, I dress well –' He would never suffer from modesty, the politicians' bane. 'I've *got* to get into parliament, Billy! Now!'

'What would you have done if Hans hadn't been shot?'

'I'd have run against you, Billy. You're almost as old as Hans was. That's why they made you only Acting Premier.'

Eustace was no stranger to cold ambition. But this young man had a freezing quality to him. The Acting Premier pressed against the leather behind him, protecting his back.

'That'll be all, Jerry.' He knew how to fight; the old union ways were not forgotten. 'Find your own way out.'

5

The three men drifted away from the gaming table and Joanna Everitt looked at the woman who remained. She was beautiful and elegant, not the sort of late afternoon player at the blackjack table. Roulette, maybe, but not late afternoon.

'You wish to play?'

'No,' said Juliet Aldwych. 'I'm just here to give you a warning. If you trouble my husband, John Aldwych, in any way I'll come in here and let your bosses know your jail record.'

Joanna gathered together the cards on the table, aware of the security guard watching her. 'I'm not in the least bit interested in your husband. Your father-in-law has been to see me and I told him the same.'

'Let it stay that way,' said Juliet.

Then the burly young guard came to the table. 'Some difficulty, Joanna?'

'None at all, Lew. Madame is making up her mind whether she will play or not.'

'No,' said Juliet. 'I was watching the game. I don't think I like it. There's no intellectual exercise to it, like bridge.'

She smiled at both of them, walked away and the guard said, 'Who is she?'

'I haven't a clue,' said Joanna.

Chapter Eight

1

The door-knocking revealed that no one in Joanna Everitt's street had been expecting a handyman to call. No one had ever used Mr June or even heard of him.

'So what the hell was he doing in that street?' Malone was clearing up his desk, ready to go home.

'You want to bring him in and ask him?' said Clements. 'Forget it. He's half a lap ahead of us, but he's gunna stumble sooner or later.'

He was lolling on Malone's couch, looking exhausted. The Premier's murder was still the Big One, but there had been another two homicides in the past twenty-four hours. Politicians were talking of zero tolerance as the law-and-order policy, but out there beyond the rhetoric guns and knives were being used with no tolerance at all.

'I had a call from Police Centre,' he said. 'The two guys tailing Janis said she had a visitor a while ago at the blackjack table. The woman had been watching Janis for ten minutes or so before she walked over and spoke to her. The air, our guys said, looked a bit chilly. One of them followed the woman down to her car, took the number. They checked it. It's a BMW750, registered to John Aldwych Junior. Is Old Jack getting Mrs Aldwych Junior to carry his messages for him?'

Malone sighed yet again: the habit was beginning to annoy him. 'We'll have a word with him. Tomorrow.'

Then his phone rang: 'Inspector Malone? Detective Constable Bianco, Police Centre. Nemesis.' The voice seemed to stumble on the word, as if from embarrassment. 'You asked for a check on a girl named Ruby Griatz. She was a prostitute, used to work the streets around the Cross. She was picked up last week, dead. OD'd on heroin.'

'Righto, thanks. Can you do a check on any bank account she might've had? We're looking for a deposit of something around fifteen thousand.'

'In a hooker's account?' The voice now sounded incredulous.

'It's a strange world,' said Malone, hung up and told Clements the news. 'Janis knew the girl was dead. I'll take a bet, too, that the girl doesn't have a bank account, not one with fifteen thousand bucks in it.'

'What do we do?'

'Right now I'm going home. I've had enough frustration for today. Go home and play dolls with Amanda.'

'She tears the head off them. Says she learned that at her day-care centre.'

'I wonder if Mrs Masson, from Happy Hours, is tearing the head off her Mr June? With Dakota and Alabama and Wombat Rose cheering her on?' He put on his pork-pie hat. 'I don't care. See you in the morning.'

He drove home, unabused by raging drivers, opened the garage doors to find the Laser parked in there. Ready to abuse, he went round the side passage, was about to go in the back door when he saw Maureen floating in the pool. He opened the gate in the pool fence and went in. 'Who had the Laser today? You or Mum?'

'I did.' She climbed out of the pool. 'Oh sorry, Dad. The garage doors were open –'

'Open for me and the Fairlane. The boss.'

'I wasn't thinking – I just drove straight in.' She took off her bathing cap, shook out her hair. She was wearing a pale blue one-piece that might have shaken up the life guards down on Coogee beach or got her a walk-on in *Baywatch* but should not be worn in front of fathers and brothers. 'I've had a bugger of a day, Dad. Sorry – I'll back it out now.'

'No, sit down. What sort of a bugger of a day?'

190

She sat down on a poolside chair and he sat beside her. She draped her towel round her, but didn't look cold. 'Peter Kelzo came to the studio today. He'd been invited to go on *State Hour*, but he'd ignored the invitation. Then this morning he rang, said he was ready and turned up for the taping this afternoon.'

State Hour was the only current affairs programme that Channel 15 ran and then only under pressure that it might lose its licence. Its argument was that infotainment was as deep as the average viewer wanted to paddle, but Canberra occasionally stumbled back on to the straight and narrow and it had insisted that Channel 15 run a current affairs programme or else. *State Hour* was run on a budget that, said those who worked on it, ran out at a dollar a minute. It was hosted by an alcoholic ex-newspaper hack who managed to stay sober for the forty-eight-minute run and sometimes asked questions that stabbed the guests in their complacency. Up till now, though, it had never made waves that rocked even the flimsiest boat.

'Why were you there?'

'Because they were working from my material. I wasn't on the show. I was behind the cameras with the floor manager, but he saw me – Kelzo, I mean – and snarled something in Greek and glared at me.'

'Did he mention you on the show?'

'Not by name. He just called me the bitch who'd been raking up muck about him –'

'I'm surprised you didn't go on camera and deck him. You'd have been on *Sixty Minutes* next week.'

'I felt like it, but the floor manager held me back. Things started to get dirty then. Larry Cotter –'

'The host?'

'Yeah. He suddenly got sharp and nasty. He asked Kelzo a couple of personal questions and Kelzo flew at him. They had a donnybrook right in front of the cameras – the whole lot is on tape – Kelzo knocked Larry out of his chair, then tried to bash the two guys on the cameras –'

191

'Was Joe St Louis there?'

'No, thank God – that would've been a real stoush. There was just George Gandolfo. He was trying to quieten Kelzo down, but for a minute or two it was like that Muhammad Ali video, *Rumble in the Jungle*. Kelzo even made a swipe at me—' She put her hand on Malone's arm as he stiffened. 'I ducked, he didn't connect. He did his block completely, Dad – he was trying to hit everyone in sight. Then two security guards came in and got him under control. George Gandolfo took him off and the producer came down –'

'Where was he while all this was going on?'

'Up in the control booth, getting it all down on tape, telling the cameramen to get up off the floor and keep rolling. Producers are never where the action is. He came down when it was all over, clapping his hands like a kid at a party – they're going to run it in full on Sunday morning – nobody will look at *Meet the Press* or anything else –'

'It was tape, not live?'

'No, tape. It's stored in a room, the Programme Room, till they run it Sunday morning. It'll be headlines on the Sunday night news and Monday morning's papers. And, hopefully, Peter Kelzo will be dead politically.'

'I doubt it.' He held out his car keys. 'Put my car in the garage. But get changed first – I don't want your wet bum on the driving seat.' Nor did he want her out in the street stirring up the blood of the male neighbours. He was turning into an almost Muslim father.

He followed her into the house, stopped in the kitchen and kissed Lisa. It might not be more than a brush of his lips against the back of her neck, but even after all these years it was not perfunctory.

'She told you about the scrap at Channel 15 today?' said Lisa.

'Yeah. I wish she could get a job at the ABC. They're never in trouble with anyone except the government. How was your day?'

192

'Lord Mayor Amberton has suddenly had a rush of blood to the head. He wants to know why *he* can't open the Games, instead of the Prime Minister. He says they are the *Sydney* Games and he's the Lord Mayor of Sydney.'

'Did you put out a press release on that?'

'No, we bound him hand and foot and gagged him. Figuratively.'

'The best way. Saves calling in the police. What's for dinner?'

'Greek meatballs.'

'I'll give Peter Kelzo a call and invite him over.'

2

At 2.50 the next morning a security guard at Channel 15 was hit on the back of the head and rendered unconscious. Five minutes later the Programme Room went up in flames and everything in it, including the tapes for Sunday's *State Hour*, was destroyed.

Maureen went to work and Malone called her as soon as he reached his office: 'What's happening? You okay?'

'I'm all right, Dad. But everyone here is in shock. This sort of thing doesn't happen to TV people – it only happens *on* TV. The local police are here.'

'There been any threats? Phone calls?'

'No. Da-ad –' Usually when Dad was split into two syllables by his offspring he was about to be asked for something. But not this time: 'Don't worry about me. I'm not going to shove my neck out, not any more. I'm not stupid.'

'What's going to happen to that story you were investigating?'

'I don't know. At the moment it's on hold.'

'Leave it there. Take care, Mo.'

'I will, Dad. I promise. I love you,' she said and hung up in his ear.

He stared at nothing, flooded with good fortune.

There were no headlines, just a secondary item on Channel 15's news that evening and a news brief on the inner pages of the *Herald* and the *Telegraph-Mirror*.

Members of Strike Force Nemesis, alerted to what was on the *State Hour* tapes, interviewed Peter Kelzo, George Gandolfo and Joe St Louis. All three of them said they were at home in bed, separately. Truth is stranger than fiction, especially when told by consummate liars.

3

'Where's Gail?' asked Malone at the morning briefing.

'Off sick,' said Clements. 'A summer cold. She sounded pretty sniffly when she called in.'

'What's the roster?'

Clements told him. Then Malone looked at John Kagal. 'You're the only one free, John. Let's go out and talk to Mr August about why he was driving up and down Janis Eden's street.'

'I thought you'd never ask.'

But Kagal grinned as he said it and Malone had to take him at face value. There was no doubt that Kagal, easily the most capable of the detectives still without rank, had so far been no more than a dogsbody on the Vanderberg case. Malone had not deliberately overlooked him; it had just happened that Gail Lee and Phil Truach had been the best in particular circumstances. Nothing would be lost by taking Kagal along with him now.

Malone went back into his office and checked with the two officers tailing August: 'He's out here at the Happy Hours Day-Care Centre, sir. He's fixing some windows – some hoons threw bricks through them last night.'

'In *Longueville*?'

'The locals are in shock. It's the end of the world, sir. Will we let our man know you're coming?'

194

'I don't think so. We'll be there in half an hour.'

It took Malone and Kagal thirty-five minutes; traffic crawled and clogged like cooling lava. Kagal, who was driving, showed no impatience, but Malone fidgeted in his seat. He tried to relax, not wanting to appear less composed than the younger man. He had come to recognize that, spoken or unspoken, there was competition between Detective Inspector Malone and Detective Constable Kagal. Though Malone had no ambition to be Police Commissioner, he knew in his heart that some day he would be reading comments by Police Commissioner Kagal and he would spit and make some sour remark to Lisa as he sat in his rocking chair and his bifocals smoked up. He was not mean-spirited, just raging against the ageing. He was certain that Lisa would grow old gracefully, but he doubted that he would.

When they drew up outside the day-care centre there was no sign of the two police officers or of August's van. But there was commotion in the Happy Hours yard and Malone and Kagal got out to investigate.

'Oh, Inspector –' Mrs Masson turned as they approached. She and her two assistants were surrounded by a couple of dozen excited children. 'Not *now*, please! We've got a problem –'

'It's Fred!' volunteered Wombat Rose, all excited relish. 'He's under there!'

She pointed at a small open door in the brick foundations of the hall. The foundations were no more than two feet high and one of the assistants was crouched down calling to Fred to come out. 'Fred, darling, come out – we'll all talk to you –'

There was no answer from Fred; he wasn't talking to anyone.

'How long has he been under there?' asked Malone.

'Three weeks,' said Wombat Rose.

'Shut up, Rose,' said Mrs Masson. 'I don't know – five minutes, ten at the most. My partner was here a while ago – he would've gone under to get Fred out of there –'

'I'll go under,' said Wombat Rose.

'Will you please be quiet!'

'Where is Mr – June?' asked Malone.

'He left, I dunno, ten minutes ago for another job – he's been repairing our windows – someone threw bricks through them last night –' She squatted down beside the tiny door. 'Fred! Come out, darling –'

There was no answer; Fred had found his haven.

Mrs Masson stood up. 'We've got to get him out of there – there could be spiders –'

'Yurk!' screamed Wombat Rose, Dakota and Alabama.

'Shut up!' Mrs Masson was on edge; Malone guessed that his and Kagal's sudden appearance had thrown her. Then abruptly she looked at him. 'Would you go under and get him? Please?'

Malone hesitated, then looked at Kagal. 'You're younger than I am, John.'

Kagal took off his jacket and tie, folded the jacket and handed it to Wombat Rose, who took it as if she had been accepting men's jackets all her young life. He looked down at his trousers as if debating whether to remove them, too; then decided against it. He was not wearing Armani, but Malone knew that whatever it was it was better than his own Fletcher Jones polyester-and-wool.

Kagal must have read his thoughts because he smiled up at Malone as he lay down on the ground. 'What the well-dressed speleologist is wearing.'

He edged his way through the narrow door, which was barely wide enough for his shoulders. There was a babble of encouragement from the children; Wombat Rose bent down and shouted to Fred that everything was going to be all right. There was still no answer from Fred, hidden somewhere in the darkness under the hall.

Malone watched Mrs Masson, who looked as if she might collapse at any moment. 'Relax,' he said quietly. 'Fred will be out of there in a minute or two. Detective Kagal can be very persuasive.'

She didn't glance at him, just said, 'I hope so.'

Fred is the least of her problems, he thought; he's just the feather that's going to bring everything down. Had the bank foreclosed on the Happy Hours?

It took Kagal five minutes to deliver Fred. He pushed the small boy, streaked with dirt and cobwebs, out of the door, then crawled out after him. 'Fred's okay. He hasn't said anything, but he's okay.'

One of the assistants clutched Fred to her and the other children clustered around them. Then Kagal looked at Malone. 'I'm going back in – it'll only take a minute. There's something interesting under there.'

Mrs Masson was paying attention to Fred, but she straightened up as Kagal dropped down and crawled back through the tiny door. 'Where's he going?'

'He's found something under there. It may be something left by those louts who broke your windows. We'll know in a minute –'

He didn't believe what he was saying. He had seen the expression on Kagal's face, the look of excitement from a man who tried never to show it. What was under the Happy Hours hall had not been left by some hoons throwing bricks at windows. It was, it had to be . . .

Kagal crawled out of the doorway, reached back and pulled out, first, a rifle and then, with some difficulty, an old-fashioned leather suitcase. He stood up and looked at Malone. 'Bingo?'

'Bingo,' said Malone, then turned to the two assistants. 'You'd better take the kids inside. No, not you, Mrs Masson,' as she moved to get the children together. 'Let your girls handle them.'

'What's that?' said Dakota.

'It's a gun, stupid,' said Wombat Rose. 'You shoot people with it.'

'Shut up!' For a moment it looked as if Mrs Masson would hit the little girl. 'Go inside, Rose, dammit! Go inside!'

Wombat Rose stared up at her, frowning. 'I was only telling Dakota what it was –'

'Inside!'

The children were rounded up and, protesting, were herded into the hall. Malone, Kagal and Mrs Masson stood above the rifle and the suitcase.

'Do you know what's in it?' Malone kicked the suitcase.

'How would I know? I've never seen it before. And I've never seen that,' she added, nodding at the rifle.

Kagal picked it up. 'A Winchester. Ballistic's report said it was a Winchester or a Tikka .308 that killed the Premier.'

He spoke almost casually, but it was brutal and Malone saw that it was meant to be. Mrs Masson reeled back without moving; the blow was inside her. They were standing under the crepe myrtle; a petal fell off the tree and landed on her brown hair like a small splash of pale blood. Kagal held out the rifle.

'Is it Mr June's?'

Out of the corner of his eye Malone saw one of the young assistants, the Asian girl he had seen on his first visit here, standing in the doorway of the hall. Wombat Rose and Dakota and Alahama clung to either side of her, faces suspended from her hips like balloons. Mrs Masson looked back, saw her and waved to her to go back inside the hall.

Then she turned back to the two detectives. She had aged; years had suddenly fallen in on her. Her voice was husky, as if coming out of a throat that had almost closed. 'I told you – I've never seen it before.'

'What about the suitcase? Is it Mr June's?'

She hesitated, then shook her head. 'No, it's mine. Or rather, my mother's. Her initials are there under the handle. It's been in the storeroom at our flats – I haven't seen it in ages –'

'Do you have a key to it?' asked Malone.

She shook her head; the splash of pale blood fell off. 'It'd be at home somewhere. I haven't used the case in God knows how long –' She stared at the suitcase, then looked at Malone with eyes that already looked bruised. 'John can explain this, I'm sure –'

198

'John, go and see if they have a hammer,' said Malone. 'A claw one. We'll force the locks.'

He squatted beside the suitcase as Kagal, leaving the rifle standing against the foundations of the hall, went looking for a hammer. The suitcase was old and scuffed; it had done a lot of travelling. It was plastered with travel stickers: P & O, Orient, Cunard, Hotel de Crillon, Hotel Pera Palas: labels from another age. Mrs Masson's mother must have had money: more than her daughter now had.

'That was all before I was born,' she said, as if reading his mind. 'The money was all gone before I came along –' She looked back at the now empty hall doorway. 'Would you believe my mother had a governess? She never needed day care –'

She was talking to shut out the present. Malone stood up. 'Lynne – I'm afraid John is in trouble –'

'Which John?'

He touched her arm. 'Snap out of it, Lynne. *Your* John. If you can help us –?'

'Help you? How? I told you I know nothing about that—' She flung a hand at the suitcase and the rifle as if she wanted them swept back under the hall. 'I can't help you. Or John—' She put a hand over her mouth; he heard her mumble, 'Or myself.'

Then Kagal came back with a claw-hammer, knelt down beside the suitcase. 'I'm sorry about this,' he said and put the claw under each of the locks and wrenched them open. Then he lifted the lid.

'Bingo,' he said for the second time, but this time it was not a question.

'More than that,' said Malone. 'A lottery win.'

The suitcase was crammed with hundreds of hundred-dollar notes. Lynne Masson uttered something between a gasp and a sob, put a hand over her mouth again. Malone put a gentle hand on her arm.

'It looks bad, Lynne.' Then he said to Kagal, 'I'll have our fellers pick him up.'

He went back to their car, rang the surveillance team. 'Where is he?'

'He's working at a block of flats in Wollstonecraft. His van is parked across the road from us. He knows we're here – he waved to us as he went into the flats.'

'Pick him up – we're going to charge him. Call me back when you've got him. Take him to Police Centre, we'll charge him there. Don't tell him what we've found. We'll lay it in front of him at Police Centre.'

'Congratulations, sir.'

'Not me. It was Wombat Rose and Fred.'

'Who?'

He hung up and went back into the play yard. Like Kagal he never gave in to excitement, but it was not a conscious urge to suppress it; it was just that experience had taught him to hold on to the excitement and the satisfaction till the trial was over and justice was done. By then there might be no excitement, but there was always satisfaction.

Wombat Rose, Dakota and Alabama stood in the hall doorway; Wombat Rose fluttered her fingers at him and gave him a smile as old as a middle-aged hooker's. Behind them he caught a glimpse of Fred, staring absently at nothing, still in his isolation. He waved at them, then crossed to Kagal and Lynne Masson.

Kagal, wearing disposable gloves, was putting bundles of notes back into the suitcase. 'I'm guessing, but I'd say there's seventy to eighty thousand in there. Enough –'

He didn't finish, but Malone knew what he meant: enough to hire a hitman to kill a Premier.

'You'll have to come into Police Centre at Surry Hills, Lynne. John will be there – they're taking him in now.'

She looked terribly fragile, a wreck held together only by her skin.

Even in the brief encounters he had had with them Malone had recognized that John August and Lynne Masson loved each other. He knew the mystery of love, but didn't understand it. No one could be more in love than he and Lisa; but the elements of it had always confounded him, he had never been able to fathom them. Lisa, better educated than he, had once told him a medieval physician had listed love amongst mental diseases: hence, madly in love. Sanity or madness, understood or not, he recognized that Lynne Masson was bound to August by more than just sex or the need for companionship. She had just been struck dead, though still living.

Kagal picked up the suitcase; with its broken clasps he had to hold it in both arms like a laundry basket. Malone took the rifle by the trigger guard, careful not to smudge any fingerprints on the stock or the barrel. Then he touched Mrs Masson's arm. 'Let's go, Lynne.'

The Asian girl had come to the doorway again, pushing the three little girls behind her. 'Lynne?'

Mrs Masson looked at Malone. 'Let me ring the parents to come and pick up their children –'

'Lynne, there's no need for that. Your assistants can look after the kids –'

'How long will I be at – what is it? Police Centre?'

'I don't know, Lynne.' She might be there for quite a while, depending on how much she was linked to August, how much she knew. He spoke to the girl in the doorway: 'Take care of the kids. I'll call you and let you know when Mrs Masson will be back. Your name is –?'

'Ailsa.' She had a small voice that seemed to go with her small pretty face.

Then his mobile rang. He let go of Mrs Masson's arm, and went over to the gate. 'Yes? Malone.'

'Sir – bad news. He's gone!'

'What do you mean – gone?'

'Pissed off, sir. We went up to the flat where he was working – the woman, the owner, said he got a phone call, told her there was an emergency and she said he ran outa the flat –'

201

'How'd you miss him?' Malone could feel the anger and frustration boiling up in him.

'He must of gone out the back way, through another back yard. His van's still down in the street –'

'Righto, start looking. Everybloodywhere. Call in the North Sydney police – Shit!' He hung up, stood a moment staring at the Happy Hours hall, everything just a blur. Then his gaze cleared and he saw the Asian girl, Ailsa, still standing in the doorway and he knew who had made the phone call to John August.

Chapter Nine

1

John August, or John June, had vanished.

Malone had come to know from past experience that a task force was as unwieldy as a small army; or a small bureaucracy. By the time a plan of action had been determined, August was well ahead of it. When detectives went to his bank to put a stop on his account, he had already been there and withdrawn the full balance of four thousand three hundred dollars, including a deposit of five hundred dollars made a day before.

'He's got enough to keep him solvent for a while, maybe to get him out of the country,' said Greg Random. 'Has Immigration been alerted? Good. Check all interstate flights, see who paid cash for their ticket. Does he have a credit card?'

'We don't know,' said Malone. 'Not yet. We're checking with American Express, Visa, all of them, asking them to block any charges. But I don't think he'd be that dumb – he's not going to let us trace him by where he uses his card, if he's got one.'

'He has a mobile,' said Kagal. He had had a wash and brush-up, but his shirt was still streaked and his trousers would need to go to the cleaners; he still looked more elegantly suited than his two seniors. 'We'll check that, in case he calls Mrs Masson. We've alerted Telstra and the other companies.'

'If he's gone interstate by bus or train, we'll have trouble picking him up,' said Malone. 'Eventually he's going to have to buy or steal a car. That'll be a lead.'

'He'll steal one,' said Random. 'Four thousand bucks isn't gunna buy him much and leave him spending money.'

They were in the task force's Incident Room. A few officers

worked at computers, but most of the force were out on the hunt for August. No press release had been issued as yet, but reporters were already making persistent enquiries as to why all the action. By this evening August would be news, his picture on all TV news and in tomorrow morning's newspapers . . .

'Do you have a good photo of him?' asked Random.

'No,' Malone admitted. 'Mrs Masson couldn't give us one. She said he had a thing about being photographed – maybe that was a hangover from his Pentridge days. We had to call RTA and use one from his driving licence application. They're about as bad as passport photos. It's a likeness, but only just. We've got some surveillance photos, but even they aren't the best.'

'Where's his partner?'

'She's out in one of the interview rooms. John and I are going in to talk to her now.'

'Do you think she was on to what he'd done?'

'No.'

'Is it ever the other way round? A man doesn't know what his partner's been up to?'

'Are we talking shooting a guy or just sleeping with him?' asked Kagal. 'There are no professional hitwomen, except in movies and TV.'

'We don't know that August was a professional,' said Malone. 'I think he took on his job to help out his partner. Now he's left her holding the bag, seventy-five thousand dollars worth.'

'You said her day-care centre was in debt,' said Random. 'Would that amount of cash have wiped out the debt?'

'And given her a bit over. He probably saw it as a good cause.'

'Okay, go in and talk to her. But don't get soft-hearted. Her partner, no matter what other cause he had in mind, killed Hans Vanderberg.'

Malone and Kagal went in to question Lynne Masson. The Surry Hills station staff were busy with their own problems: a battered wife seeking protection, a teenage heroin addict who had fallen off the edge of the world, a teenage hooker brought in for rolling a drunk. The strike force, though necessary, was a distraction, a hindrance to the local station staff. It was an invasion of the territorial imperative, bureaucracy's golden rule.

Lynne Masson was being minded by a young uniformed policewoman: the Surry Hills Day-Care Centre, thought Malone. He nodded to the policewoman to remain. 'You're –?'

'Constable Elsa Tennyson, sir. Surry Hills.' She was plain-faced and sturdy, a no-nonsense girl. But she appeared sympathetic to Mrs Masson.

Malone and Kagal sat down opposite John August's partner. 'Lynne, if you co-operate, this shouldn't take long. You can get back to the kids –'

'I'm not worried about them – they're well looked after –' She had aged, as if all the muscles in her face had suddenly gone loose. The thick hair was a mess, fingers entwined in it as she held up her head. 'Where's John?'

'A good question,' said Kagal. 'Maybe you can tell us. Do you have a hideaway, some place out of town where you go for a break?'

She took her hand away from her head, straighened up, uttered a dry harsh sound that might have passed for a laugh. 'A hideaway? A break? We couldn't even afford to go *camping*.'

'We know things are tough for you, Lynne,' said Malone. 'The day-care centre's debt –'

'How do you know that? Jesus!' She was indignant, genuinely so. Women's debts, Malone had noted, were always more private than men's. As if, more than men, they showed shame about debt.

He ignored her question: 'The money in the suitcase would pay off the Happy Hours debt and leave you some over. Enough for a break,' he added, trying not to sound malicious.

'Did John ever discuss finding some way to help you out?' asked Kagal. Then, as if remembering his manners, he said,

'Would you like some tea or coffee? Will you get her some?' He smiled at Constable Tennyson, who half-rose.

'Stay where you are,' snapped Mrs Masson. 'Let him get it for me.'

She stared at Kagal, who stared back at her. Don't play the bad cop, thought Malone. Then Kagal smiled again, working his charm: 'Later, Lynne. Now – did John ever discuss finding some way of helping you out?'

'Such as?' She was pulling herself together.

'Oh, robbing a bank. Kidnapping someone for ransom. Joking, of course.'

'You or him?' She was altogether now.

He smiled again, but the charm wasn't working. 'Did he ever mention a woman named Janis Eden? Or Joanna Everitt?'

She frowned. 'Who are they?'

Malone took over, putting Janis Eden into the background. 'Did he ever mention a man named Peter Kelzo?'

She frowned again, but this time not in puzzlement. 'I remember the name. I think John did some work for him.'

'Did John belong to any political party? The Labor Party, for instance?'

'You're joking again!' She was fine now; the muscles of her face had strengthened. 'He always voted informally, he said. The donkey vote, as one of our Prime Ministers called it. That was all he knew, the Prime Minister, I mean. John said the donkey vote was the middle-finger salute to the politicians. He wouldn't have belonged to a political party if they'd paid him.'

'*Someone* paid him,' said Kagal. 'Seventy-five thousand dollars.'

'What's his relationship with Ailsa?' asked Malone.

'Ailsa?'

'The Sri Lankan girl, your assistant. She phoned him, told him what we'd found under the hall. A couple of our women detectives are out there now questioning her.'

'They'll scare the hell out of her . . . There was no relationship!

206

God, what you try to read into things—' For a moment it looked as if she was going to fall apart again; then she visibly took control once more. She turned to the young policewoman: 'I'd like a cup of tea, Elsa, if you wouldn't mind? Weak black with sugar.'

Malone nodded to Constable Tennyson, who stood up and went out of the room. 'Lynne, we're not suggesting *that* sort of relationship. But why did Ailsa rush to warn him?'

'How do you know she *rushed*? She might have called him just to tell him what you'd found – how would she know you thought it belonged to him? John was very helpful to her when she arrived from Sri Lanka. He's sympathetic to people – he does Meals on Wheels –'

'He wasn't symathetic to Hans Vanderberg,' said Kagal.

She shook her head stubbornly. 'You're wrong – he didn't do anything like that –'

'Oh, come on! We have the gun – the money –'

But they couldn't budge her. The young policewoman came back with the cup of tea and a biscuit. Lynne Masson thanked her, sipped the tea, ate the biscuit and stonewalled her way through the rest of the questioning.

At last Malone sat back. 'Righto, Lynne, you can go now. We'll give you transport back to the Happy Hours. Don't try and leave Sydney – we may want to talk to you again.'

'You're wrong, you know,' she said. 'About John.'

'I don't think so. If he gets in touch with you, tell him to come in. It'll save us and him a lot of time and trouble.'

Constable Tennyson escorted her out and Malone looked at Kagal.

'We got bugger-all out of that. Get a tap on her phone, at home and at the day-care centre. August is going to try and get in touch with her sooner or later. They're as close as I am to my wife. That's going to be his downfall in the end.'

'I'll never understand love.'

Kagal was bisexual, but lived with an ex-member of Homicide's staff. Malone had wondered if the relationship would last, but it had gone on for two years now and seemed to be solidifying into permanency. Whether it would lead to marriage was anyone's guess, but that was not the standard these days. It surprised Malone that Kagal would confess to not understanding anything.

'Do you and Kate talk about it?'

'No. Do you and your wife?'

He tried to remember, but couldn't. 'No. Maybe it's not meant to be understood.'

Kagal stood up; smiled, not charmingly but wryly. 'Maybe they should've given us a course in it at the police academy.' Then he looked down at his trousers. 'These are Hugo Boss. They're ruined. I'll need a reimbursement chit.'

'I'll sign it. Can you get Hugo Boss at K-Mart?'

2

John August had been surprised when, two months ago, George Gandolfo came to see him as he worked on a Kelzo job at the Olympic complex. It was a small job, putting new glass into windows that had been smashed, but August took anything that brought quick money, cash in hand, no taxes deducted.

'John August?'

'No.' August put down his tools; carefully, as if he felt they were to be re-possessed. He was abruptly tense, but he showed no sign of it. 'John June. You know that.'

'I know that, John. But I also know who you were.' George Gandolfo was also tense; but then he was never relaxed. 'A guy working on the site, from Allied Trades, he recognized you a coupla months back. He was in Pentridge with you.'

'He should of kept his trap shut.'

'He was just chatting, John, he's not gunna broadcast it. But he said you did some chatting yourself in Pentridge. You told someone you'd intended to kill the guy when you were acquitted. That your plea of self-defence was all bullshit. That right, John?'

August was cautious. 'It might of been. You big-note yourself in there – it helps clear your space.'

'You had quite a reputation in there, he said. Nobody ever tried to ride you.'

'What's this leading up to, George? Did Peter Kelzo send you?'

'He dunno I'm here and I'd appreciate it if you didn't mention it when you see him.'

It had been raining all week and great shawls of dark clouds still hung in the south. Pools, small lakes, of water were everywhere; in the stadium, when August had looked in at it this morning, the running track looked like an oval ring of dried blood. If it rained like this in September the IOC would go back to Lausanne wondering if it was punishment for sins of commission. August, though he was an Olympic supporter, had grinned at the thought. He knew that many of the corporate suits of Sydney looked on venality as a virtue.

'So why are you here, George?'

Gandolfo looked around, ears and eyes as alert as a frightened rabbit's; it was obvious that he was not enjoying whatever had brought him here. There was no one within earshot. With the rain, most of the workers employed outdoors had gone home; just a few, like August, remained under cover. 'During your, er, chatting in Pentridge, you talked about how much you knew about guns.'

'That guy who recognized me –'

'No names, John, no pack-drill.'

August laughed, more relaxed now; though Gandolfo would not have recognized the difference. 'George, you've never done an ounce of pack-drill in your life . . . But this guy, he must of done a bloody lot of listening. Yeah, I know a bit about guns. I belonged to a gun club up at—' He named a country town in Victoria. 'We used to go shooting in the duck season. The wildlife

209

do-gooders, they'd come out and you'd wanna shoot them instead of the ducks.' He grinned. 'I never did, but I was tempted. What's this leading up to, George? You wanna know where to buy a gun? Or have you got one and you want my opinion on it? You gunna shoot someone? A voter or a do-gooder?'

'No, John.' Despite the humidity Gandolfo was wearing a suit, his jacket still on, tie and collar neat beneath his pointed chin. He looked like a door-to-door salesman, a fidgety one selling untried goods. 'My client wants you to shoot someone.'

'Your *client*?' August laughed as if Gandolfo had told him a good joke. 'What are you running, George? A hitman agency?'

'No bullshit, John. This is on the level. My client wants someone – eliminated.' He paused before the last word, as if it were foreign. He was certainly in foreign territory, the country of murder. 'I've been told to offer you any price within reason.'

'How much?' At that point August had not been interested, merely intrigued.

'Fifteen –' Gandolfo saw August's deadpan reaction, mistook it: 'Twenty thousand. Five down and the rest on completion of the job.'

August studied him for a minute or more. Two hard-hatted workmen walked by; one of them looked at August and laughed: 'He trying to sell you insurance, John?'

August waited till they had passed on, then he said, 'You really are fair dinkum about this?'

Gandolfo nodded, fidgeted from one foot to the other.

'How much is in it for you?'

'You don't have to worry about that. Are you interested?'

August took his time again; he had felt like murder once, but it was not habitual. Then he took up his tools and turned back to the window he had been repairing. 'Not at that price, George. Go and tell your client I'm not some cheapjack kid who'd do it for drug money.'

'But you're interested?'

210

August took his time again; then he nodded. 'Who's the target?'

'I can't tell you that till we come to a deal.'

'Okay, you go back and tell your client I'm interested. But I've got problems, debts that have gotta be cleared up. The price is seventy-five thousand dollars.'

Gandolfo took a step back as if he had been pushed. 'Ah shit, John! This isn't some fucking joke – it's a business deal –'

'Seventy-five thousand, George.' Now that he had named the sum, worked out what it would do for him and Lynne, he was comfortable with the idea of murder. 'Your client must have a big problem if he wants someone hit – tell him I've got a big problem, too. Seventy-five thousand, George, or I go to Peter Kelzo and tell him what your client's got in mind. He's the one you want bumped off, right?'

Gandolfo took another backward step, almost fell over. 'Christ, no! Don't even *think* that way!' He looked as if he wanted to run away into the thick curtain of rain sweeping towards them. 'No, it's –'

'Who?' said August when Gandolfo suddenly stopped.

'It's –' Then he shook his head, gathered himself together like a man scooping up scattered coins; for a moment he had fallen apart with fear. He's scared of Kelzo, August thought. 'I'll go and see my – my client. I'll tell you the – the hit when I see you again. I'll get you on your mobile. But I gotta tell you – I think you're asking too much –'

'That's my price, George. Tell your client – take it or leave it.'

'You'll keep your mouth shut? You could get yourself killed, John.'

'I could, George. But who would your client get to do it?'

It was another week before Gandolfo came back to him. August hadn't expected him. He knew the price he had quoted was high, probably too high, but it would get Lynne out of debt. He was, he guessed, what they called a mercenary; but in a good cause. Though he would never be able to tell Lynne that.

211

It was a fine sunny day and he was delivering Meals on Wheels. He came out of a block of flats in Wollstonecraft, having taken in chicken-and-leek pie with two veg and bread-and-butter pudding for dessert to an old duck who thought he was Jesus Christ Himself, to find Gandolfo standing beside his van, a green Ford Falcon parked behind it. Today the thin fidgety man was in grey slacks and a green polo shirt, as if the formal approach had been made and now they could get down to talking terms like old mates.

'You got a minute, John?'

August had enough sense of humour to appreciate the situation: 'To talk about a killing and seventy-five thousand bucks? Sure, George, go ahead. Shoot, as they say.'

Gandolfo winced, but managed a weak smile; he had some humour but he always had trouble getting it to the surface. 'I've talked to my client. The seventy-five thousand is okay, but it's still only five thousand down, the rest when the – the deed is done.' He stumbled again, as if this time embarrassed by being self-consciously literary. 'It's gotta be done soon.'

'How soon?'

'A coupla months at the most. Give you time to prepare.'

'Do I get to meet the client?'

'No.'

'Is it a he or a she?'

'It's not necessary you know. Why would you wanna know, anyway?'

'I'd never do a domestic. I knew a guy in Pentridge, he did one and he was never sure who was right, the husband or the wife. Domestics are never cut-and-dried.'

'Yeah, you're right there,' said Gandolfo, sounding like a man who was drowning in a domestic. 'Well, waddia you say? Is it on?'

'Who's the target?'

Gandolfo leaned close to him, gave him the name. August showed no expression, just nodded. 'I'll need time, get a fix on his movements. I'm not gunna do a drive-by, that's for knuckleheads. It'll be professional. How will I be paid? Cheque or cash? I don't take credit cards.'

'Cash, of course!' Then he saw that August was grinning and he said lamely, 'Are you always a joker?'

'It's the only way to survive, George. It's a shitty world –' He opened the back door of his van, gestured at the hot-boxes containing the meals he was delivering. 'I take them in to some old ducks, some old fellers, they never see anybody but me and the community carer comes in twice a week. Is that what we grow old for, George? You wanna grow old?'

'Yes,' said Gandolfo, who was afraid of dying.

'Okay, I'll put your name down for Meals on Wheels. Maybe I'll still be delivering, we can grind our dentures at each other. You got the five thousand down payment?'

That had been almost two months ago and now he was on the run. He had not panicked when Ailsa, Lynne's assistant, had called him on his mobile. She had just called to say there was some trouble at the Happy Hours and he should get down there quickly and help Lynne.

'What's the trouble, Ailsa?'

'The police are here and they've found a suitcase and a gun under the hall.'

'Thanks, Ailsa. Tell Lynne not to worry.'

But of course Lynne would worry; she was a born worrier and he had always felt good when comforting her. His first wife had never been a worrier and had never needed comforting; that had been the difficulty between them because there was part of him that was a born carer. He had tried to kill his wife's lover because he cared, or so he had told her. She had not believed him and he had only half-believed himself. He knew the cold current that occasionally surfaced through his caring exterior.

As soon as he had left the flat, where he had been hanging a new bathroom door, he had gone down and out the back door of the building, over a fence and through the back yard of a neighbouring house into the next street. Already thinking ahead he had gone up to the main road and caught a bus to North Sydney, where his bank was. There he had withdrawn almost all his cash, then come out of the bank and gone to a public telephone.

'Lynne's not here, John.' It was the other assistant, Beth. 'The police have taken her away – she said she'd be back.'

'Where's Ailsa?'

'There are a couple of policewomen here interviewing her. She's scared stiff, John. Do you want to talk to her?'

'No.' He tried to keep the panic out of his voice. What were the police doing with Lynne? Christ, she knew nothing about the money and the gun. 'Don't say I rang, okay? How did they find the suitcase and the gun?'

'One of the police went under the hall after young Fred Norman. Do you know anything about it, John?' Her voice was cautious, as if afraid of offending him.

'No, Beth, I know nothing about any of it. Tell Lynne –' He was about to say, *Tell Lynne I love her.* 'Tell her I'll call her. How are the kids?'

'Fine. They've never seen so much excitement. Wombat Rose is sitting on a policewoman's lap, giving her a rundown on everything.'

'I'll bet.'

He hung up, walked out into the lunchtime crowd. He looked at them, wondered what sins and crimes lay behind their chattering faces, their pensive expressions, their laughs. He heard a siren and stiffened, but it was a fire engine heading for someone else's disaster.

Then he began to wonder where he would run to.

3

Inspector Clarrie Binyan came across from Ballistics at Police Centre and walked into Malone's office. He sat down, taking his time. As, he would say, his Aboriginal forbears had been doing for the past forty thousand years. He ran a hand through his thick greying curls and gave Malone his slow smile.

'The prints on that Winchester matched those of this bloke August?'

'Yes,' said Malone. 'They were on the suitcase, too, and on some of the money.'

'Well, I've got some bad news for you, mate. That Winchester isn't the gun that killed The Dutchman. It's a .308 and so's the bullet they took from his neck. But they don't match. There's no way you could offer that gun as evidence.'

Malone sucked his lips. 'So he's got another gun somewhere?'

Binyan nodded. He had an encyclopedic knowledge of weapons, from the boomerang and woomera through to the latest developments of honest, God-fearing employees of honest, God-fearing nations. 'Probably. There's another thing. I noticed in the report someone mentioned a night-'scope. I went down there last night, to that sewing centre where he stood to fire the shot. The lady who owns it, she says it's knocked the bottom outa her business. All the well-knowns, they don't want it known they come to her to get their trousers and their skirts let out.'

'Get on with it, Clarrie. You didn't go down there to have a yarn with her.'

'Patience, Scobie.' He always sounded as if he'd had forty thousand years of it. 'At night it's almost like bloody daylight down there. Too much light for a night-'scope. This bloke knows guns, knows what he's about. He wouldn't of used a night-'scope. He'd of used a "twilight"-style – the Germans make one, a Schmidt and Bender, or there's an Austrian one, a Swarovski. They're not large. Did they search every inch under that hall?'

'Every inch, Clarrie. There was nothing else under there but the suitcase and the Winchester. Where would he buy the guns? How much would they cost?'

'He could buy 'em in any gun shop, if he had a permit. They, the Winchester and the Tikka, if that's the other gun, they cost just on a thousand bucks each. If he had to buy 'em without a permit, they'd cost more. Maybe he's had 'em for years. That Winchester we've got is a 1985 model. I went downstairs from my office to the blokes on the task force, they gimme a look at his form. He belonged to a gun club before he went into Pentridge, but there's nothing in the report that they confiscated any guns. He could still have 'em. Or anyway, the second gun.'

'Why do you always come bearing bad news? Is that an Abo custom?'

Binyan had the most charming smile, a real reconciliation smile. 'Mate, don't you think it hurts me, I can't come in here and lay all the evidence you want there on your desk? I had a lotta time for The Dutchman. He did a lot for our mob – it might of just been politics, but sometimes it made him unpopular and he still did it. He had more guts than all of those who are gunning for him. *Were* gunning for him.'

'What's your guess? Someone in politics hired the hitman?'

Binyan spread his hands. 'Your guess is as good as mine. Russ Clements told me you had a girl in mind who might of hired him, going after Jack Aldwych or his son. That right?'

'I've got even money on her.'

'And anyone else?'

'Two or three. And maybe I could be dead wrong. It could be someone way out there in right field –'

'Left field.' Binyan knew his baseball.

'Right field.' Malone knew his politics. 'There are some nutters on the Left, blokes still living in the 1930s, but they would never knock off The Dutchman. He protected them from the go-getters of the nineties, the economic rationalists. He never agreed with them, but he protected them. Nobody from the Left did him.'

'That's taking economic rationalism a bit far, isn't it? Knocking off a State Premier.'

'Get outa here. Where do you get your ideas?'

Binyan stood up, still smiling; but Malone often wondered

216

how much pain it hid. 'Our mob are always on the sidelines, mate. That's where you get the whole picture. Good luck. I'll let you know if I get any more bad news.'

'Do that.'

But Malone always enjoyed his meetings with Clarrie Binyan. The dark-skinned man had a macroscope in his Ballistics office that, he claimed, could tell the difference between a white man's single hair and an Aborigine's single hair: the split hair would be the white man's. It was a joke that Malone, faced almost every day with men who split hairs, could appreciate. But he sometimes imagined that Binyan, staring into the macroscope, looked at more than the lands and grooves on a bullet. He saw life with a macroscopic eye that amused him. It was a way of surviving.

4

'You like literature, Gert?'

'Not literature, Billy. Literature is what critics and academics run around in. I like *books*, that's what ordinary readers enjoy.'

'Did Hans read much?'

'Only political histories. I don't think he ever picked up a novel. That's what I read. Novels. I learn more about people from reading novels than I would from political histories.'

'Hans knew people, backwards and forwards.'

'Personal experience, Billy. Not from reading books.'

Gert Vanderberg and Billy Eustace were in her study; though she still thought of it as Hans' study. Eustace had rung her and said he wanted to see her privately, then he had come out here, accompanied only by his driver, to the Vanderberg house in Rockdale. They had bought it twelve years ago when Hans had taken over the Boolagong electorate. It was a blue-brick California bungalow, built in the twenties, on a double block; it was the largest house in the quiet street, but not pretentious. There

217

was a tibouchina tree in the front garden, a huge purple bouquet like a reminder that death had recently come to this house, and there were four peach trees, with the fruit of longevity, in the back yard. There were security doors and bars on the windows, but no high security fence; it was the home of the State's most powerful politician, but there was no one on guard duty; the voters would have considered it an affront to themselves. That was the Australian way; or had been up till a week ago. Now there was 24-hour police surveillance, something that made Gert Vanderberg uncomfortable.

'The police know who the hitman was,' said Eustace, coming to the point with unusual brevity.

'I've read the papers, Billy. I'm waiting to hear who paid him. It was someone in our party.'

She knew, as well as anyone, that in this State, political parties were firing squads standing in a circle.

Eustace shook shook his head, but not in denial. 'It's a different world to what you and I knew, Gert. We had bashings, that sorta stuff, but a killing –' He shook his head again.

'Are you afraid you might be next?'

'Gert, I'm just a fill-in.' He had no conceit, a political handicap. 'When we get back in, they'll let me lead for a while, then they'll dump me.'

'Who's *they*?'

'I'm not sure.' But she was sure he was. 'Of course, the shot might not have been meant for Hans. There's a rumour it was meant for Jack Aldwych.'

'Jack Aldwych?' she said innocently. 'Oh, the ex-criminal.'

'You don't call him that, not these days. It doesn't take long, you got enough money, to become respectable, not these days. I thought you knew him?' he said innocently.

'I've met him once or twice, just casually. Why would anyone want to shoot him?'

'The police are working on a theory that an ex-girlfriend of Jack Aldwych's son might of paid for the killing.' He was not

218

yet accustomed to being Acting Police Minister; he liked to show what he knew. Gert Vanderberg had been privy to all of Hans' secrets, both as Premier and Police Minister, but she was his wife, for God's sake. Billy Eustace, she guessed, would spread secrets like patronage. 'She could afford him, they think. The hitman, I mean. Seventy-five thousand dollars.'

'That was the price?' She was suddenly angry at the price, as if Hans had been devalued. She sat quiet for a long moment, then she settled back in her chair: 'Billy, what did you want to see me about?'

He took his time; one could almost see him putting the words together like play-blocks: 'Gert, this is the only electorate left that hasn't decided its pre-selection. We've got everyone else everywhere else all lined up for the election. All except Boolagong.'

'No problem, Billy. Barry Rix is going to be our candidate.'

'He's not endorsed –'

'He is, Billy. By me.'

'Gert, Barry is the one I want to talk about –'

'Ah!' she said and waited, like a mother confessor.

'Barry is the problem. He's – he's dull, Gert –'

She managed not to laugh. Charisma was a word she doubted Billy Eustace could spell. Political columnists had compared him variously to plain wallpaper, an empty bottle and a wet day in Hobart.

'He's a good bloke, a hard worker, honest – honest as the day is long. But he just doesn't *have* it, Gert. We want someone from here who's got git up and go –'

'I like that,' said Gert Vanderberg, as if she had never heard it before. 'Git up and go. Have you got it, Billy?'

'I don't need it, Gert. The voters *know* me –'

Indeed they do, she thought. 'Who've you got in mind? With git up and go?'

She could see him arranging the play-block carefully: 'Jerry Balmoral.'

219

She took her own time, put off by the gall of the suggestion. Then she said, 'No way, Billy. He's arrogant, conceited, ambitious –' Then she laughed at herself: 'What am I saying? I've just described ninety per cent of the politicians in this country. Politicians in any country. Except you, Billy,' she added and sounded gracious.

Eustace was not dumb; he knew compliments for him were few and far between. So he was not offended. 'Okay, he's all those things, Gert. But he's what voters want, someone they can identify with. Not you and me, Gert, and all the baby-boomers –'

'I was never a baby-boomer, Billy.'

'I don't mean you were. Look, Gert, the voters under thirty-five, forty, they're not interested in all the old values. They want someone who's in tune with today. *Today*, Gert, not yesterday. That's Jerry Balmoral, he's just right for the under-forties.'

'When did you change your mind about him?'

'How do you know I had any opinion on him?'

'Billy, I'm like Hans was –' She paused for a moment, like a catch in the breath. 'There's nothing in the party I don't know.'

Bloody Roger Ladbroke, he thought. The bastard was still working for his dead boss. He would kick the shit out of him tomorrow, he would sack him . . . But he knew that he wouldn't. He needed Ladbroke, the man who knew all the shoals and rocks in the media sea.

'We're not gunna walk in with this election, Gert. The voters are getting shirty towards us. All that Olympics mess, the hospitals breakdown, law and order – the other mob won't do any better than us –'

'But?'

'But the voters are sounding as if they might get rid of us.'

'Not in our electorate, Billy.' She almost said *my* electorate. 'No, you have to look after yourself and the party. Boolagong gets Barry Rix as its candidate. It's what Hans would've wanted. Would you like some tea?'

Eustace knew now that tea was all he was going to get. 'No, I better be getting back.' He stood up. 'Do you still make your pumpkin pavlovas?'

'Occasionally. I'm getting on, Billy, I don't have the energy I used to have. Not since Hans has gone.' Not two weeks yet, but it seemed like two decades.

'Well, look after yourself. I'm sorry you don't see my point about Jerry Balmoral.'

'Don't worry, Billy. You'll survive without him. He's a back-stabber if ever I've seen one, you're better off without him. The one you have to watch out for is Peter Kelzo.'

He hesitated, then said, 'Do you think *he* might have paid the hitman?'

She looked up at him, face expressionless. 'He's on my list, Billy.'

He let himself out of the house and she sat on in the book-lined room. She picked up the book she had been reading when he arrived, one by Mary Wesley. She and the author were much the same age, old enough to have come to know men and their failings.

Billy Eustace, she was sure, knew more than he had told her.

Chapter Ten

1

'They got a phone trace on our man,' said Greg Random over the phone. 'He called his partner, Mrs Masson, from a public phone box in Rockdale.'

'Crumbs.' Some of the slang of his childhood still clung to Malone's tongue. It sounded soft beside four-letter words, but it was only an expression anyway. 'I thought he'd be miles away –' Then *Rockdale* abruptly hit him: 'Shit, he's not after Mrs Vanderberg too!'

There had been reported sightings of August in Albury, Warialda and Coonabarabran, all hundreds of kilometres from each other. Criminals on the run multiply their images in the ever-helpful public eye. Law'n'order was a heated subject in the coming election and, by God, the public was going to help.

'We're doubling the surveillance out there. She's not going to like it, but she'll have to put up with it.'

'What did he have to say to Mrs Masson?'

There had been the regular morning conference of the task force, then Malone had come back to Homicide. Other murders, like traffic accidents, were still occurring; he was not investigating them, but he had to confer with Clements on how they were handled. The phone intercept on August had happened ten minutes ago.

'It was a love call, I guess you'd call it. Said he loved her and was sorry for what had happened, that he had hoped the money would wipe out their debts. We've got the Rockdale police down to where he made the call, but so far they haven't reported in. I doubt that he's hung around. He'd guessed the line was tapped.

After he'd said goodbye to Mrs Masson, he said cheerio to the blokes on the line. He's a cheeky bastard.'

'I don't think his cheekiness is going to last. He really loves that woman of his, Greg. His life's over and he knows it. But what was he doing in *Rockdale*?'

'I don't know, Scobie. I don't think he would've been out there to do Mrs Vanderberg, but he might have another contract to do – what's his name?'

Malone had to think: politics these days was full of vague shapes, vague names. The back benches were stocked with anonymity: 'Rix. Barry or Harry Rix. He used to be The Dutchman's branch secretary. He was the one Joe St Louis was supposed to do over, but Joe got the wrong feller.'

'Well, Mr Rix might be August's next target.'

'He won't be if our main suspect, Janis Eden, was the one who paid August.'

'Anyhow, we've sent extra men out there, they're going to comb the neighbourhood. We might have some luck.'

'You don't sound hopeful.'

'It's the Welsh in me. You want me to quote you a Welsh poet? *I stuffed my life with odds and ends –*'

'Take your ear away, Greg. I'm hanging up –'

'Hold it! I want you to go out and talk to Mrs Masson, see if you can get anything further out of her. Use your Irish bullshit.'

'We call it blarney.'

'Same thing. Good luck.'

Malone took Gail Lee with him out to Longueville. He had become comfortable working with her; there was an ease between them that slipped round rank, though she never abused the relationship. It had taken the Police Service almost a century to acknowledge that women had their place in law enforcement. One day there would be a woman Police Commissioner and in graves all around the country there would be bones trying to break out of coffins as they had once broken in doors.

'We treat her gently, Gail. This woman has had the bottom

223

fall out of her world. I don't want to be around when we have to pick up the pieces of her when she totally falls apart.'

'That's when she may tell us where we can find Mr August.'

'Is that feminine pragmatism?'

'No, it's feminine logic. A woman will often sacrifice a man to save him for herself.'

He looked sideways at her as she drove, fast but competently as usual. 'Now I understand why I've never understand a woman's logic.'

She glanced at him, smiled. 'Leave Mrs Masson to me, okay? You're not an unsympathetic man, but I think we need a woman's touch here.'

'I'm glad you think I'm not unsympathetic. I must tell my wife and daughters.'

The opportunity presented itself much sooner than he expected; at least to tell it to one daughter. But what he would tell her would not be sympathetic at all.

When they drew up outside the Happy Hours Day-Care Centre there were four other vehicles parked at the kerb. A marked police car, two cars with press stickers on their windscreens, a Channel 15 van with a transmitter dish on its roof: enough excitement to have drawn a small crowd of onlookers. Even in well-bred Longueville curiosity was sometimes let out of the house.

Malone cursed as he got out of the car, pushed his way through the crowd into the yard. The first thing he noticed was that there were no children: Wombat Rose, Dakota, Alabama, Fred were all gone. And with them, he guessed, were gone the Happy Hours.

The second thing he noticed was Maureen interviewing Mrs Masson. He turned to the young uniformed officer who approached him. 'What the hell's going on?'

'Who are you, sir?' He was one of the local cops, not from the strike force.

'Inspector Malone, Homicide. Where are the surveillance fellers, supposed to be keeping an eye on Mrs Masson?'

'They're further up the street, sir.' He introduced himself as Constable Raine. He was tall and big, with bushy black eyebrows a broken nose and a very thick neck which suggested he was either a rugby forward or was heading for a goitrous old age. 'They called us to come down when the media guys turned up. They didn't want to be identified.'

The two of them had moved away from the crowd and now were joined by Gail Lee. The television crew and Maureen didn't appear to have noticed the new arrivals. One of the newspaper reporters recognized Malone and moved towards him, but Malone shook his head, mouthing *Later*.

Gail said, 'She's giving Mrs Masson a hard time.'

'I'll give her a hard time when I get her home.' He saw the bushy eyebrows go up and he said to the young officer, 'She's my daughter.'

'I was gunna break it up, sir –'

Gail, one eye on her boss, said, 'Where are all the kids?'

'The parents took them out of the centre,' said Raine. 'It's gunna be closed down.'

Malone, holding in his irritation, was watching Maureen talking to Mrs Masson. He couldn't hear what was being said, but it was evident that Mrs Masson was not enjoying the interview. Then it came to an abrupt stop: she snapped something at Maureen, turned away and in a stumbling run went up into the hall. The cameraman and the soundman went to follow her, but Maureen stepped in front of them and shook her head. Then she saw her father and froze.

Malone said nothing, just strode past her and up into the hall. Gail Lee followed him, but she turned in the doorway and looked straight at Maureen and the television crew.

'I would advise you to leave now.'

'That's up to us,' said the cameraman. 'Not you.'

Gail looked at Maureen. 'I think you'd better talk some sense into your colleague. You're in enough trouble as it is.' She nodded back into the hall.

'Who with?' The cameraman was young, overweight, belliger-ent; three beers and he would take on the world.

Gail ignored him, continued to look at Maureen. The latter hesitated, then turned away. 'Let's go. I'm finished.'

'Why, for Crissake? Fucking police stand-over –'

Then Constable Raine stepped forward. 'Maybe you'd like to come up to the station and lay a complaint? You can give the camera to your mate here –' He nodded at the soundman, a youth who looked as if he wished he were deaf. 'He can take our picture as we go out the gate. The press guys can follow us and write a story about you and me and your abuse of a woman detective. Okay?'

'You're a fucking smartarse –'

'It takes one to know one. Come on, Jack, just piss off before I have to run you in –'

The soundman was tugging at his cable, like a dog-owner trying to get his charge away from a pole. 'Come on, Barney, let's get outa here –'

The cameraman backed away, still muttering and glowering, and Constable Raine grinned up at Gail Lee on the doorstep. 'They think they own the world. Good luck with Mrs Masson. She's a real nice lady. It's a pity –' He gestured vaguely, said nothing more and turned away.

Gail went into the hall where Malone was sitting opposite Lynne Masson amidst an empty carnival of tiny desks, toys and bright paintings on the walls where the children's images of themselves and their world hung like innocence itself. But an empty mask leered evilly at the two detectives, like a death-mask of an ancient Wombat Rose.

'What upset you?' Malone was asking.

'That bloody girl –' Lynne Masson was a shattered woman; she seemed hardly aware of the two detectives. 'Jesus, you wonder where they come from! Have they no – no sympathy for people?'

'I'll ask her,' said Malone quietly. 'She's my daughter.'

Mrs Masson blinked and looked at him as if he had sworn at her. 'What? Your daughter?' He nodded. 'Good God, is that how you brought her up? Jesus, I try to teach these kids here –' She swept an arm around her at the absent children, gone probably forever from her. Then she blinked again, as if realizing for the first time that the children were no longer there. 'I try to teach them to respect people –'

'My wife and I thought we'd done that,' said Malone. 'I guess we never anticipated foot-in-the-door journalism. What did she say that upset you so much?'

'She wanted to know was the money you found under here –' She tapped the floor with a nervous foot, as if it were mined. 'Whether it was to pay off my debts, the day-care's debts. They'd found that out –' Then she seemed to freeze herself together, stared at him: 'Did you tell her about my debts?'

'No, believe me I didn't.'

'Then how –?'

'Lynne, you've been drawn into a mess . . .' He looked at Gail, though he didn't know why; unless it was for support he suddenly needed. Then he turned back to Mrs Masson: 'Channel 15 were working on a story about internal fighting in the Labor Party – that was before Premier Vanderberg's assassination.' She frowned when he used the word, but said nothing. 'When John killed the Premier –'

She shook her head, but it was difficult to tell whether it was in denial or stupefaction.

'It's a whole new ballgame, Lynne. You're in it – Detective Lee and I are in it – Channel 15, the whole media . . . They're not going to leave you alone till we find John.'

'Lynne,' said Gail, leaning forward on her chair, as solicitous as an aid worker, 'where can we find him?'

'I don't know! God, I want to find him as much as you do – I still can't believe he – he shot –' The words choked her like smoke from a fire she could not believe was now just ashes.

'He did it, Lynne,' said Gail gently. 'If he calls you again, tell him to turn himself in. He can't run forever. Does he have any other relatives or friends besides you? You mentioned his mother down in Victoria?'

'They're not – they don't speak, haven't for years, he said. They never got on – she's a religious crank, he said –' She looked around the hall again, as if only just realizing she still had another problem: 'I worked so hard for all this. I really enjoyed the kids – so did John – I told them it was going to be great to grow up –'

'They'll survive,' said Malone. 'Especially Wombat Rose.'

She nodded, but looked unconvinced.

'Do you have a recent photo of John?' Gail asked.

Again she blinked; her thoughts were like marbles in a barrel. 'Photo? John hated having his photo taken – he used to say it was bad luck – he'd say it as a joke, but he would always turn away when someone produced a camera –' She concentrated, looked at them both: 'I suppose –?'

Malone nodded. 'He didn't want his past to catch up with him, Lynne.'

'I saw that awful one of him on TV last night – the prison one – I couldn't believe it was the same man –'

'Even the Pope would look bad in a police photograph.'

She tried for a smile, but it was too much effort. Then she said, 'If he calls again – you're tapping my phone –'

'I'm afraid so, Lynne – we have a warrant.' Malone stood up. 'John knows it. He may not phone again, but if he does, tell him to give himself up. It will be easier for you, tell him.'

'You think so? Seeing him go to jail for – how long? Fifteen, twenty years?' She shook her head so vigorously her hair fell down over her face; she pushed it back. 'No, I think I'd rather he just disappeared.'

Malone understood her thinking; but he couldn't agree with her. 'Don't obstruct us, Lynne. We don't want to put you in jail.'

Gail Lee said nothing, just patted Mrs Masson's shoulder as

228

she stood up. She looked around the cluttered room, picked up a Banana in Pajamas doll and put it on one of the low tables, where it instantly fell over. 'What happens to all this?'

'The bank takes the lot. What happens to the money in the suitcase?'

'The court confiscates it and it goes into general revenue.'

'So it gets lost? Can I claim it? It would save Happy Hours.'

'I think you'd have a hard time proving it was yours,' said Malone. 'I agree with you, it could save all this, you could bring the kids back –'

'No.' She shook her head again, facing facts. 'The parents would never bring their kids back. Not after –'

Malone and Gail walked to the door. There Malone turned back, saw the bent-over figure that looked for a moment like nothing more than a large child. Then she raised her head and said, 'What are you going to say to your daughter?'

'I don't know,' he said. 'Unfortunately, she's long past day care.'

2

John August had no intention of stalking Gert Vanderberg; he had no idea where she lived nor did he care. He had been in Rockdale by sheer accient. After he had spoken to Ailsa, Lynne's assistant, yesterday he had debated where he could run to. He was dressed only in a shirt and overalls and he was carrying his metal tool-box; he was not exactly dressed for catching a bus or plane to some distant destination. He had not panicked; that was not in his nature. He knew his picture, the old police photograph of twelve years ago or whatever they dug up, would not be displayed till the first of the evening's television news at five o'clock. He went into the McDonalds at North Sydney and over a cheeseburger and french fries he pondered where to go from here.

He took his work diary out of his tool-box. There was a job

for next Tuesday, putting in some new bookshelves; the job was originally for tomorrow, but the woman, Mrs Milo, had cancelled, saying she and her husband would not be back from Noosa till next Monday. The address was in Neutral Bay, twenty minutes walk from here. He finished his cheeseburger, put the carton and the greasy napkin in the waste-bin, neat as always, offered his table to a woman with three children, winked at the kids and left.

The Milo residence was a two-storied house on a narrow block; he had come looking for it last week when he had been in the neighbourhood. No one saw him enter the house. There was a side entrance and he went down it and round to the back of the house. He checked to see if there was an alarm system, found none and five minutes later had opened the back door and was inside the house.

He spent the night there, turning on no lights, feeding on biscuits and tinned fruit and black coffee; there was nothing in the big refrigerator. He was careful to leave no fingerprints, once looking ruefully at the finger with the missing joint that had given him away at the Sewing Bee. He slept fitfully, Lynne moving in and out of his restless mind, then he got up early and went into the bathroom. He found a pair of scissors and cut off most of his dark hair, then with Mr Milo's electric razor he trimmed it down to a short stubble. Before he shaved he looked at his face; it was nondescript, a face in the crowd. He had not shaved for two days and there was a dark shadow on his long upper lip; he decided to grow a moustache. Still standing in front of the bathroom mirror he put on his gold-rimmed glasses. The disguise was minimal, but he would pass. There are advantages to being average.

He had breakfast of honey on dry cereal and black coffee. Then he went into the main bedroom to rummage through the closets. The Milos evidently spent a lot of money on clothes; expensive labels swung round on hangers like calling cards. Mr Milo, it seemed, was about the same height as August, but beefier; the jacket and trousers he chose were a size too

230

large, but he was being chased by police, not tailors. He smiled at the thought of taking the jacket and trousers back to the Sewing Bee for alteration, but the smile was just the faint echo of a hollow laugh. He was past humour, at least for the moment.

He left the house the way he had entered it. He was wearing a tan sun-hat with a green-and-brown ribbon, one of Mr Milo's Ruffini & Brooks' oxford blue shirts, a brown custom-tailored sports jacket and a pair of Daks cavalry twill trousers, the extra width drawn in by an expensive leather belt with Mr Milo's initials on the buckle. He had never been so well dressed in his life. The effect was spoiled only by the tool-box he carried.

He debated whether he should head north or south. For some reason most fugitives, if they did not flee the country, headed north, as if Queensland were a habitat where a leopard could change his spots without anyone's noticing. True, not so many years ago, southerners had thought of the Gold Coast as a habitat where white-shoed leopards sold swampy spots to any sucker who came north, but now it seemed that every second retiree was heading north. The region had become respectable to a point where even *Baywatch* had been invited to settle.

August decided to head south. He walked to Milsons Point railway station, caught a train to Town Hall and changed to one for Sutherland; there he would steal a car and drive maybe even as far south as Victoria or even Tasmania, the island State so often left off maps, even those drawn by mainlanders. It might be an ideal state in which to get lost.

Just before the train reached Rockdale he saw the two transport police officers coming through from the carriage in front. The train drew into the station, he got up and stepped out as the doors opened. He didn't hurry, took his time, a well-dressed handyman on his way to work; he even paused to give a hand to an old lady having difficulty stepping on to

231

the platform. In the carriage the two officers had paused by a youth in T-shirt and jeans, baseball cap on back to front, who had his feet up on the seat opposite him. He was in trouble.

Still haunted by what he had done to, and for, Lynne, August had gone into a public phone-box and called her. He had guessed that the police would have a tap on her phone; but he *had* to speak to her. When he hung up he felt worse.

Then he went looking for a car; or rather, a pair of number-plates. In Pentridge a professional car thief had given him a course in car-stealing – 'Think of it as a rehabilitation course, mate. Don't leave here without learning nothing.' He found a street lined with cars and in five minutes, after opening his tool-box, he had removed the front and rear plates from a Subaru. He put them in his tool-box and moved off, glancing right and left out of the corners of his eyes to make sure he had not been observed.

He went back to Rockdale station, caught a train to Sutherland and found the sort of car he was looking for – 'Never pick one with a distinctive colour, mate, not unless you got an order for it.' It was a light grey Datsun, a commuter's car parked in a street across from the station. Again unobserved, he changed the plates, opened the driver's door as he had been taught, hot-wired the car and drove away, heading south but with no particular place in mind.

At seven o'clock he pulled into a motel in Narooma, two hundred miles down the coast, registering as J.W. Milo, the initials on the shirt he wore. There, on Channel 15's late news, delivered by a woman newsreader whose claypan make-up rendered her expressionless, he saw the encounter between Lynne and the young bitch who, in the sign-off, identified herself as Maureen Malone.

He went to bed seething with anger at what they were doing to Lynne. In the middle of the night he woke determined on revenge.

'I've resigned,' said Maureen. 'I leave on Friday.'

'You resigned or they sacked you?' Malone had arrived home, bringing his irascible temper with him like an office workload.

'Both.'

'Lay off her, Dad,' said Claire.

The two of them had been waiting for him, like ambushers, as he came round the side passage from the garage. He had seen Claire's car, a Honda Civic, parked at the kerb and he had wondered why she was here this evening. They had jerked their heads at him and escorted him – like cops? – in through the pool gate and sat him down in one of the chairs beside the pool. Then they had sat opposite him.

He had looked towards the house. 'Where's Mum?'

'We told her to stay inside. This is between you and us,' said Claire.

'How did you get into the act?'

'I rang Mo this afternoon to tell her Clizbe and Balmoral were withdrawing the suit against her and Channel 15. She asked me to come home and give her moral support.'

'You're not here as her legal adviser?'

'Pull your head in, Dad. This is no time for jokes.'

'I think I need Mum here. For moral support.'

'No, you don't. Now shut up and listen. Tell him what happened, Mo.'

The evening air was still, a faint tinge of autumn to it. From a back yard further down the street there came the shouts of children: a happy family careless of moral support or legal advice. Malone looked towards the back of the house and saw Lisa standing at the kitchen window. She raised her hand and gave him the thumbs-up sign. At least there was moral support there.

Maureen said, 'I didn't want to do that interview, Dad.

Honestly. I knew what it might do to Mrs Masson. But Justin, my producer, was sold on it or else – if I didn't do it, I was back to being a researcher, nothing more, I'd get all the little shitty jobs. He gave me that dickhead Barney as cameraman – he knew Barney would shove the camera in her face, he's that sort. A real blokey bloke, can't stand women – but can't stand poofters, either. A real pain in the butt, I hated working with him . . . I was between a rock and a hard place, Dad.'

'Basically and at the end of the day. Skip the clichés, Mo.'

Maureen looked at her sister. 'He's not going to listen –'

'I'm listening,' said Malone. 'You haven't given any evidence yet to excuse you.'

Then Tom, wheeling his bike, came round from the side passage. 'Hullo, what's going on?'

'Get lost,' said Claire.

'Sounds like you need some help, Dad –'

Malone waved a gentle hand of dismissal. 'Go in and help Mum lay the table or something.'

Tom went to say something, then thought better of it. He was learning the vibrations that come earlier to girls than they do to boys; he was not insensitive but he was still struggling out of the membrane of youth. 'Just yell, Dad –' he said and went in the back door.

Maureen was struggling to hold in her feelings; she was on the verge of tears. 'Jesus, Dad, haven't you had to do things you thought were wrong! I told you – I didn't want to do it –'

'Are they running the item tonight?'

'Yes. Look, I'll go back and tell Mrs Masson I've resigned, that I didn't want to do it –'

'The damage is done. Leave it for a while, till we see how things turn out.' He was softening, but not by much. He turned to Claire: 'Why are Clizbe and Balmoral dropping the suit?'

'We don't know – they wouldn't tell us. Just told us to forget it and send them the bill. Which we'll do, with pleasure.'

'Dad –' Maureen leaned forward, put her hand on his knee;

he hesitated, then put his own hand over hers. 'I'm really sorry. The trouble is, Channel 15 have got more to follow. I didn't dig it up, one of the other researchers did. Clizbe, Balmoral and Peter Kelzo have got together –'

He frowned: wolves and bears mixing?

'I know,' she said, squeezing his knee. 'But it's true. Last week they were cutting each other's throats – well, Joe St Louis was bashing Mr Clizbe . . . Now . . . Now they've got a deal where Kelzo drops his man from the Boolagong pre-selection and he gets behind Balmoral. They're out to toss Mrs Vanderberg –'

He shook his head at that. 'They've got Buckley's chance of that. They might just as well try for pre-selection in Serbia.'

'Well, they're going to try. And there's another thing. Channel 15 have found out that Jerry Balmoral has been taking out that Chinese girl in the Olympic Tower partnership –'

'Camilla Feng,' said Claire.

'I remember her,' said Malone. 'Quite a dish.'

'I'll tell Mum.'

'The suspicion is,' said Maureen, 'that the two hundred and fifty thousand that's supposed to have been given to Boolagong came from Olympic Tower. They're after something –'

'What?' asked Malone.

'We ' Then she remembered that she and Channel 15 were no longer *we*. 'They don't know. But there's a rumour of a casino being built at Coffs Harbour – nothing definite yet – they could be after the licence –'

'Rumour, suspicion –' He looked at Claire.

'What we think, our firm, is that Clizbe and Balmoral have gone to someone on the Channel 15 board and made a deal. No suit, no more story. We think the deal's been made, but no one's telling us. Just drop the suit, we were told, and send them the bill. It stinks.'

'It gets your sister off the hook.'

'Yeah, that's the good part. But it still stinks.'

'It really does,' agreed Maureen.

'Girls,' said their father, 'welcome to the real world. That's how it's held together. By deals.'

'You don't sound – *disgusted*?' said Claire.

He turned aside and spat into a nearby bush, then turned back to them. 'That's how I feel, every time. Then I spit, get the taste out of my mouth and try to get on with the job. Which in this case is finding out who paid John August to bump off the Premier.'

'There's another rumour –' said Maureen.

He sighed. 'There always is.'

'That the Premier might not have been the target, that it could've been Jack Aldwych or his son.'

So far the task force had managed to be silent on its suspicions about Joanna Everitt; even the veteran police reporters had not been told. The media had concentrated on the killing of Hans Vanderberg, the *political* murder, and though there had been one or two suggestions that Aldwych, though never naming him, might have been the target, there had been no follow-up. Janis Eden, if anyone remembered her, was not in the cast of characters.

'We've thought of that,' said Malone non-committedly.

'And are you chasing it up?' asked Claire.

'We are pursuing our enquiries –'

His two daughters looked at each other. 'Wouldn't he give you diarrhoea?' said Claire. 'Putting it politely.'

Then Lisa came to the back door. 'All right, you've had long enough – the conference is over. Have your shower, darl, and we'll have dinner.'

'What's for dinner?' asked Maureen.

'For you two, humble pie.'

Again the two girls looked at each other. 'They should be on *Australia's Funniest Home Videos*,' said Maureen.

'How did we ever deserve them?' asked Claire.

Malone stood up, slapped the behinds of both of them and went ahead of them out the pool gate and into the house. He winked at Lisa as he passed her and went on into their bedroom to strip for his shower. The girls could be pains in the arse, like all offspring, but he loved them dearly.

And couldn't express his relief that Maureen had got herself out of the firing line.

4

Billy Eustace had come here to the boardroom of Olympic Tower, bringing with him Roger Ladbroke, on whom he was relying more and more. He had been massaged, polished, done over as much as the rough original had allowed; Ladbroke had brought in the image-makers and Billy Eustace had surrendered. He had never been a poor dresser, as his predecessor had been, but just nondescript. Now he had a new wardrobe, which, he had to admit as he looked in a mirror, made him look good, if not impressive. The shine was taken off the image by how much it had cost him. He still counted pennies, even though they were no longer minted.

The visit was an unofficial, non-governmental one; skulbuggery, as Ladbroke's old boss would have called it. The others in the room: the two Aldwyches, Leslie Chung, Madame Tzu, General Wang Te and Camilla Feng: all recognized it as such. There was no moral atmosphere to spoil it. They all, even the *young* Miss Feng, knew this wasn't just a chat over coffee and biscuits.

'Iced Vo-Vos,' said Jack Aldwych, holding up the national icon. 'My favourites.'

'Mine, too,' said Eustace, not to be outdone in patriotic fervour. So far the conversation had been no more than ping-pong, the balls bouncing lightly and no one making a smash. So far all the balls had remained on the table, but Aldwych and Co. were waiting to see what was under it.

Roger Ladbroke, no patriot he, had passed on the Iced Vo-Vos and just sipped his coffee. He had, with hand on heart (or rather his wife's: he had been fondling her breast in bed at the time), sworn to leave politics and go back to journalism; there had been no shortage of offers, the media falling over themselves and each other to get him on their payroll and dish out the dirt of the past twenty-two years. Then the light on the road to Damascus had blinked, faded, gone out like a faulty traffic light; then abruptly it had turned red and turned him back to politics, or sin, call it what you liked. It would even be worth staying on as Billy Eustace's minder to remain where he was, in the swamp of politics that smelled, to him, like a garden of poppies. He couldn't resist the drug.

Madame Tzu was drinking green tea, not coffee, and had turned her nose up at the biscuits. At last she grew tired of the ping-pong and whacked the ball at the corner of the table: 'Are you going to win the election, Mr Eustace?'

'Can't lose,' said Eustace, glad the game was at last warming up, and looked at Ladbroke for confirmation, if a little apprehensively. The bloody polls were still predicting the voting would be too close to call. Line-ball, said the commentators, some of whom hadn't a clue what a line-ball was.

'We are succeeding in convincing the voters that Mr Eustace is the natural successor to Hans Vanderberg –' Ladbroke almost said, *I am succeeding in convincing . . .* But he knew as well as anyone that acolytes with arrogance beyond their station might just as well cut their own throats because sooner or later their bosses would do it for them. Nothing has changed in the upper galleries of history. 'Our government will be returned. The margin will be less, we'll lose some seats, but we'll retain power.'

'How can you be so sure?' Madame Tzu didn't trust, or had contempt for, democracy.

'The other side has been out to lunch for the past four years. They have just woken up, too late.'

'So you'll be the Premier?' said Aldwych.

'No doubt about it,' said Eustace and managed an air of confidence rather like a threadbare overcoat. He was well-dressed now, but he was still wondering if the wardrobe of Premier would fit him.

'So what do you want from us?' said Aldwych, putting away the ping-pong balls.

Even after two years here amongst the barbarians Madame Tzu was still surprised at the bluntness of the Australian approach. Even in the mad, mad days of Chairman Mao circumlocution had still been practised; the Red Guards might give one a punch in the face, but they had been an aberration and soon disappeared. She remarked that Chairman – no, Premier Eustace did not appear put out by the bluntness.

'We understand,' said Billy Eustace, 'you would like a bill introduced setting up a casino somewhere.'

'Coffs Harbour,' said Les Chung, who had been silent up till now.

'Wherever,' said Eustace; if the price was right, he'd give it to them in Macquarie Street, right across from Parliament House. 'We understand Hans was going to promote such a bill.'

'Where did you get that understanding?' Aldwych looked at Ladbroke.

'He told me,' said Ladbroke. 'If he were still alive, it would have been my job to sell it.'

'And can you still sell it?' asked Camilla Feng.

So far General Wang-Te was the only one who had remained silent, but he had missed nothing and behind the designer glasses his eyes were flickering like an accountant's calculator. He would never be Westernized, or Australianized, but he enjoyed the education.

'We can sell it,' said Ladbroke confidently. The years had taught him what kites would fly and he knew this one would. The voters now looked on gambling as one of the higher pursuits in life.

'How much will it cost?' asked Jack Junior, chairman and keeper of the books.

Eustace looked at Ladbroke, who had to carry the night-soil;

even The Dutchman hadn't quoted the price. 'Two hundred and fifty thousand.'

'What a coincidence!' said Camilla Feng. 'Exactly the same price – I mean amount – we gave to the Boolagong electorate.'

'Not an *extra* quarter of a million,' said Eustace. 'The same money. It stays with Boolagong – at least till the election is over.'

'Mrs Vanderberg won't like it,' said Les Chung and looked again at Ladbroke: 'She'll be disappointed in you.'

'Disappointed, yes, but no more than that,' said Ladbroke. 'Gert is a pragmatic woman. She can still run Boolagong, be Mother Teresa out there, and we'll see that Barry Rix, her man, gets pre-selection and is elected.'

'We'd heard that you were backing Jerry Balmoral.' Les Chung looked at Eustace this time.

'Where did you hear that?' But Eustace was not surprised. Radar in State politics was more advanced than anything the Pentagon had yet developed.

'He told me,' said Camilla Feng. She had been out with Balmoral again, just once, and let him kiss her, promising that next time her mother wouldn't be waiting up for her. He had gone away satisfied with that, satisfied, indeed, with the whole night. They had gone to the Golden Gate where, she told him, Mr Chung had insisted the dinner should be on him.

'That was yesterday's news,' said Ladbroke, who, like a good minder, was already into next week's news. 'Balmoral and Mr Clizbe, from Trades Congress, and Peter Kelzo, whom I think you know, have got together and think they are going to take over Boolagong. It won't happen. Barry Rix will be pre-selected, we'll get behind him and see he's elected and he will then put forward the casino bill, then the Premier –' he nodded at Billy Eustace, who nodded in acknowledgement – 'then the Premier will take it up and it will go through.'

'What about the Upper House?' asked Aldwych.

240

'A mix of hacks, nuts and time-servers. We have the majority there and the bill will go through.'

'Who is your majority? The hacks, nuts or time-servers?'

Ladbroke smiled. 'We have no nuts in our party.'

'And what will happen to the two hundred and fifty thousand?' at last asked General Wang-Te.

Billy Eustace looked at him as if he had only just arrived. He was not at ease with Asians; they all looked alike to him. Even Les Chung was a stranger to him; he was not to know it, but Chung was a stranger to many people and Chung didn't want it otherwise. But this feller was a Chinese general and represented the face of an army of millions. True, he was an ex-general, but Billy Eustace knew there were no ex-generals.

'It comes back to the Premier's Fund.'

'What's that?' said Madame Tzu.

'Don't ask,' said Aldwych and winked at the Premier.

'It's agreed then?' said Eustace.

'If it can be done without holding a gun at Mrs Vanderberg's head,' said Chung. 'We don't want any bad publicity. We don't want *any* publicity.'

'It can be done,' said Ladbroke and knew he would be the one sent to do it.

'There's still unfinished business, though,' said Jack Junior. 'We don't know who killed Hans Vanderberg.'

'Yes, we do,' said Eustace. 'A man named August. The police are after him now. It's been on all the news –'

'I don't mean *him*,' said Jack Junior. 'Who paid him? The reports said the police found a suitcase full of money.'

'I thought you had your own suspect?' said Eustace.

'Oh?' said Jack Senior. 'Who told you that?'

'I'm the Police Minister as well as Premier.'

He's no longer *Acting*, thought Ladbroke. He's going to be harder to mind than I thought.

'You can forget the woman you had in mind,' said the Police Minister and Premier. 'Hans was the target, not you.'

Where did he get that from? Ladbroke wondered. He definitely is going to be hard to mind.

'You're sure?' Aldwych was surprised that he felt disappointed. Surprise was new to him: he must be getting old.

'Absolutely sure. You were not the target. Nor you,' he told Jack Junior.

The latter didn't try to hide his relief. But: 'How much more do you know?'

Eustace could be voluble, but now he was trying for a new model: the Sphinx. He had no idea who or what the original Sphinx had been; Peter Kelzo might have told him, but he would not ask the time of day of Kelzo. His model was the Sphinx in Egypt and when he had told Ladbroke, the latter had at first been relieved, grateful that he would not have to write corrections for a mouth that too often had run off the road. Then he had begun to wonder how you wrote press releases for a monument.

'I know enough, Mr Aldwych. Just take it for granted, you've got no worries.' He stood up. Somewhere in the past couple of days he had gained a semblance of dignity, of authority. The image-makers would have been encouraged, though he was still in the developing fluid and the desired image still was fuzzy. 'Thanks for the Iced Vo-Vos. Pity they're now owned by the Americans.'

'The Americans own *everything*,' said Madame Tzu spitefully.

Eustace looked at Camilla Feng. 'Will you be seeing Jerry Balmoral again?'

'There's no point now, is there?' she said. 'He was getting nowhere and now he's going nowhere.'

'You have so much good sense for a young woman,' said Madame Tzu. 'I was like you when young.'

'I'll bet,' said Aldwych.

'The old make better use of youth than the young.'

Ladbroke raised his eyebrows. It sounded like old times, The Dutchman mangling the language into aphorisms that sounded like sense.

Jack Junior had no time for philosophy, not if it got in the way of business: 'Nothing that's been said in here will get outside this office, will it?'

'Of course not,' said Ladbroke and sounded annoyed it should be suggested that a minder would not know when lips were sealed.

'You should of worked for me,' said Aldwych with a grin, 'before I retired.'

'It would have been easier,' said Ladbroke and gave Billy Eustace a smile to say he didn't mean it. Not much.

Eustace straightened his tie; he was always in fashion round the neck. Two years ago ties had looked like regurgitation; last year they had all been yellow, like an outbreak of sartorial malaria; this year it was the Olympics tie, a squiggle on the chest. 'It will be a pleasure working with you all.'

When Eustace and Ladbroke had gone, Aldwych went into the outer office, told the two secretaries to go for a walk and sat down at one of their desks. Then he called Homicide: 'Scobie?'

'Jack. What's on your mind?'

'Scobie, just to prove we're mates, I'm telling you what I've just learned. Forget Joanna Everitt – Jack and me were not the targets.'

'You're sure? Where'd you get this?'

'You sound disappointed. So'm I, in a way. I'm sure, Scobie. I got the drum from the horse's mouth. Well, he's a horse's arse, actually.'

'You're not going to tell me where you got it, who he is?'

'Just take my word.'

'Then do you know who paid for the hit?'

'No, I don't. If I knew that, I'd tell you.'

'You don't know, but you're making an educated guess?'

'You're a hard man to be mates with. No, I dunno and I'll leave the guessing to you. But forget the bitch.'

'Well, thanks, Jack. Yeah, I'm disappointed, it was never an odds-on bet that it was her. Take care.'

'You too, Scobie.'

Aldwych hung up, sat a while pondering who had paid the hitman. He was sure that Billy Eustace knew; or had made an educated guess. Whether, as Police Minister, he passed that on to the Police Commissioner was another matter. Aldwych remembered police commissioners who had passed nothing on to their political bosses. But those had been the good old days . . .

Aldwych stood up as the two secretaries came back to the outer doorway. 'Finished, Mr Aldwych?'

'Not quite, girls. But don't go, just one more call.' He took a small diary from his pocket, checked a number, then called it. 'Joanna? Jack Aldwych. You gunna be home the next half-hour?'

'I'm leaving for work in half an hour –'

'We'll give you a lift. Don't argue, Joanna. Just be waiting for us.' He put down the phone, smiled at the two secretaries. 'The wife's sister. Too independent for her own good.'

5

Aldwych and Blackie Ovens waited in the Daimler outside Joanna Everitt's apartment block. Across the street Aldwych had seen the parked car with the two plainclothes men in it. 'Cops, Blackie. They'll be following us when we pick up our girl.'

'Just like the old days, eh?'

Then Joanna Everitt came out of the block and Blackie got out and went across to her. She turned towards the unmarked police car, as if she might call for help; then she changed her mind and came across to the Daimler with Blackie. She got into the back seat, where Aldwych sat.

'I usually drive myself to work –'

'We'll do that for you,' said Aldwych. 'You can catch a cab home.'

As Blackie took the car away from the kerb Joanna said, 'What do you want? I can scream my head off and those guys back there will come to my rescue. They're cops —'

'I know, Joanna. No one's gunna hurt you. I'm here to tell you you're not gunna be hurt. Relax.'

She sat back in the seat, but still looked suspiciously at him. She was dressed in a green suit with a yellow blouse; she wore expensive shoes and carried a matching handbag. She looks like a top-price hooker, thought Aldwych, but that was only because he hated her.

Instead he said, 'You look like a million dollars. Don't she, Blackie?'

Blackie Ovens just nodded, keeping his eye on the road. He hated these buggers who thought that a couple of old coots in a Daimler shouldn't be on the road. Twenty, thirty years ago he would have chased them and ironed them with a tire lever. There was no fun to growing old.

'Thanks for the compliment,' said Joanna. 'Some day I'll have a million dollars, maybe more. Like you.'

He grinned. 'I'm still a battler at heart. Ain't that right, Blackie?' Then he looked back at Joanna. 'Girlie, I picked you up to tell you you're off the hook.'

She was puzzled; not by the term but at what looked suspiciously like benevolence. 'Off the hook? What do you mean?'

'I've had it on good authority that you didn't hire that bloke August to hit me or Jack. Or both of us.'

'I told you that!' She leaned forward, then gathered herself and sat back. She said nothing for a while, even turned and stared out the window. Then she looked back at him: 'Look, Jack, I've started a new life. I've changed my name — everything in the past I'm putting behind me — you, Jack Junior, the time I spent in jail —'

'Listen to me, girlie. I'm letting you off the hook, but I'm not giving you absolution or whatever it is the priests dole out. If ever you come near me or Jack again, I'll have Blackie call on you –'

'Boss,' said Blackie Ovens, eyes still on the road, 'I don't do women, you know that.'

'I know that,' said his boss amiably. 'I'm just trying to frighten the shit outa her. I've done that, haven't I, Joanna?'

'No, you haven't. I'm not afraid of you, I never was. And you can tell that to Jack Junior and that stuck-up bitch of a wife of his.'

There was no ferocity to what she was saying; they could have been discussing the weather or the traffic. Aldwych just sat studying her, deaf to what she was saying. He disliked her; no, hated her. He had never hit a woman, not out of any gallantry but because he had feared Shirl. If ever she had learned he had hit a woman, even one of his brothel girls, she would have left him. Shirl would not have liked Joanna, but she would have protected her.

At last he said, 'What are you gunna do with your new life?'

They were riding over the Bridge, the police car two cars behind them. Blackie eased the Daimler into the transport lane, heading for the southern toll gates; the cab between him and the police car blasted its horn, telling him to get a move on. He ignored it, kept to his usual steady sixty kilometres an hour; the days were long gone when, as the getaway driver in several of Aldwych's bank hold-ups, he hadn't known what a speed limit was. The cab swung over into the inner lane and went past in a rush, the driver yelling abuse at him. Twenty, thirty years ago, Blackie thought . . .

'Fucking wog,' he said, then looked in his driving mirror. 'Excuse me, miss.'

'We're both racists,' Aldwych told Joanna. 'Too old to change. What are you gunna do with your new life?'

'I'm establishing myself at the casino. Then –'

He waited, then said, 'Then?'

She was relaxed now. She turned in the seat and looked almost friendly. 'There's a rumour there may be another casino licensed to operate, out of Sydney –'

'Where?' He succeeded in looking genuinely curious.

'The rumour is Coffs Harbour. I'd like to finish up there, managing the floor. I understand the gambling game now, every aspect of it, and I'm a good manager.'

'I'm sure you are. Well, well. Coffs Harbour. I thought of retiring there once. Nice place, lots a nice friendly people. All waiting to be fleeced.' He grinned at her.

'It's their money,' she said. 'Casinos just provide a service.'

'Like ambulance stations?'

'When did you become anti-gambling? You robbed people right, left and centre.'

'I robbed banks, not people.' He managed to sound pious, St Aldwych of Assisi throwing crumbs to the battlers.

When they dropped her at the casino, Blackie got out of the car and opened the door for her, like a real chauffeur. The parking valets looked at her, wondering if she had been making a bit on the side with one of the high rollers.

'Been nice meeting you, Joanna,' said Blackie. 'Look after yourself.'

'Oh, I will, Blackie.' She looked back into the car. 'Goodbye, Jack. I hope we don't meet again.'

'Oh, we'll meet again,' said Aldwych, but under his breath.

They drove away and he sat in the back of the car chewing his cud as if it were candy. He looked up and saw Blackie eyeing him in the driver's mirror. The two old men smiled at each other.

'Well, Blackie, waddia know? I never tasted revenge before to see if it was sweet – I just done it. But up in Coffs Harbour –' He laughed, a hearty sound from from the belly, a sound that would have frightened the birds out of the trees around Assisi. 'I'm gunna be licking my lips.'

6

George Gandolfo couldn't believe what he was hearing:

'We'll do lunch with Clizbe and Balmoral,' said Peter Kelzo.

'How do you *do* lunch?' asked Joe St Louis.

Kelzo did his best to look patient. 'Joe, for Crissakes, it's just an expression. When I get elected, I'm gunna be spending a lotta time with the high life around town, the smart-arses with university degrees and all that. I'm gunna have to use words like incredibly this and that, or basically or at the end of the day. It's the way the smartarse end of town talks.'

'I wouldn't trust that Clizbe,' said Gandolfo.

'George, that's what democracy is all about. That's what Socrates said – you gotta grab democracy by both ends of the stick.'

One of these days, when he slowed down, George Gandolfo was going to look up everything Socrates had said. In the meantime: 'Why are we gunna have – do lunch with them?'

'We're gunna bring 'em into our camp. I've got the buzz – Billy Eustace is kicking them outa Boolagong. We can't get Jerry Balmoral inna there – that old witch Gert Vanderberg isn't gunna let democracy in the gate.'

'Meaning who?' asked Joe St Louis.

'Meaning us, for Crissakes. Shut up, Joe, while I explain the facts of life to George. Balmoral ain't gunna get inna parliament this election, but we promise to take him over and groom him for the future. He's got what it takes for this new century – he's got bullshit all done up in a new shiny package. While we're taking over him we take over Trades Congress.'

'I gotta admire you, Peter,' said Gandolfo. 'You take the long view.'

'It's the Greek in me.'

The long view backwards? But Gandolfo kept that question to himself.

And now they were doing lunch at the Summit, the revolving restaurant at the top of a tall tower in the heart of the business district. Kelzo had booked a window table and the five men sat there and looked out at Sydney as it slowly, ever so slowly, changed below them. The weather was perfect and any politician, or would-be one, could stretch his imagination up here and see as far west as the State's boundaries. It was the closest most of them could come to the long view.

'It's all ours,' said Kelzo, gesturing. 'All we gotta do is plan.'

'I don't know I'm prepared to wait that long –' said Balmoral.

'Jerry, Athens wasn't built in a day –'

Rome, said Gandolfo under his breath, all at once protective of his heritage.

'– you're young, Jerry, we'll build you up –'

'What about me?' said Clizbe in the tones of a man who could see himself being pushed aside. 'I'm young. Well, half-young.'

'Norm –' Kelzo was practising sounding patriarchal. 'We need your experience in union matters. You don't wanna get into parliament, do you?'

'I dunno, I wouldn't mind. Maybe down the track. I'd like to retire into the Upper House. It's a nice retirement.'

'We'll look after you, Norm – down the track. Jerry, I promise you, ten, fifteen years down the track, we'll have you in The Lodge in Canberra. You and your lady friend. I saw you the other night out at dinner. She's one of them Olympic Tower people, isn't she? A nice touch, her being Chinese. You'll be the first multicultural couple in The Lodge.'

'You're a bit premature, Pete –'

'Peter.'

'– she's a bit stand-offish at the moment. But I'm getting there.' You knew that, if he had been there at other times, he

249

would have got there with Queen Elizabeth the First or with Marie Antoinette. 'Like you say, she'll be an asset.'

'You see, Jerry, that was what I was saying. All we gotta do is plan.'

'In the meantime,' said Clizbe, 'who does the donkey-work? The planning, I mean.'

'Why, me and you,' said Kelzo, but sounded like a general, or Pericles, inviting a corporal in for a chat.

'Who'll look after the finances?' asked Balmoral.

'George will,' said Kelzo. 'You're good at that, aren't you, George?'

'I used to be,' said Gandolfo.

Kelzo raised his glass of Hunter red '95, a classic year, the waiter had told him. 'Here's to us, a brotherhood.'

'How's your nose, Norm?' asked Joe St Louis. 'I'm sorry I decked you that time. Pete told me it was in a good cause –'

'Peter,' said Kelzo automatically, and smiled at Clizbe. 'Bygones are history. Socrates said that.'

Bloody Socrates, thought George Gandolfo and looked at Balmoral, wondering whom he would be quoting when he got to the Prime Ministership and The Lodge.

Chapter Eleven

1

In the morning August paid his motel bill, wished the woman owner a beautiful day and drove back north. It was a good day for driving, too bright for murder but otherwise perfect. He switched on the car radio and heard Alan Jones, king of the talk-back, say, 'There's a coincidence in this latest development – the Channel 15 reporter is the daughter of the Homicide inspector on the August case –'

He switched off the radio, slowed down the car, blinded by fury. He could see the Malones, father and daughter, comparing notes at the end of the day: *How next can we pressure Mrs Masson?*

He pulled off to the side of the road, waited while the fury abated. He had always been subject to rage, but in the past it had been a cold rage. There had been the chilling anger at his father, the man with big ideas and no talent who had gone away to jail for the third time and never come back; there had been promises, promises, promises, but in the end there had been nothing, not even love. He had turned to his mother, but she had turned to God and there had been no love there, not for him. There had been several women, then his wife, and there had been no love there. Perhaps it had been his own fault, perhaps they had seen the emptiness in him and had not trusted it. Then he had met Lynne and suddenly there was love and no rage, cold or otherwise, at all. Now it was all over.

He drove on into the city, allowing it to swallow him so that he swam beneath its surface, as in a sea. He parked the car in the Goulburn Street parking station and walked up to the cinema complex almost opposite the Olympic Tower. He and Lynne had been only occasional moviegoers; he had never kept up with the latest offerings. He had time to fill in, so he turned in to the box-office, looked at the titles on the board above the window, named a movie and bought a ticket. Despite his rage he was a patient man; he could not move further till late at night. He sat through a coming-of-age film that, as far as he could remember, bore no relation to his own youth; he sat between two teenaged couples, who were coming but not of age, and felt embarrassed. He was glad when the interminable credits began to roll, when such creative artists as accountants and stand-by drivers got credit, and he stood up and escaped.

He went out and into the nearby McDonald's. Lynne, who loved to cook, had never allowed him to eat junk food; he smiled at the thought as he waited to kill two people for love of her. He was flirting with danger being so close to the Sewing Bee and Olympic Tower – 'Criminals too often return to the scene of their crime' – but the adrenaline kept him going. He ate two hamburgers, having had no lunch, and drank two cups of coffee and, as usual, cleaned up after himself. Coming out of McDonald's he almost bumped into two uniformed police, but they just stepped aside, said 'Excuse me, sir', and passed on. In the clothes of Mr Milo he obviously looked like a man to be respected. Clothes maketh the man, as a tailor on the make once said.

He went back to the parking station and took the car out and drove over the Bridge to the Lower North Shore. He found a parking space in a side street and left the car there. He walked to a small reserve, sat on a seat and watched the happy ones, those without a care in the world (though he knew that was not true of anyone) going into the nearby small restaurants. Darkness slid down, the lights came on round the small reserve and it was time to move.

The building where the local Meals on Wheels was headquartered was in a nearby street. It was two-storied and single-fronted,

252

with a serving counter in the front shop and a kitchen and storeroom at the back. Above were lock-up offices. Because he was the service's volunteer handyman as well as a volunteer delivery-man, he had a key to the front door. There was no alarm system, on the presumption that only the lowest shit would break into a volunteer organization. So far the presumption, or delusion, had held.

He let himself in and closed the door behind him. He turned on no lights but he had brought his torch with him from his tool-box. He went through the shop and the kitchen and into the storeroom at the back. There, behind a stack of jumble, the sort of stuff that accumulates as if by the design of unknowable forces, he had hidden the rifle case. He took it out, checked that the dismantled Tikka, the Schmidt and Bender twilight 'scope and the five-cartridge clip were still in it. Then he put the stack back in place, switched off his torch and left the building, locking the door after him. When he had hidden the case there, smuggling it in past the other volunteer workers, he had expected it to be there only for a day at the most while he collected his hit fee. Then he would have taken it and the Winchester and gone somewhere out into the bush and buried them. Lynne's problems would have been solved and they could have got on with their lives, enjoying the happiness that they had both found. That was how it would have been had not the fingerprints on the dusty window-sill of the Sewing Bee given him away.

Now he had to wait through another night. He had no idea where the Malones lived. He had looked up all the Malones in the phone book: too many of them. He had called all the S. Malones; none of them responded when he asked, 'Scobie?' He was not to know that Scobie Malone had an unlisted number, but he guessed that might be the case. The only alternative was to go out to Channel 15 on the Epping Road and wait till the daughter Maureen put in an appearance. He would kill her first, then wait for her father to come out into the open.

If he died himself in any return fire it would not matter.

253

'I'll drive you out to the studio this morning,' said Malone.

'There's no need, Dad – Mum's not using the Laser –'

'I want a word with your producer.'

They were at breakfast: Malone, Lisa, Maureen and Tom. The latter had an assessment test coming up this morning at university and had a folder spread out beside his plate as he slurped muesli into his mouth.

'Could we have a little less noise down that end?' asked Lisa.

'Who, me?' Tom looked up; then, as if he had at last caught an echo of what his father had just said: 'Why do you want a word with her producer? Are you going to do him? The bastard wants a kick up the bum.'

'Shut up.' Maureen was in a dark mood; she even appeared to have aged. 'Dad, what are you going to say to Justin?'

'First, I'm going to give him a piece of my mind about exposing you the way he did. Then I'm going to tell him to lay off Mrs Masson or there'll be some legal interference, we'll take out a restraining order against him and the channel –'

'Da-ad, come *on*! Why have you got to stick your nose in? Let police public relations do it. Or Police Headquarters. Someone – *anyone* else. God, I don't want them thinking I've had my daddy come out there to pick on the producer because he got Little Maureen into strife –'

'Pull your head in,' said her daddy. 'I'm going out there, not only because of you, but because Greg Random told me to. He's my boss, he's in charge of the strike force. Channel 15 are muddying up the waters, they've over-stepped the mark. It's our job to find John August, not the media's. And that's what I've been instructed to tell Justin Whatshisname. Now if you don't like it you can stay at home and I'll tell them you finished up yesterday and not today.'

'I think Dad's right,' said Tom.

'Mind your own business –'

'Hey, wait a minute, Mo! I'm not taking sides here, but that bastard made you carry the can. Who do you think the TV viewers will remember putting the boot into Mrs Masson – you or your mate Justin?' Tom closed the folder beside his plate; the assessment test could wait. 'You're the bunny, the one on camera. When you go looking for another job, the other channels will say, Hey, wait a minute, here's that trouble-maker –'

'No, they won't,' said Lisa. 'They'll think of her as an asset. TV stations aren't interested in soft-soap interviewers – she'll have no trouble getting another job. She's made her name – the wrong way, but there's no wrong way in television if you get the ratings –'

'Thanks,' said Maureen, but didn't attempt to defend her industry. 'I still don't want Dad going out there –'

Malone could see how upset his daughter was and he made a concession: 'Righto, I'll hold off when I'm talking to Justin about you. But I'm going to put the boot into him if he wants to keep interfering in our chase after Mr August. You don't have to be there when I do that.'

After breakfast, while Malone was getting the Fairlane out of the garage, Lisa walked to the front gate with Maureen.

'Mo, it's not the end of the world. Put it down to experience.'

'Why is it parents always give that sort of advice?' But she wasn't resentful.

'Because we've been through it. I've made blunders, so has Dad. Let's go out to dinner tonight. We'll put another dent in his American Express card.'

'I'll be in that,' said Tom, wheeling out his bike. 'Try him on Ampersand or Level 41.'

'He'd leave home,' said Lisa and kissed them both.

Driving out to Channel 15 through a day spoiled only by the traffic, Malone said, 'When we nab August, that's when you're going to get the *big* story. Who paid him.'

'I'm not going to get it. I'll be out of a job.'

'We'll try and hold off till you get a job.'

'Don't joke, Dad. I'm not in the mood.'

So they drove on in silence, turned off the Epping Road and into the side road that led to Channel 15. The studios were set in ten acres that backed on to a reserve of thick bush, where there was a small colony of koalas. A high wire fence separated the parking lot from the reserve, the fence itself partly obscured by a line of oleanders. Malone slowed down at the gates, Maureen waved to the security guard and he motioned them to go on through. Malone headed for a parking space between two top-of-the-range BMWs.

'Not there, Dad – that's for executives only.'

'If I were on my own . . . Okay.'

He drove on past a line of lesser cars, found a parking space and pulled in. He and Maureen got out.

In the bushland reserve August raised the Tikka, nodding appreciatively at his luck. Two at once . . .

3

August had reconnoitred the area in the darkness of very early morning. He had driven out here and parked the Datsun half a kilometre down the road from Channel 15. The entire bushland reserve was fenced off as protection for the koalas. August remembered Lynne telling him stories of conservationists and animal lovers coming out here to demonstrate against the building of the studios, to protect the koalas against the ravages of game shows and sitcoms and other crimes against nature's own. A compromise had been reached with Channel 15 paying for the whole reserve to be enclosed and to be responsible for the welfare of the koalas. It appointed a 'nature officer' who, when she wasn't making coffee and running errands for producers, conducted groups of schoolchildren around the reserve to observe

256

the koalas at home. The koalas, as disdainful as cats but not as selfish, turned their backs on the kids and clambered higher up the eucalypts.

He had brought his rifle-case and a pair of wire-cutters from his tool-box. He made an angled cut in the wire, peeled it back and squeezed through; then he pushed the wire back into place so that the cut was not apparent to any jogger who might come trotting by in the morning. He went on into the bush, stumbling in the darkness and sometimes walking head first into a tree. Something scurried away from beneath his feet and above him a bird uttered a cry, as if annoyed at being disturbed. Then he was at the fence looking out on to the parking lot. The board of Channel 15 was notoriously skinflint and after midnight all lights in the lot were turned off. But there was enough moonlight for August to see that he had a 180-degree vision of the parking lot, even allowing for the oleanders on the other side of the fence. He cut a hole in the fence at shoulder height, took out the Tikka and assembled it, affixed the 'scope and set it down against a tree. Then he sat down against the tree, wrapped his arms across his chest and went to sleep. *Lynne used to laugh at his ability to sleep anywhere, any time . . .* Once, during the night, she slipped into his mind and, in his sleep, he uttered a long dry sob.

He woke when a currawong shat on him; the dollop landed right in the middle of the crown of Mr Milo's hat. He took off the hat and looked up at the bird; was it some sort of omen? But all his life he had ignored omens; his mother's religiosity had turned him against any warnings that contradicted reason. He threw the hat away, then turned to find a koala, sitting in the armpit of a eucalypt, staring at him like one of the kids from the Happy Hours. The same look of shrewd innocence that – was it Wombat Rose? – used to show.

He stood up, awkwardly, as if all his joints had aged during the night. He leaned against the fence and peered out through the wire and, beyond the oleanders, saw the parking lot was already half-full. He looked at his watch: seven-thirty.

He would have slept on had the currawong not given him a wake-up call.

He was hungry and thirsty and cursed himself for not having thought to buy some sandwiches and a Coke. He watched the koala chewing on a gum-leaf; then became aware of three others all having breakfast. He grinned, good-naturedly cursed them for their cruel manners, wished for a Meals on Wheels van to go by and turned back to watch the parking lot.

His eyes were strained by the time the blue Fairlane drove in. For an hour and a half he had stared at every car and truck that came into the lot, the rifle held at the ready. He had begun to wonder if the Malone bitch was coming to work today. He had seen two news vans drive out, but he was sure she was not in either of them. He had begun to fret with frustration and was angry at himself for the weakness.

Then he saw the Fairlane come in, drive right round the line of parked cars and pull into the space not more than seventy or eighty metres from him. He could not believe his luck when both Malones, father and daughter, stepped out of the car.

He raised the Tikka, took aim on the daughter, who was nearer to him. Then, as he began the pressure on the trigger, the koala fell out of the tree right beside him.

4

The bullet whanged off the top of the Fairlane and went ricocheting away to embed itself in the BMW of one of the executives. It missed Maureen only by inches and she stood stiffened more by puzzlement than by fear. Then her father yelled, 'Down!' and she dropped flat to the ground beside the car. Malone himself dropped down as the second bullet hit the car's side window.

'Stay where you are!' he yelled under the car.

He rose, crouching low, and began to move along the line of cars, taking out his .40 calibre Glock pistol and easing his finger on to the trigger safety catch. He saw the security guard come out of his post at the gates and he yelled at him to take cover; the guard instantly turned and went back into his post, ducking down out of sight. A car came through the gates and, seeing no one on duty, came on down towards the line of cars where Malone was. Taking advantage of the distraction, certain that August (who else could it be?) was not intent on random shooting, he raced, still crouched over, towards the line of cars nearest to the bushland and the wire fence. He had identified from which direction the fire had come, though so far he had not seen the marksman.

Then through the oleanders he saw the figure on the other side of the wire fence. He was not sure that it was August, but, again, who else could it be? He yelled, 'Drop the gun, John!'

He was answered by a bullet that splintered the windscreen of the car behind which he crouched. He straightened up, took quick aim, fired and dropped down again. He had no real hope of a hit: he was still thirty or forty metres from August and he knew it was only Clint Eastwood who could hit a man at that distance, quick firing with a police pistol.

He yelled again at August and was answered by another shot. Back across the parking lot Maureen had run across to the entrance to the main building, shouting at those who had come out to see what all the hullabaloo was about; they stared at her, then abruptly scuttled back inside. The man who had just driven his car into the lot had got out and stood looking at Malone as if wondering if this was an action scene from some future telemovie.

Malone, still crouched behind a car, saw August searching for him through the screen of oleanders. August began to work his way along the fence towards the road, ending up in the angle of the fence and opposite the security gates. He was exposed for a moment beyond two oleanders, but he was too far away for a safe shot from Malone.

Malone lifted his pistol, held it with both hands, took careful aim. He saw August staring towards him; then abruptly he turned and ran back into the trees. Malone waited a moment, then started running, bent over, towards the gates. He was in reasonable condition for a middle-aged man, but this was a young man's game. He came to the spot where the fence turned at right angles and ran back down the side road. He paused, took a deep breath, steadied himself, then turned the corner.

August all at once had lost the urge to kill; the fury ran out of him, turned to despair. He raced down the inside of the fence, came to the opening he had cut, pulled back the wire and slipped through. Then the wire caught on his jacket, held him firmly; it was as if the absent Mr Milo had put a restraining hand on him. He struggled, heard the jacket rip, slipped through and outside the fence, then turned back and saw Malone only thirty metres away, gun raised and aimed.

'Drop it, John!'

August looked down at the Tikka, as if he had forgotten it. There was one cartridge left in the magazine. He stared at the rifle, then he raised it and put the end of the barrel in his mouth.

'Don't, John! Don't make it worse for Lynne!'

5

'Why did you stop me?'

The two of them were seated in a small office that Malone had commandeered from the studio. There were large photos on the walls of actors from the channel's soap operas, all with smiles a mile wide. A young uniformed officer stood just inside the doorway and Malone was waiting for Greg Random and some of the task force men to arrive. Maureen was in her producer's office, he suddenly solicitous of her, while they waited for a doctor and a counsellor who had been summoned. Channel 15 had got an exclusive on the arrest of John August, the fugitive hitman, and the producer was trying to persuade Maureen to front the camera and report the item. She was refusing, something that her father, at the moment, did not know, but for which later he would hug her as he had not since she was a child.

'John, I've been with women who had to identify their husbands who'd committed suicide. You wouldn't have wanted that for Lynne, not with the top of your head blown off.'

August thought about that for a long moment, then nodded. 'I guess not. Is this an interrogation?'

'No, that'll be done back at Police Centre, by senior men to me. No, I'm just keeping you company till my boss arrives. You glad it's all over?'

Again the long pause: 'Yeah, I guess so.'

'Who paid you, John?' The question was almost too casual.

August smiled, but there was no humour to it. 'That's just it – I haven't a clue.'

'Come *on*, John –'

'No, true. *I don't know.*'

'Who paid you the money? Was there a middleman?'

This time there was a little more humour to the smile. 'I think he thought of himself as an agent. But I'm not gunna give you his name. Like you said, it's over.'

'It isn't, John. Not till we find who wanted the Premier killed.'

'Well, don't expect anything from me. I went into this with my eyes open. I give you someone's name, you think it's gunna help me?' He shook his head. 'What d'you reckon I'll get?'

'Probably life, never to be released. You killed a political leader, John. Every politician from the PM down is going to want you to get the maximum, in case you've inspired someone else to have a crack at one of them.'

August sat quietly for a while, then he said, 'I'm sorry I tried to kill you and your daughter. I was just so shitty about what you were doing to Lynne.' He was silent again for a moment, then he said, 'Tell Lynne –'

'Tell her what?' Malone's voice was kindly.

'No, I'll tell her myself.' Then he closed his eyes and the tears ran down his cheeks, not for himself but for her.

Chapter Twelve

1

'You're not gunna nail this to anyone,' Clements had said two days after August's arrest. 'We've checked bank accounts of everyone. Nothing, no big withdrawals, except for Bev Bigelow buying ten thousand shares in Telstra.'

'Nothing on Kelzo?' Clements shook his head and Malone said, 'What about Billy Eustace? He's the heir.'

'Mate, do you go and ask the Premier and Police Minister permission to look at his bank account? In any case, I don't think he'd be vicious enough to have someone shot. He might stab 'em in the back, but that's no crime.'

And so the murder of Hans Vanderberg went into the files and now the Sydney Olympics are about to be opened. Around 110,000 people, including 24,373 official guests, are waiting for the final runner to come into the stadium with the torch to light the Olympic flame. Who will it be? everyone is asking: an athlete, a swimmer, a boxer, an IOC official running from corruption? The human brass on the official dais, polished for the occasion by anticipation, shines with blinding self-esteem.

The Malones, all five of them, have good seats, courtesy of Lisa's role with the City Council. Malone looks for Police Commissioner Zanuch amongst the brass, but the glare is too much. He does see Billy Eustace, who appears to be waving individually to the 110,000 spectators, some of whom are voters.

Bygones have become history, as Socrates or his mouthpiece Peter Kelzo said. Labor won a crushing victory at the elections last March and Billy Eustace is now acknowledged as more than just a stop-gap. Ladbroke and the image-makers have scrubbed

262

him and shaped him and occasionally he looks and sounds like a leader. His personal stinginess is now tolerated as economic rationalism and the Big End of town picks up tabs as if they were redeemable. He has just collected the first six months' interest on the seventy-five thousand dollars he lent Jerry Balmoral's private company, Ambition Proprietary Limited, when Jerry wanted a second mortgage on something or other.

Gert Vanderberg still runs the Boolagong electorate with a firm but benevolent hand, pushing Barry Rix through the political traffic as if he were in a perambulator. She still misses Hans, but in her thoughts he is still alive, still bigger and better than those still in the Bear Pit in Macquarie Street.

Jack Aldwych and the Olympic Tower consortium have been promised their casino at Coffs Harbour and Aldwych is waiting for the day when he and Jack Junior interview Janis Eden. But he is feeling his age now and reads the obituaries before he reads anything else in his morning newspapers. He has begun to appreciate the sweet irony that as one approaches one's own death one becomes more interested in the departures of others.

John August, still on remand in Long Bay and waiting to be brought to trial, still refusing to say who brought him the hit fee, watches the Olympic opening on television and wonders if there is someone in the crowd who paid the money. Once a month Lynne Masson comes to visit him and they both weep when she leaves. She is working as an aide at the Clontarf Gardens nursing home, finding the elderly more calming than the infants.

Peter Kelzo made Greek meatballs of his opponents in the March election. He is now Minister for Multiculturism and has introduced Socrates, Demosthenes, kaccavia, moussaka to Chinese, Lebanese and a dozen other assorted nationalities in his domain, not all of whom are appreciative of the cultural hand-out. George Gandolfo and Joe St Louis are working in Macquarie Street with him, where Joe St Louis has established a new standard as a minder.

Norm Clizbe and Jerry Balmoral are running a stronger, better financed Trade Congress and are often seen in the company of the Minister for Multiculturism. Balmoral also pays private visits to the Premier. Still occasionally impatient but learning to take the long view, he has a new girlfriend, a lovely Italian girl whose grandfather is a 'Ndrangheta *capo* in Calabria and, says his granddaughter, takes a deep interest in politics. Balmoral does not correspond with him.

Malone is still in charge of Homicide. Lisa is still at Town Hall, but will within the next two weeks be no longer in charge of Olympics public relations. Claire and Jason are engaged, Maureen now works as a researcher on *Four Corners* at the ABC and Tom is getting merit passes in Economics and girls and is in the State cricket squad.

There is still no one in the country, whether university-educated or illiterate, who can make a statement without two points of reference: *basically* and *at the end of the day*. There are several websites that refuse to accept messages that do not begin with: *Basically* . . .

Sydney went off the rails for two weeks, but the rest of the world did not notice. The voters have lost interest in who paid for Hans Vanderberg to be shot and their interest, more lively, more focused because it is on sport, is on who will bring the torch into the stadium . . .

'Here he comes! Who is it? Who is it? Ohmigod, isn't that incredible? It's –'